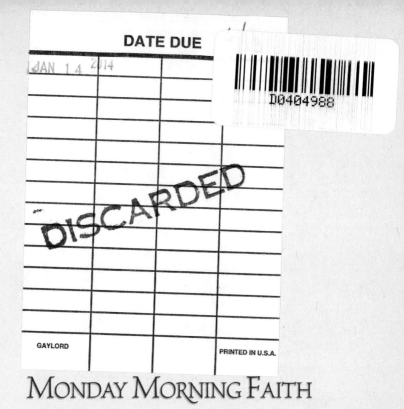

MONDAY MORNING FAITH

LORI COPELAND

MONDAY MORNING FAITH

ZONDERVAN®

GRAND RAPIDS, MICHIGAN 49530 USA

ZONDERVAN.COM/
AUTHORTRACKER

We want to hear from you. Please send your comments about this book to us in care of zreview@zondervan.com. Thank you.

ZONDERVAN®

Monday Morning Faith
Copyright © 2006 by Lori Copeland

Requests for information should be addressed to:
Zondervan, *Grand Rapids, Michigan 49530*

Library of Congress Cataloging-in-Publication Data

Copeland, Lori.
      Monday morning faith / Lori Copeland.
         p. cm.
      ISBN-10: 0-310-26349-2
      ISBN-13: 978-0-310-26349-4
         1. Women librarians—Fiction. 2. Papua New Guinea—Fiction.
  I. Title.
  PS3553.O6336M66 2006
  813'.54—dc22

                                  2006010171

Interior design by Michelle Espinoza

Printed in the United States of America

06 07 08 09 10 11 12 • 15 14 13 12 11 10 9 8 7 6 5 4 3 2 1

To the men and women who serve the Lord on the mission field

MONDAY MORNING FAITH

PROLOGUE
◎◎◎

I manhandled my carry-on luggage and an oversized umbrella down the long jet bridge, aware of the *thump thump thump* of my rubber-sole shoes against the carpeted floor. I sounded like a butter knife caught in the disposal.

As I entered the plane, my heart rate accelerated. *This was it.*

No turning back now.

The point of no return. The real thing.

I squeezed past the smiling flight attendant, passed the stairway on· the plane to the upper lounge, and made my way through first class into the cabin section. I paused, overwhelmed by the sheer size of the 747 Boeing aircraft. My eyes traveled row upon row of cabins. How would they ever get this thing off the ground? They would—I knew from prior experience—but right now my fact meter had blown a fuse.

Moving along, I passed the galleys, glancing at my ticket and excusing myself when I stepped on toes or bumped into a fellow passenger blocking the aisle. I eased through business class, past even more galleys, the lavatories, and the coach/ tourist/economy section. I studied my ticket. My seat was in the back of the plane. So were the majority of bathrooms.

At long last, I spotted my row. With my purse on the end of an armrest and my oversized umbrella tucked underneath my arm, I swung around—almost knocking a man unconscious with the clumsy rain gear. When I heard the solid *thwack!* I spun, horrified. The wounded passenger clutched the side of his head. For a heartbeat my voice failed me, but I managed to sputter out a weak, "I'm *so* sorry!"

I turned back to store the umbrella in the overhead bin, but the burdensome wood handle nailed a woman seated next to the aisle and flipped her spectacles two rows up. She grabbed for the flying missile and missed. Squinting, she glared up at me.

By now all I wanted to do was crawl in a hole and pull the dirt in behind me. Everything I did drew more attention to my clumsy entrance. Glasses were passed back, and the hostess appeared with an ice pack for the passenger's smarting injury. I tried to stuff my carry-on in the overhead bin; the hostess took the umbrella and assured me she'd give it back when we landed.

I sank into my seat and wanted to die.

And I figured I would. This monstrosity—this jumbo jet—would never get off the ground, let alone fly thirteen hours over land and sea. Had I done that once before? Me. Johanna ... Johanna ...

What *was* my last name?

I brushed at crumbs on the front of my suit jacket. I had yet to walk through O'Hare and pass a hot dog stand without indulging. Chicago Dogs.

Starbucks.

See's Candies.

My nerves and I hit them all; I was eating my way to the hereafter. I pushed my glasses up on my nose. Contacts would be impractical where I was going. The climate was far too hot. I'd left them at home with my wool coat.

I glanced out the window a final time. Saginaw, Michigan—and Mom, Pop, and Nelda—was eons away. My entire existence had been marching toward this moment in time. Would I measure up?

Of course, since this man-made contraption would never get off the ground, I wasn't sure it mattered whether I did or not.

Sniffing the faint scent of wieners in the air, I settled back to await my death.

ONE

My descent into madness began in the fall—October 13, to be exact, which happened to be my birthday. The dreaded fortieth. I was old enough for the bloom to be off the rose, but still young enough to shrink from the AARP card coming my way in another ten years.

How I reached the milestone so fast and how I could feel so young on the inside and so ancient on the outside still puzzled me. I used to be a brunette, but my hair was showing touches of silver, and if those were laugh lines around my eyes, I must have been having a better time than I'd realized.

I dried my hands on a paper towel and gave a final glance in the restroom mirror. Johanna Holland, old maid. A tag I hadn't planned on when I charted my life. I'd counted on the bungalow, picket fence, loving husband, and two perfect children. But here I was, aging so fast I couldn't catch my breath, and so wrapped up in work and other things that marriage was the last thing on my mind.

Sighing, I prepared to face my birthday festivities. Never mind that I was the one who'd set up the community room at the Holfield Community Library, where I'd worked for twenty years (crepe paper, obligatory balloons that read *Half Dead, One Foot in the Grave*, and the old standby *Over the Hill*). I'd also helped address the party invitations and ordered the refreshments, which was one way of getting what I liked, I suppose.

My aunt Margaret, Dad's sister (a sweet lady, but nutty as all get-out) had ordered my birthday cake, so there was no telling what I would be stuck with this year. She'd indicated a surprise. *Surprise* and *Aunt Margaret* were words that I never wanted to hear in the same sentence. The last time she "surprised" me, I ended up on a blind date with a widower named Harvey. He had ten kids and was looking for a live-in babysitter. He did offer marriage, on the first date, which I declined. I realized he was desperate, but I wasn't. In fact, I wasn't even needy, and for a forty-year-old woman that was doing okay.

I pushed my glasses farther up my nose.

The noise level grew louder as I approached the library community room. I smiled, spotting the balloons dangling from the ceiling. One for every year I'd graced the earth with my presence—forty big, round, shiny helium globes, announcing to the whole world that I was hopeless.

Not.

I still had a little spunk left in me, but I got the point. Forty and still single. Aunt Margaret equated the condition with death. According to her, the battery was about to expire on my biological clock. In fact, she'd stage-whisper, she suspected it had already ticked its last tock.

Any misgivings I might have had about tonight's festivities vanished in a chorus of well-wishers greeting me. Friends and family, two of life's greatest blessings. Truly, I was rich in the things that counted.

Threading my way through the packed room, I shook hands, shared hugs, and basked in the affectionate glow of love. What wonderful people who cared enough to help a lady celebrate her birthday.

Mom and Pop were by the window; I ended up beside them. "Hey, you two. Having a good time?" As always, they wore the demeanor of Ma and Pa Kettle—long, solemn faces. Pop never liked parties. Mom, frail and thin, suffered from osteoporosis; my father was confined to a wheelchair, the victim of emphysema. But they both were dressed in their Sunday best, here to celebrate with me. I was proud of them. I lived at home, looking after their needs. I didn't mind a bit. Despite their no-nonsense approach to life, they were a joy to be around, seldom complaining. And their love for each other and for me was the cornerstone of our lives.

Mom, seated on the sofa, reached up to pat my hand. "It's a good party, dear. Fun."

"The best." Oh yeah, a real blast. Thank goodness in an hour it would be over.

"Have you seen your cake yet?" Pop's tone indicated trouble on the way, and my antennae shot up with the speed of a push-button parasol.

"What is it this year?"

"Nothing." Mom glowered at Pop. "It's a beautiful cake, Clive."

I groaned. What had Aunt Margaret done? I looked at Pop in time to catch a fleeting grin. "What?"

The faint twinkle in his eye did *not* calm my nerves. "Ole Margaret strikes again."

I *knew* I should have ordered my own cake.

Mom's older sister was one of those people who knew how everyone should live but was blind to her own shortcomings. When Millie Treybocker asked Margaret if she was making

New Year's resolutions, my aunt said she had intended to, but after thinking it over, she couldn't think of any areas where she needed improvement.

Pop shook his head. "You'll have to see it to believe it."

Standing space around the table had cleared, so I hopped up and made my way over to take a good look at the culinary centerpiece. My tongue coiled in my mouth.

My cake was shaped like a *shoe*?

A high-topped, buttoned-up, old-fashioned shoe. The monstrosity on the cake board must be Aunt Margaret's symbol of my life.

She materialized beside me. "Well, what do you think?"

"It's ... creative."

"Isn't it? I thought it might give you a push in the right direction."

"And which direction might that be?" Off a cliff? Fleeing the building, screaming?

"Johanna Holland! You can't be that dense. It's the Old Woman Who Lived in a Shoe."

"Oh ... okay, but what does that have to do with me? If you recall, she had a number of children. You may not have noticed, but I have none. Nada, Aunt Margaret. Zippo."

"No, but Harvey has a peck."

"Harvey?" She was still harping on the widower? The man who wore his outdated polyester suits a size too small?

"He's willing to give you another shot. The cake was his idea."

I looked up to see Harvey waving at me from across the room. I closed my eyes and then opened them again. Oh, no! He was working his way through the crowd in my direction.

"Aunt Margaret! I am *not* interested in marriage, and if I were, I'd like to pick my own candidate, if you don't mind."

"But you're too picky. You're about to miss the boat—"

I walked off in my flat-heeled shoes, counting under my breath. I wasn't *about* to miss the boat—I *had* missed it. Couldn't she see that?

I headed for the door, anywhere to get away from Harvey and the gleam in his ferretlike eyes.

"Johanna! Where you off to?" Nelda Thomas, fellow librarian and best friend, waved at me. Tonight her mocha skin glowed against the soft rose of her blouse.

"Hi, Nelda. We're running out of plates and cups. I'll be back in a jiff." I had to get out of here before I strangled someone. Heaven help me, but Aunt Margaret brought out the devil in me.

When I stepped into the main lobby, library patrons were going about their business. I spotted a Wet Floor sign and frowned. Who'd spilled something? And what had they spilled? Coffee? Soda? The coffee shop was a trendy addition, but the once-immaculate library could do without the sticky messes that too often showed up. I slowed my pace, but the second my slippery soles hit the slick, my feet gained a mind of their own.

My arms flapped, and I balanced, struggling to catch myself. But one foot went one way, the other slid a different direction ... and right there in the lobby of the Holfield Community Library, Johanna Holland did the splits. Granted, I used to have the move down pat. I'd performed the maneuver (both right and left split) on a regular basis as a high school cheerleader. Though that had been many moons ago, I remembered the move.

What I didn't remember was the pain!

I managed to drag one leg back toward me, thinking I might never walk again. A plan formed in my pain-hazed mind: just crawl to the restroom and stay there until feeling returned to my lower limbs. As far as I could tell I'd not broken anything, but I'd knocked everything out of joint.

In the middle of my panic, firm hands took hold of my forearms and I became airborne as someone I couldn't see lifted me to my feet. Somehow I managed to stand erect.

I took a deep breath and turned around to come face-to-face with Tom Selleck. My hold tightened on the rocklike biceps, hanging on while I stared up at warm brown eyes, rugged, handsome features, a silky mustache.

I blinked and shook my head. When I looked back, Tom Selleck had disappeared, leaving in his place a man who had to be his twin. "Thank you," I managed. My face had to be the color of the burgundy drapes hanging in the reading rooms. I shoved my glasses up on my nose.

He smiled, and the effect was stunning. "You're welcome. Name's Sam Littleton. You work here, don't you?"

"Yes. I'm Johanna Holland, head librarian." I straightened, touching my hair. "Have we met?"

It was all I could think to say, but I knew the answer already. We hadn't. Believe me, I'd have remembered this man if I'd seen him in the library. I'd have remembered him if I'd seen him in a dark alley.

"No, but I'm here often. I've seen you around." He indicated the stack of books he'd dropped when he came to my rescue. "I'm researching Papua New Guinea."

I struggled to regain my composure. Bending over, I began to pick up the scattered reading material. "I must have made quite a spectacle."

His features sobered. "You took a bad spill. Sure you're okay?"

"I'm sure." I'd have aches and bruises tomorrow in muscles I didn't know existed, but I'd choke before admitting it. "Papua New Guinea? You're going there?"

"January 15th." He smiled, indicating the stack of books. "I have a lot of reading to do."

"Yes—it would appear." *Think, Johanna, say something intelligent.* But the mental well had run dry. I was as blank as a cleaned slate. What were we talking about? Oh, yes. Papua New Guinea.

"You sure you don't need to see a doctor?"

"No." If my face got any warmer I would ignite. "I'll be fine."

He picked up his books, smiled at me, and walked on. I sized him up as he walked away. Maybe midfifties, prime physical condition. A weird tingling zipped up my spine. Must have been because of the fall . . .

Shaking off the sensation, I returned to the party. The fun and festivities were going strong, but thank heaven both Harvey and Aunt Margaret had disappeared. Facing the inevitable, I reached for the knife and approached the cake. "Okay, who gets the first piece?"

Nelda held out her plate. "A shoe cake?"

I managed a smile. "There's a joker in every crowd."

"Where did Margaret go?"

"Who knows? Off to pester someone else, I assume." I hadn't intended to sound so sharp, but Nelda caught it, of course. She caught everything.

"She on your case again?"

"Always."

"She hates the thought of you being single, doesn't she?"

I licked buttercream frosting off my finger. "You should see the candidate this time. He comes equipped with ten children, so I wouldn't have to do a thing but rear them and tolerate him."

"Ten?" Nelda set the plate down and fanned her face. "Nobody today has that many kids. Think how much it would cost to buy shoes. Reminds me of that nursery rhyme about the old woman who ..." Her gaze fell to the table. "Aha! The cake!"

I whacked a hunk of heel and slid it onto my plate. "It's supposed to give me ideas."

Nelda snorted, spraying punch on her new rose silk blouse. "Oh, I'll bet it gives you ideas, all right."

We looked at each other and promptly collapsed in a fit of laughter. We'd no sooner regain our composure when I'd catch Nelda's eye, and we were off again.

She wiped her eyes, still chuckling. "Want me to talk to your aunt?"

"Would it do any good?"

"Not a bit, but I could make the effort."

"Save your breath." I slid a fold of a paper napkin under my eyes to wipe away remaining tears, hoping my mascara hadn't run. "She's harmless, I guess."

"But irritating." Nelda handed me her plate. "It's late. I need to be getting home. The kids will have torn the blinds down by now."

"I need to be going too. I'll see about Mom and Pop."

Pop had wheeled to where Mom and my cousin Mack were waiting. Mack was acting as chauffeur today, and I appreciated it. He'd see my parents got home all right. The party was over, but I still had to clean up.

I stared at the huge bunches of balloons. "What am I going to do with those?"

"Leave those to me." Nelda grabbed the party favors. "I'll get Jim Jr. to help, and we'll drop them off at The Gardens. The residents will love them."

"Do you think the messages are appropriate for an assisted living facility?"

"Don't worry about that. Trust me, they'll love them, and if it isn't someone's birthday now, it will be soon. Birthdays roll around there faster than cockroaches on rollerblades."

Nelda and her son, Jim Jr., did volunteer work at The Gardens; I was delighted to let them take the balloons. We carried the leftover cake and punch to the break room for the library staff.

Jim Jr. arrived by the time we'd emptied the trash and run the vacuum. We carried the balloons out to his van, and he and Nelda drove off, balloons whipping around in the backseat.

I got in my car and drove to the Video Barn, where I rented a couple of Tom Selleck movies. Sam Littleton's face surfaced to mind, but I pushed it back into the recesses. Yes, he was attractive. Yes, he'd made my heart flutter. But that's all there was to it. A chance encounter on my birthday.

I didn't want—or need—any more than that.

I enjoyed my life as it was, thank you. Taking care of my parents, what with their varied health problems, took time—time I didn't begrudge. I enjoyed being with them.

If I lacked anything emotional, Itty Bitty, my two-year-old Maltese, was there to give me Itty kisses, which always made me feel better. I wished my little dog needed outdoor exercise, but he required indoor exercise, so we'd run through the house chasing a ball or playing hide-and-seek. Itty would find me every time, and every time I had to laugh. He'd sit back on his short little body, cock his rounded head, and stare at me with those black-rimmed, close-set eyes. His feathered ears would droop while his black nose twitched. His high-set tail, covered with a long coat and carried over the back, made a funny sight, indeed. I kept him clipped short for convenience, though I was sure he'd prefer to retain a silky long coat.

Mom and Pop loved the dog, and loved having me with them. I knew they worried that they were putting a crimp in my social life, but I wasn't interested in a relationship at this point. Just give me a good book, or let me visit with Mom and Pop or watch the Discovery Channel, and I was happy. And with my job, I didn't have to buy books retail. I got them from library sales.

Yes, indeed, life was good.

Over the next few days, though, I caught myself wondering if Sam Littleton would be in. He never was — or I didn't spot him. Just as well. He'd already disrupted my routine more than I liked.

One morning I finished reshelving Daniel Baker's stack of books. He'd retired as head foreman at the handle factory and was indulging in a lifelong goal: reading every Western in the library.

The little man with a bushy mass of snow-white hair grinned at me. "You need to get in some new Louis L'Amour titles." He pointed to a volume. "That's one I've read."

"Mr. L'Amour isn't writing anymore, Mr. Baker."

His eyes bulged. "Why not? Man's got talent. Real talent."

"Mr. L'Amour has passed on."

He shook his head, shock reflected in his eyes. "All the good ones do."

I smiled. *And the bad ones too.* "Oh, there are a lot of good writers around; you'll discover them." I handed him the stack of reading material. He was still grumbling when he left the desk.

Nelda approached, pencil wedged behind her right ear. "We're sending out for pizza. You in?"

"Of course."

This was my life: books, old men, and an occasional pizza.

Late that afternoon, I drained the last of my green tea and shut off my computer. Sitting in one position for three hours had left me stiff. A glance outside my window revealed a light drizzle icing the trees. Michigan winters could be arduous; the late fall storm system had crept in when we weren't looking. In the two weeks before my birthday we'd enjoyed Indian summer with temperatures in the low seventies. But the cold air this morning foretold change.

The hands of the office clock pointed to five thirty. I collected my purse and coat and exited the side entrance. The ice wasn't thick, just enough of a coating to make walking hazardous and unprotected windshields a real pain. I slipped on my leather gloves, thinking about the ice scraper Pop bought me for Christmas last year. One of those fancy automatic things you plug in the cigarette lighter. Clearing the windshield should be a snap.

The traffic kept the roads clear of ice, so I wouldn't have any trouble getting home once I made it out of the parking lot.

Making my way across the slippery asphalt was a little tricky, but since I wore sensible shoes—not those high-heeled horrors Nelda favored—I made good time. I grabbed the ice scraper out of the trunk, opened the driver's side, and plugged it in the receptacle. Within seconds the gimmick was doing its job.

I moved from the windshield to the side window on the driver's side—and then it happened. My right foot hit a slick spot. I made a grab for the side mirror, missed, and went down hard, ending up flat on my back on the asphalt, my feet and legs halfway underneath the car.

When the jarring pain cleared, I lay there, stunned from the fall. I would have to scoot backwards far enough to get my feet clear of the car to sit up. I placed my hands flat on the pavement.

Lord, if you love me, don't let anyone be watching.

I yelped when strong hands reached under my arms, hoisting me to my feet. I was still standing on ice, so I grabbed the mirror and turned to face my benefactor. My heart dropped to my toes as once again I found myself staring at Sam Littleton. He looked as I remembered. Kind (albeit a little bemused). Picture of health. Handsome.

He stood there on the ice as if he were Superman.

And I had just been caught in another clownish fall. I was *never* this clumsy!

He grinned. "Miss Holland. Enjoying the first bout of bad weather, are you?"

Assessing the physical damage I'd incurred, I decided I was bruised, but not broken. I straightened, shoving my glasses up on my nose. "Mr. Littleton, I've about decided you're detrimental to my health."

He laughed, a rich warm sound in the cold air. "My apologies."

I stared at the library's treasured tomes scattered across the icy parking lot and winced. "You dropped your books."

"I'm sorry. I was afraid you'd broken something." His eyes focused on the volumes. "They look to be all right." He bent to pick up the hardbacks, and I recovered enough to help. He dumped the armload in his car with a careless abandon that set my teeth on edge. What was he thinking, treating books like that?

He offered a gloved hand and I accepted it. "You still look shaken. Let me buy you a cup of coffee."

The thought of a hot mug of something in the library coffee shop was tempting. Mom and Pop wouldn't wait dinner for me. They ate at six o'clock on the dot regardless of who was there.

"Oh, I mustn't. I ..."

His grip tightened on my arm. "I insist. Take a minute to relax, recover from the fall before you drive home." He propelled me across the parking lot, ignoring my protests in a way that brought about a slow burn. Who did this man think he was? Maybe I didn't *want* coffee.

The cozy coffee shop embraced us. Aromas of fresh-brewed beans and warm spice muffins filled the air. Sam steered me to a table by the window as a young girl approached, eyeing Sam like a dieting woman eyes a supersized cheeseburger. "May I help you?" She didn't look my way.

Apparently the fall had rendered me invisible.

"Two black coffees, please." Sam lifted a brow. "Cream?"

"No, just coffee." I wanted a latte or hot tea, but I wouldn't quibble. Mostly because I was afraid my tongue wouldn't work right. Clearly, I was out of my element here. Coffee with a man. Not a common occurrence for me. And with him smiling at me that way, his hand next to mine on the table . . .

The whole thing seemed almost too intimate.

The waitress smiled at Sam and left while I searched my mind for something to talk about. My love life? Hardly. For one thing, it was nonexistent, unless you counted Harvey, Aunt Margaret's candidate. For another, it wasn't exactly a proper topic of conversation for a man I didn't even know. Maybe sports. Then again, maybe not. Sports had never been a favorite of mine, so if I wanted to sound intelligent, that was out. I steered clear of politics on general principles. People could get too impassioned about their personal choice in candidates.

So what did that leave me? I mustered a smile. "You haven't left for Papua New Guinea yet?"

Well now, that was clever since he was sitting across the table from me, clear brown eyes brimming with interest.

"January 15th."

Color flooded my cheeks as the date struck a chord. He'd mentioned it at our first meeting. I grappled for an intelligent response. "Why Papua New Guinea?"

He picked up his napkin and polished a spoon. "I'm a retired surgeon. I'll be running a clinic in a remote village, and I'll be working with a couple of missionaries and their wives. We're trying to break the communication barrier with these particular villagers, learn more of their ways, help improve their quality of life."

"And introduce the gospel?"

"Probably not. We don't speak their language or understand more than just a few basics of their culture. What we want to do is provide friendship, medicine, and health care in hopes that the people will begin to trust us. The gospel is still many years away for this tribe."

He bent forward, dark eyes intent. "What about you? Do you have a church affiliation?" Our coffee arrived. Sam thanked the waitress, then awaited my response.

"I accepted Christ at an early age, but I've never felt led to the mission field."

He reached for the sugar. "Not everyone is. I'm sure you do your share of God's work."

"I like to think so." Often my work with the children at the library was a ministry of its own. In addition to my other duties, I took time to oversee story hour every afternoon. That was a library tech's job, but I enjoyed watching those eager young faces come alive when I read stories of faraway, exciting places. I went on to explain that my actual "calling" was the care of my aging parents. Mom and Pop needed me, and I had dedicated my life to meeting their needs. "And I spend one Saturday a month at the hospital doing volunteer work."

Sam stirred sugar into his coffee and tested the temperature. "I'm a member of Sandstone. You might be familiar with the church?"

"I know where it is." Everyone knew Sandstone, the largest nondenominational congregation in Saginaw. I'd always thought they were flamboyant and somewhat flaunty with their work. They had a three-hundred-and-fifty-voice choir, the biggest fleet of buses in the area, and well over five thousand members — three thousand of whom came every Sunday.

He picked up the thread of conversation in a nice, easy-to-listen-to baritone. "I'd been peripherally involved in mission work for years, but when I lost my wife a couple of years ago I plunged in headfirst."

I studied the rugged planes of Sam's face, the crisp wave of graying hair across his tanned forehead, the well-muscled forearms, the all-around American male good looks, and tried to imagine him in a jungle living in a mud hut—or whatever missionaries lived in. The picture didn't fit.

"Belinda died of leukemia. She was a nurse—we married in our early twenties and worked side by side all our married life."

I offered the trite. "I'm so sorry. That must have been a terrible ordeal for both of you."

He nodded, eyes distant. "Watching someone you love die is difficult."

I resisted the impulse to reach out and lay my hand across his. After all, I didn't know this man. He would think I was being forward. "You mentioned you're involved in missions. Have you made trips before?"

"Short-term ones. Honduras. Guatemala. Mexico—Papua New Guinea a couple of times. New Guinea is a far deeper commitment. I'll be spending much of my time there the next few years—or those are my immediate plans." He smiled. "God could change them anytime."

I stared deep into my cup. "It would be difficult for me to leave the familiar behind."

He fell silent for a moment. Then, "A wise man once said that everything he gave up was worthless compared to what he gained from serving God. Since Belinda's death I've developed a real heart for missions. I believe this is my purpose in life."

"And that wise man was?"

"The apostle Paul."

"Yes, of course." Clearly I needed to devote more time to my Bible reading. "So you're going to save the natives?" I regretted the nerves-generated, flippant remark the minute it came out of my mouth. A slow heat stained my cheeks. "I didn't mean that the way it sounded."

He didn't appear offended. "I understand. At this point, I don't know the exact nature of my work other than to conduct a free medical clinic. One couple that I will work with has been on the field for twelve years and has yet to have any real progress with the language. It takes time—incredible amounts of time and patience—to reach these people."

Somewhere over our second cup of coffee we became Sam and Johanna. I sat back and pondered my good fortune. *Dr. Sam Littleton.* He'd had a large practice but retired when Belinda fell ill. He'd assumed her full care in their home for the duration of her illness.

"What do you do in your spare time?" He sounded interested, not just polite.

I laughed. "Spare time? What's that?"

When he lifted a brow I elaborated. "I work full time, and my parents are in poor health. Taking care of them can be time-consuming."

"Social life?"

"Nonexistent."

"What if I invited you to a church concert? Would you come?"

For the oddest reason I wanted to say yes, but I'd avoided dating—or developing friendships at all—for too many years. My parents came first.

"That's very nice, but I can't."

His eyes held mine. What did he see? A middle-aged librarian? Graying hair, large glasses (that could use a good tightening), and rather plain features? I'd been told that my eyes were my unique feature—hazel-colored with black spiky lashes. A man as handsome as Sam Littleton could have his pick of ladies. The coffee shop waitress had made that clear. Sam wasn't really interested in me. He was just being nice.

He smiled. "Maybe another time."

"Maybe." I didn't want to close the door, though I knew the chances of seeing him other than in the library were slim to none.

He walked me to my car and I drove home, my mood as treacherous as the icy highways. I seldom wasted time wondering if I was missing out on life, but tonight the thought entered my head. I was forty. Single. Mom and Pop wouldn't live forever, and when they were gone I would have no close family other than Aunt Margaret, if she was still alive. I shivered in the car's interior. *Aunt Margaret.*

Images of the shoe cake made me queasy.

Nelda phoned around nine. "I saw you walking across the parking lot with that good-looking man who's been checking out all the books on Papua New Guinea."

"You've seen Sam in the library? Why haven't I noticed him before?"

"If you'd come up for air once in a while, not be so buried in your computer, you might see what's going on around you. Half the females at the library are in love with that man. The other half haven't noticed him yet."

I made my voice casual. "Oh? Is there something special about him? I hadn't noticed."

Nelda's silence was eloquent.

Undaunted, I went on. "He's very nice, dedicated to his church. He's going to Papua New Guinea in January for an extended mission project."

"Gone for a long time?"

"He didn't say." Might as well be eternity. By the time he got back he'd have forgotten all about Johanna Holland and tonight's brief encounter.

Nelda sighed. "Isn't that the way it goes? All the good ones are either taken or running."

"He's not running; he believes God's calling him to the mission field."

Another sigh. "Well, a mere mortal woman cannot compete with God. Best you mark this one off the list."

"What list is that?"

"The mental list every woman carries around in her mind. The one where we evaluate every man we meet — oh, come on! Don't try to tell me you don't do the same thing. You're not dead!"

"Nor am I preoccupied with the male gender." Nelda was married, for heaven's sake! But she wasn't *dead*.

"So you say." I heard the telltale crunch of chips. "Well, can't win them all."

We said good night, and I opened my Bible to stare unseeing at the pages. Itty Bitty gazed up at me, eyes alert. I kept seeing Sam Littleton's face instead of Holy Writ. Was that blasphemy? I laid my head back and closed my eyes. Now why was I even thinking about a man I'd seen only twice? And why did I feel ... well, almost saddened that he was leaving?

Doctor Sam Littleton would never in a million years be of interest to me.

Papua New Guinea. Mission field. The man might as well be going to Mars.

TWO

Sunshine streamed through my bedroom curtains Sunday morning. I woke to warmer temperatures, if midforties could be considered warm. After breakfast, I drove Mom and Pop to church, thankful for muddy traces of last night's ice melting along the roadside. If this kept up, Saginaw was in for a hard winter.

The church parking lot was half filled when I pulled into the handicapped space. Pop maneuvered himself into his chair, and I pushed it up the ramp and into the church. Our seats were halfway down the left side, center aisle. Pop's chair fit against the pew, and Mom sat in the end seat next to him. I sat on her right side. I'd made a confession of faith and been baptized at this church. I'd been young—seven—but I can still remember the peace I found that night when I came forward during the pastor's invitation.

I studied the narrow aisle and decided it had shortened since those many years ago. To a frightened, shy seven-year-old, it had looked as long as a well rope.

Sighing, I focused on the attendance board: 136 in Sunday school. Last week's offering: $368.32. The big mausoleum across town where Sam Littleton attended would be running over this morning. Our church was tiny in comparison. Gosh, I knew everybody in attendance and 90 percent of their problems. That's a small congregation. We were family. Our nondenominational church was mission-oriented, and the members cared for each other. Seldom was our kitchen counter without a fresh-baked pie or Pop's favorite coconut cake, still warm from the oven of a thoughtful member.

We sang classic hymns: "Amazing Grace" and "There Is a Fountain." This morning we sang my favorite, "Oh, How I Love Jesus." Contemporary songs left me cold. One repetitious phrase sung over and over until it lost its meaning seemed a waste of good time. Nelda, who loved all music except for some of the more brash pop songs, labeled me an old fuddy-duddy who needed to change with the times. She might be right, but I'd stick to the proven.

John Richard Haddock, Hillsdale's pastor for the last fifteen years, strode to the pulpit. He had a deep, full voice and a somewhat dramatic delivery. Goodness, I was more holy just listening to him. Okay. I knew it didn't work that way. I couldn't claim God's blessings because I enjoyed listening to John Richard preach, but it was nice not to be distracted by Pop's snoring during sermons.

John began, speaking on personal spiritual growth—but I couldn't get on his wavelength. Expanding my spiritual territories just didn't connect with me. Believing God had called me to work in some faraway place—say, Papua New Guinea—was as foreign to me as believing God wanted me to start a church on the moon.

Sam believed he had a calling. That was fine. I hoped he was right. But I couldn't help a surge of gratitude that God had never seen fit to call me to foreign lands. My rut was comfortable.

After services, we stopped by The Steak House on the edge of town for Sunday lunch. For once we got there ahead of the people from Sam's church. Several of our own members were already seated. Amid a flurry of waves and second greetings, we settled at a table next to the window so Pop's chair would be out of the way and he could see outside. Unable to get out much anymore, he enjoyed his Sunday outings, and today the bright sunshine held little hint that the holidays were fast approaching.

The parking lot was full of men and women in their church finery working their way toward the steak house entrance. "You ever notice how many church members eat out on Sunday?" Pop asked.

Mom fished the lemon slice out of her water and gave it a good squeeze before dropping it back into the glass. "Ever notice how many of them brag about how they don't work on the Sabbath and then they come here to eat and shop Wal-Mart afterwards and make the employees work?"

"Mom . . ." True, Bay Road was a popular route on Sunday afternoons, but I didn't want to ruin lunch with one of her pious lectures. I shopped the Super Center on Sunday. Working forty-plus hours a week left little time for personal errands. "It's not our place to judge."

Pop winked at me. "And if I'm correct, I believe we're contributing to the problem."

Mom eyed him over the menu. "At least we're not bragging about how we don't work on Sunday."

"We don't work anymore, period." He switched out a tank of oxygen; the cylinders were getting bigger these days. "Maybe we should eat at home next week. You and Sis can get up an hour earlier, put on a roast, peel some potatoes, and whip up a batch of hot rolls to rise, churn some butter. That would be nice."

Mom took his ribbing in stride. "And make poor Johanna work on her day off?" She perused the menu. "I'm having fried chicken and ohhh, heaven help me. They have that chocolate mousse I like so much."

The waitress appeared, pen poised over her notepad. I handed her my menu. "Fried chicken, mashed potatoes and gravy, blue cheese dressing on the salad, and corn. Oh, and a cup of green tea."

I'd started drinking green tea after reading about its health benefits — how it's supposed to help you lose weight. I suspected that last benefit was a stretch since I'd been drinking it for six months now and hadn't lost an ounce.

Pop ordered the eight-ounce sirloin, medium rare, and a baked potato with sour cream. I knew I needed to nag him about his cholesterol, but there were so few things that he could enjoy anymore. If it were me in that chair, I'd eat lard sandwiches and lace my coffee with bacon grease. I wasn't going to live forever and neither was Pop.

Nelda waved from a corner table. Jim, her husband, was as big as a house. His skin was a couple of shades darker than Nelda's, and he had the gentle personality of a Saint Bernard. The man was a gem. All Nelda had to do was look like she might want something and Jim delivered. The man spent a month last spring building a sunroom on the east corner of their house so she could have a place to keep her plants through the winter. Marriage wouldn't be bad if I could find a man like Jim Thomas.

Their honor student, sixteen-year-old son, Jim Jr., was polite, well mannered, and a sweet kid. He was athletic too.

Natasha was thirteen and already showing signs of becoming a real beauty. My friend had it all — all that mattered, anyway — and was smart enough to know it.

After lunch, I passed the Thomases' table on my way to the ladies' room. Nelda hailed me. "You want to come over this afternoon and watch a two-hanky old movie? I'll make popcorn."

I thought about the invitation before I declined. "I'd better stay close to home. Pop's emphysema is acting up. He tries to hide it so we won't worry."

Nelda patted my hand. "Sure. You're a wonderful daughter, Johanna."

Jim buttered half of a roll. "You need anything, girl, you let us know, all right?"

"I'll do that, and thanks." He meant it too. Call him for anything and he'd be there before I hung up.

Later, I settled Mom and Pop for their Sunday afternoon naps before retiring to my room with a book. Nelda's compliment kept running through my mind. *A wonderful daughter.* I tried to be, but when I looked at all she had with Jim, a niggling twinge raised my curiosity. Were Nelda and Jim right? Was I allowing life to pass me by while I maintained my "wonderful daughter" status?

Johanna, for shame!

I let the book rest on my chest. I couldn't believe I'd had that thought. What was happening to Johanna Holland, beloved daughter of Clive and Harriet, the woman who was so content with her simple life? I couldn't put my finger on what bothered me, but since the night of my birthday party I'd been on edge. Maybe my restlessness came from the fact that I was no longer a teenager. I was forty years old. *Forty.*

It wasn't all that long ago that I thought a person my age had one foot in the grave and another on a banana peel.

Why did weekends go by so much faster than weekdays? Close to ten Monday morning, I glanced through the plate glass separating my work area from the main library. Traffic was brisk this morning, and I recognized several of our regulars. The library served as a meeting place for friends as they browsed the shelves, looking for something new to read and recommending their favorites.

I looked back at my monitor and then paused, frowning. Had that been Sam Littleton's tan overcoat disappearing around a corner of the shelves in the geographical section? My pulse accelerated. That's where the New Guinea research books were shelved. Soon he would've checked all we had and then what would he do?

He'd be in New Guinea, Johanna.

I frowned. Missionaries were gone for long periods, returning for short furloughs. How could they leave friends and loved ones and be away for so long? But then Sam didn't have family and he hadn't mentioned children.

I placed my hands on the keyboard, ready to resume typing, but then I stopped short, deep in thought. He might need help. I didn't assist the patrons but left that up to my assistants, but in this case ...

I left my desk and strolled toward the center section of the building. Aisle one was empty, as was aisle two. But on the third aisle I hit pay dirt. Sam was down on his hands and knees, cheek pressed to the floor while trying to read the titles on the lower shelf. He was facing me, but he was so absorbed in what he was doing he didn't notice my presence.

I didn't mean to startle him, only to clear my throat to relieve the sudden dryness. The doctor jumped as if he'd been shot. He jerked upright to face me.

"I'm sorry ..." His eyes met mine, and I lost all coherent thought. My heart jackhammered against my ribs. I could swear the air had left the room.

Goodness! You'd think I was sixteen years old and meeting a rock star.

He flashed a warm grin. "You startled me."

Reining in my sudden and most mystifying reaction, I returned his smile. "Sorry. Are you finding everything you need?"

He rattled off a title. "Do you know if it's in?"

The librarian arm-wrestled the starstruck teen to the ground. "I can check."

He handed me a Post-it note where he'd written *New Guinea Tribes and Culture.* I returned to my desk and checked the computer system. Sam had trailed me. "Yes, it should be there." We returned to the shelf and I dropped down on my hands and knees, thumbing through the titles on the lower shelf. We needed to do something to make the place more user friendly. Like eliminate the bottom row. I was getting too old for crawling on the floor. We must have made a strange sight, both of us creeping down the row, heads bent to the floor.

It took a few minutes, but I located the material. "Here it is!" I waved the prize.

He moved in closer to look and we smacked heads. Sitting up straight, I saw stars for a few seconds. I rubbed the smarting wound, grinning like an idiot. He was so close I could smell his aftershave, and I assumed I looked as startled as he did. What *was* that heady fragrance he was wearing?

We held the awkward position for a full minute, staring eyeball-to-eyeball. We'd still have been there at closing time if Nelda hadn't turned the corner and slid to a halt.

"Well, well, what have we here?"

I jerked upright, still on my knees. "We're looking for a title." The words came out in a guilty stream: *We'relookingforatitle.*

She smirked. "Is that what you call it?"

It's a good thing I wasn't on my feet. I might have slugged her. She wiggled her eyebrows—her imitation of Groucho Marx—and walked on. Judging from the wink she gave me, my face must have been a flaming cherry.

Sam got to his feet and helped me up. I accepted his hand; he met my self-conscious expression. "Got time for a cup of coffee?"

I thought of Nelda and her smirk ... and realized I didn't care what she thought. A pox on them all! If I wanted a cup of coffee, I'd have one. "Make that green tea and you have a deal."

"Just let me check out this book."

"I can take care of that." He followed me to the desk and I did the work, then walked around the counter. He tucked the book under one arm, linked the other through mine, and winked. "Shall we go, my lady?"

"After you, sir." I knew Nelda's eyes were falling out of her sockets but I didn't care. A cup of tea.

Big deal.

We swept through the doorway and I didn't look back to see if Nelda's mouth was gaping (it would be). She'd demand to know everything we discussed, and I thought maybe I'd tell her and maybe I wouldn't. It's a wonder the woman's beak wasn't worn off, the way she stuck it in everyone's business.

But I loved her anyway.

Coffee shop business was slow at this hour. The waitress —different girl from last visit, same reaction to Sam— waltzed to our table.

My voice was cold as crushed ice. "Hot green tea, please." She looked at me.

"And he'll have coffee. Black."

She nodded and stuck her order pad in her apron pocket. When she walked away Sam grinned. "I like a decisive woman."

Decisive.

Or big-mouthed?

Ill-mannered seemed more appropriate. My mother did not approve of bad behavior. Shame crept over me. Being so assertive wasn't like me. Sam Littleton brought out an alien side of me—one I wasn't sure I liked.

We lingered over the drinks. Sam leaned across the table and I couldn't pull my eyes off him. He was mesmerizing. "Johanna, I'd like to take you to dinner some night this week. Would you allow me?"

I gulped. Dinner? With him? "Oh, I don't know," I sputtered, almost rejecting the notion. A cup of tea was innocent enough, but an actual dinner date? Far more intimidating.

He gripped my hand in a firm clasp, as if afraid I'd bolt. His touch was warm and calming. "We'll make it an early evening so you can get home to your parents. We can eat here, if you like. There appears to be a good selection of soup and sandwiches."

Excuses formed in my head. I couldn't be gone from Mom and Pop ...

Didn't hold water. I left Mom and Pop alone every day.

How about I was coming down with a cold?

Nope. Wouldn't fly. I was healthy as a horse and looked it.

Previous commitments? Nah, he'd see through the excuse. Aunt Margaret was my only commitment other than Mom and Pop.

Feet hurt.

Iron-poor blood.

I tried a few others, then decided to go for it. I was forty years old, not a juvenile with a curfew. I could handle a dinner in a bright coffee shop with a very nice library patron. When I looked in his eyes and saw the sincerity, the likability, I knew I was going to accept.

"Thursday night this week would be fine." That still gave me time to come up with an excuse if I decided to back out.

"Thursday it is. What time do you get off work?"

"Five thirty."

"I'll be waiting in the outer hallway." He nodded, placing my hand back down on the table. "I'm looking forward to it."

To tell the truth, so was I. A thrill—an adolescent thrill —shot clean to my toes. *Sam wants to have dinner with me. In the library coffee shop.*

So, okay, I caved. Gave in to an impulse I knew I'd regret.

Again, I didn't care.

Then I made my first serious mistake. "What are you looking for? Maybe I could help?"

He took out a pen and jotted the information on a napkin. "I appreciate this, Johanna. Seems I can't learn enough about the subject."

What had I gotten myself into? The list would take personal time, but I wasn't here for decoration. My job was to assist patrons whenever I could.

"I'm sure I can find additional helpful information."

"I'd appreciate anything you come up with. There's so much I don't know. A lot of it will come by experience, but I like to be prepared."

I could understand that. I liked attentiveness, and organization was my middle name. He walked me back to the library a bit later. The encounter had been pleasant — even more than I expected. Sam was a wonderful conversationalist, and despite my apprehension we had managed to find common topics of interest. He liked my personal favorites, old movies and hot chocolate chip cookies; I shared his love of books and learning.

Nelda was working the checkout desk when I sailed through the arched doorway. "Well, look who's back. Thought you'd gone home for the day."

"Without my coat and purse?" I tsked. She was dying for information, but for some reason I didn't want to share the past hour. Not yet. Besides, what was there to tell about a cup of tea?

"Notice you left with Sam." She leaned on the counter, white teeth flashing. "Have a good time?"

"Very interesting person." I marched past her into the office. She followed, bright-eyed and bushy-tailed, as Pop liked to say. All ears. Tongue hanging out.

Well, not really. But as eager as she was, it could have been.

She loomed over my desk. "What were the two of you doing crawling on the floor?"

I thought about telling her we were practicing an aboriginal New Guinean dating ritual but then thought, *Nah, she'd believe me.*

"We were looking for a book."

"Humph. I figured you were looking for a contact, but if that's your story, you stick to it."

"That's my story." And she didn't need to know about the dinner date on Thursday, even though I figured it would consist of research talk in the coffee shop. That's why Sam Littleton asked me out. He wanted unlimited access to material, and I held the key to success.

I didn't care. Sam was a great conversationalist. I liked him. I'd enjoy his company while he was here and then, when it came time for him to leave, I'd wave good-bye, grateful for the opportunity I'd had to know him.

"Hey." Nelda paused in the doorway. "I saw this great pair of heels today—spiky, strappy, outrageous, and overpriced. Want to go try them on before you head home?"

"Sure." Not that I would buy them; I generally wore flat heels. But looking was fun, and I could always use a new blouse.

"You're on." She left, and I got my coat and purse and followed on her heel. A good shopping trip was just what I needed to get my mind off Sam ... er ... my work.

THREE

Even a new blouse failed to lift my spirits. My zip had zapped. Thursday arrived, and I was a train wreck!

I'd both dreaded and anticipated the dinner date with Sam. A small part of me still wanted to call him and cancel. Had I lost my mind? Why was I bothering to go to all the trouble to have a manicure, my hair styled by a professional, and, lo and behold, Nelda would not *believe* (if she knew) the *I'm-Not-Really-a-Waitress* red crowning the tips of my pedicured toenails. I'd blown more money in the past two hours in preparation for this date than I had spent on clothing in the past six months.

Of course, I wasn't interested in Sam, like romance-novel interested, but I liked him. Maybe too much. I hadn't much practice in matters of the heart, and I wasn't sure if Sam was interested in me as a person or a research source. What if the latter were true, and he was just giving the old-maid librarian a thrill by asking her out to dinner?

The thought sent my blood pressure soaring. Throwing me a bone the way you would a hungry dog, was he? I'd call him right now and cancel, that rotten —

My practical side stopped me. Sam had been every inch the gentleman. He hadn't requested my personal services; *I* had volunteered them. He appeared to enjoy my company, and I enjoyed his. He was a single man; I provided a little company. Yet I couldn't keep my eyes off the clock. I stepped to the window twice to check the weather. Still raining.

Library business was brisk all morning. I kept busy with paperwork. A new shipment of books arrived and had to be processed. Nelda stopped by my desk, hands full of magazines she'd culled from the shelves.

"Want to go to the Burger Barn for lunch? They've got killer salads."

"Salads? We're dieting today?"

She sighed. "I couldn't button the top of my slacks this morning. South Beach, Atkins, high fat, low fat, you name it. I've tried them all. Nothing works."

"Hmmm. Tried them all? No cheating?"

She stiffened. "I'm not saying I've been perfect. I had to cheat to survive. Name me the person who can live on what those diet books allow you to eat. Do you know a serving is considered a half cup? Let's see you eat a half cup of mashed potatoes and gravy."

"What kind of diet allows you to have mashed potatoes and gravy?"

"The Nelda Thomas Diet. I'm thinking of marketing it."

"I'll buy the first copy. Okay, Burger Barn it is." I shoved back from the desk and stretched my neck and back. We left the library and took Nelda's car to lunch. The Barn was packed, but we got a waitress's attention.

"Hey, how you all doing today?" Our regular waitress, Sally, grinned at us.

Nelda perused the menu. "Starved, girl. What's good today?"

"The loaded potato soup. Hey! Have I told you I'm leaving?" she asked.

I glanced up. I hoped not before she took our order. "You're quitting?"

"Leaving. My husband and I are going to Kenya. To be missionaries! We've talked about it for years, and we finally made up our minds to go."

Missionaries. I stared at the woman, trying to decide if she was serious. All of a sudden there seemed to be an epidemic of zealots.

Nelda closed the menu. "When are you leaving?"

"Next week. At first it seemed to take forever to get everything done, but now it's all falling into place. You know, I thought I'd be scared, but I'm not; I'm looking forward to going. If this is what God wants me to do, I'm ready."

How confident she sounded. Was I ever that certain about anything?

Sally took our orders and left. Nelda and I eyed each other.

"Kenya," she repeated. "I'd like to visit there someday, but not live there. What gets into people?"

I rearranged the saltshaker a few inches to the right. What indeed—and why the sudden rash of callings? A pang of resentment—or was it guilt?—hit me. Why wasn't I as fired up about God as others seemed to be? Sure, there were times when I sensed something was missing in my spiritual life—when I wanted to be more spiritually tuned in—but somehow I didn't have the hunger the pastor spoke about last Sunday. That limitless drive.

I shook my head. "I don't get these people who leave everything and travel halfway around the world in order to serve

God. Can't they find anything here to fulfill their spiritual quest?" Poverty. Injustice. The downtrodden were everywhere you looked. "I bet Sally will be ready to come home after the first week."

Nelda leaned forward, ebony elbows on the table. "I hear there are a lot of flies over there. And sickness. You know, Sam Littleton is a missionary. New Zealand, I think."

"Papua New Guinea."

Her expression changed, deepened. "Monday morning faith."

"Monday what?"

"Monday morning faith. The gospel sounds real good sitting in a pew on Sunday, but living it come Monday morning is hard."

I nodded, fearing I was afflicted with the same struggle.

Sally brought the salads and drinks. Nelda waved her back when she was about to leave. "Hold on a sec. Let me ask you something."

"Sure, what?"

"This mission trip—did you do a lot of research?"

"Did we ever! I know more about Kenya than most people who live there. The information won't mean much once we get there. We'll have a lot to learn about everyday life. Want some lemon meringue pie for dessert?" Sally tucked the pen in her pocket.

I laughed. "She's on a diet."

"Yeah. The Nelda Thomas Mashed Potatoes and Gravy Diet. What's one little piece of pie?"

"Another inch on the hips."

Nelda sighed. "Bring on the pie."

The afternoon ticked by; I counted the minutes until Sam picked me up. When I wasn't fussing with my hair, straightening the collar on my blouse, or changing earrings, I stayed busy at the computer typing in new purchases. Nelda paused, eyebrows cocked.

"How come you're wearing your new blouse to work? You don't dress this fancy."

"Oh, just in the mood to wear something nice." Nothing said I had to tell her about my plans. Besides, it wasn't a date. A sandwich at the coffee shop wasn't a date.

She slanted a narrow look at me. "Something doesn't add up. You wouldn't be trying to pull my leg, would you?"

"Would I mislead you?"

"In a heartbeat, and it wouldn't be the first time."

"Go on. I have work to do."

She left, but I knew my blouse had whetted her interest. I'd have been better off telling the truth.

Five thirty took its good sweet time rolling around. I shut down my computer and shrugged into my good gray suit jacket that complemented the new mint green blouse with matching embroidery on the color and cuffs. I was being pretty obvious.

Sam was waiting in the corridor. He turned and smiled as I approached. "There you are, right on time."

"I'm always punctual." *Get a grip.* That sounded like something an old-maid librarian would say. What was I doing here? It had been so long since I'd been on a date, I didn't know one line of sparkling conversation.

I caught a flutter of movement out of the corner of my eye. Nelda, all smiles and self-satisfied expression, sauntered by, lifting her hand in a saucy little wave. "Y'all have a good time, y'hear?"

I shot her a threatening glance. She'd been hiding in the walls, spying on me. We'd have a long talk tomorrow.

Sam took my arm and ushered me through the corridor to the coffee shop. From there I led the way back to "our" table.

New waitress tonight; same Sam fascination. The man drew women like honey draws flies. We scanned the menu, made our choices, and gave our orders. He leaned back against the seat. "I've been looking forward to this all week."

My resolve to keep this on a business level melted in the warmth of his smile. So how was I different from the waitresses? He seemed oblivious to the effect he had on the opposite sex. I'd never met anyone with his understated charm.

We chatted—about my job, my parents, my hobbies, my interests. I couldn't remember ever talking so much about myself, but then, no one had ever been interested before. I pushed my plate aside and reached for my dessert, double chocolate brownie with a scoop of vanilla ice cream topped with caramel sauce. I thought about the pie I'd eaten for lunch and pictured my side button blowing and hitting Sam in the temple. I scooted, angling my body toward the doorway. Picking up my fork, I smiled. "What do you do besides research Papua New Guinea?"

"Oh, lots of interests. I read, mysteries and Westerns for fun, nonfiction on a lot of subjects, I like to fish, golf once in a while, and work in my church."

"Yes ... your church work." I laid the fork aside, appetite suddenly gone, and cleared my throat. "How do you know it's a true calling and not something *you* want to do?" Obviously, any child of God wanted to serve him. But thousands of miles away from home in a terrain so crude bugs had a hard time finding the place?

I wanted to do more for the Lord, but with my job and Mom and Pop, when would I find time? I'd joined the choir once but made it to so few Wednesday evening practices that I dropped out.

Sam pushed his plate aside, easing his chair back from the table. "When I started working with missions I didn't intend to get so involved, but something kept pulling me in deeper. One thing led to another. Belinda and I planned to go on longer trips—to test mission waters—and then she got sick. We weren't sure at that time of the Lord's calling, and when she fell ill we aborted the plans."

"Of course." Hard for me to picture him with a wife; he was never with anyone when he came to the library. The topic changed to Papua New Guinea, and I listened as he told me about the country, a land of crotons, coleus, and other ornamental plants. Where papaya and pineapple bordered thatched huts, and the invigorating smell of rolling surf filled the air.

The man was already an expert. Why did he need my help?

Coffee shop employees started mopping the floor, stacking chairs on top of tables—a subtle hint they planned to close. Sam paid the bill and walked me to my car. I unlocked the door and turned to face him. He took one hand and bent toward me, his lips brushing my cheek in a gentle kiss— almost an afterthought. "Good night, Johanna. It's been a wonderful evening."

"Thank you, Sam. It has been nice." Perfect. I would have few others like it, and I knew it.

I got in my car and drove home in a daze. His kiss had been polite and impersonal. That was Sam. Kind. Sold out to the Lord.

How I envied his trust.

I refused to give significance to the evening. The nonevent was a pleasant ending to a hectic day. Nothing more.

But a kiss. Now *that* was unusual from a patron.

I bumped into Sam twice more that October—both times in the research section, and once down on his hands and knees. It is hard to concentrate with such distraction.

Friday night, I was late getting away; it seemed everyone wanted new reading material. Maybe because a drizzle-snow had fallen all day and they all planned to stick close to home.

Close to seven I came home to find my mother in a mild state of panic. "Thank goodness you're here!"

I froze. "What?"

"It's your father. He's having trouble breathing."

I trailed her into the den, where Pop sat in his wheelchair, face pale, chest heaving with the effort to get his breath. One look told me all I needed to know. "We're going to the hospital."

"I'll be all right," he wheezed.

"Don't bother arguing. We're going." I shouldered my purse and pushed his chair out to the car. With Mom's help I got him loaded in the backseat. She climbed in the passenger's side, and I backed out of the driveway and threw the transmission into drive. The emergency room staff knew us by sight. Pop was whisked out of the car and onto a stretcher. Mom and I ran behind the gurney as staff wheeled him to the pulmonary unit.

While the ER staff worked on stabilizing Pop, Mom and I sat in the small waiting area adjacent to the emergency entrance. She gripped my hands so tight I could feel my circulation slow. Her lips trembled. "I'm so worried about him. It seems each spell is worse than the last."

I patted her arm. "He'll be all right. The doctors know what to do."

Her eyes filled with tears. "I don't know what I'd do if anything happened to him. We've been together for so many years. He's my anchor in life."

"Nothing is going to happen, Mom." But I knew my words were empty. He wouldn't always be all right; Pop was getting worse all the time. He'd confided one day that trying to breathe was like having a straw up one nostril and pinching the other closed. That was his constant struggle. I didn't know what would happen to Mom when he drew his last labored breath. But I did know this: he was living on borrowed time.

The door to the waiting room opened and an older woman entered. My mouth dropped open. She was leaning on Sam Littleton's arm.

I sat up straighter. There he was, large as life. I'd gotten used to seeing him around the library, but what was he doing here? Tonight? And who was the lady he was supporting on his arm?

He spotted me and concern spread across his wind-dappled features. I shook my head, the irony hitting me. I got up and walked toward him. "Hello. Seems we can't go anywhere without bumping into each other."

"Hello, Johanna." His gaze indicated the older woman. "Clarisse has come down with the flu, and there wasn't anyone to bring her to the hospital, so I volunteered."

Yes, he would do that.

I introduced him to Mom, then returned to my seat while Sam checked Clarisse in and helped her fill out insurance information. Moments later they followed a nurse down the hall.

"Who'd you say that is?"

I glanced at Mom. "A library patron."

"Nice-looking man. Clean-cut."

"Ummm?" I picked up a *Reader's Digest* and turned to the humor section. "Is he? I hadn't noticed."

I might not be called to the mission field, but I was finding there was one gift I had in abundance.

The gift of misleading.

<hr />

Between the first week in November and Thanksgiving, it seemed that I bumped into Sam around every corner. We'd go for coffee or get in a long discussion over Papua New Guinea's main income source: copra, which was produced from stands of coconut palms. I knew little about it other than what I'd read, but Sam was well acquainted with the villagers' method of acquiring cash, and I found his knowledge fascinating.

We'd gotten pretty cozy until the morning he set a stack of books on the return counter. "Did I tell you I'm leaving for a couple of weeks?"

I didn't look up. If I had, my eyes would have been gaping. Papua New Guinea? Had the trip been moved up? I went light-headed. Had trouble catching my breath. "Leaving?" I managed the right touch of polite indifference. There was that gift of misleading again. I really was getting good at it.

"One of the leaders had to back out of a mission trip because of family problems, so I'm taking a group of nurses to Matamoros for a week. I'll be supervising a medical clinic—"

Matamoros. Mexico. Suddenly I could breathe again. "How nice!"

My sheer exuberance blew him off his feet. Never had I shown such enthusiasm for his work. *Mexico!* He wouldn't be gone nearly as long as the Papua New Guinea trip! Would he be back before the holidays?

My enthusiasm knew no bounds. I wanted to lasso my tongue and lash it to my hip. "But I understand they're not encouraging tourists in Matamoros—too dangerous anymore."

"We'll be staying close to the border. It's not as threatening—"

"Oh, I'm sure you're very cautious. Nurses, huh?" I leaned closer. "Pretty ones?"

"Not as pretty as you."

"How nice! You are a good man, Sam Littleton." And *blah* and *blah* and *blah*, until I'm sure the man's head was spinning like Carrie in *The Exorcist*. Sam ceased trying to interject and in the most polite way allowed me to make a complete idiot of myself.

Finally, he leaned against the counter. "It's a short, unexpected trip. I'll be back before you know it." His eyes searched mine. "You know me, Johanna. I'd always wanted to do more than fill a pew."

The simple declaration hit me square between the eyes. Pew filling was what I did best.

"I hope you have a good experience, Sam. You'll have my prayers."

I meant every word. He was an exemplary person. God had done a good work in this man. Sam would be as dedicated in Matamoros as he would on the Papua New Guinea mission field: as caring, sympathetic, and determined to do what he believed God wanted him to do.

Most important, he would be away from Saginaw. Which meant I could get my priorities straight.

"Thank you. We'll have a lot to talk about when I get back."

Was that a hint of relief I heard in his voice? I shoved my glasses up on the bridge of my nose.

He leaned closer and I caught a whiff of his cologne. "I'll bring you back something special. Painted gourds? Twenty-dollar Rolexes?"

I laughed. The man had a sense of humor. My breath caught. "Oh, Sam. I do hope you have a wonderful time and the trip is all you pray it will be."

He smiled and his eyes looked deep into mine. "I'll miss you, Johanna. Your prayers and support mean a lot to me."

"I'll miss you too." My support? He'd miss my support?

Well, of course. I didn't expect more.

He straightened. "Well, I'd better go. Got a lot to get done before I leave."

I had a great need to give him something, like women in historical times giving their knight a memento to carry close to their hearts into battle. I fingered the scarf at my throat, then cold reason stepped in. I'd scare him to death if I gave him a personal item. He'd think I'd lost my mind. *Support*, the man had said. We hadn't reached the commitment stage, and I had no reason to think we ever would.

I held out my hand. "Go with God." How easy the platitude rolled off my lips. Before I would have thought nothing about the phrase; now I asked myself if I believed the blessing.

He held my hand a fraction longer than necessary, his eyes looking deep into mine. "Take care. I'll be back before you know it."

He left and I stared after him, depression closing around me. A week wasn't all that long, but it seemed like an eternity. I'd miss our discussions over cups of green tea. I'd even gotten Sam to switch from coffee a couple of times. I'd miss seeing him pop in and out of the library, miss this gentle, good man who had become a very dear friend.

Good heavens! I was about to burst into tears! Horrified at the thought, I retreated to my office, where I closed the door and sat in the silence for a good long while.

I'd known I'd miss the good doctor, but I'd never imagined how much. I'd be working in my office and see a flicker of movement, then look up expecting to see him walking by. The stab of disappointment when I remembered he was gone worried me. Sam was a tempting diversion, but even if he should show more than a hint of interest in me, Mom and Pop had a prior claim.

On Friday, Nelda paused in the doorway. "Heard anything from Mr. Good Looking?"

"Of course not. Why would I hear from him?" And why would I tell her if I did?

"Thought he might call or something."

"He's deep in Mexico. He's not thinking about me."

She wiggled her eyebrows and pursed her lips. "He doesn't have e-mail?"

"How should I know? He's in the boonies—I don't think they make an extension cord long enough to reach him." I was being stubborn and facetious—and loving it.

She flicked a nonexistent speck of dust off her lavender sweater. "Are you sure he's only interested in the research?"

I laid a folder on my desk. "Have you seen my pair of scissors?" Someone was always taking my stuff.

Nelda laughed. "Changing the subject, are we?"

"We are. Have you seen the scissors?"

"They're on my desk."

"On your desk. I hate it when you borrow and don't bring back."

She shrugged. "Don't have a cow. I'll get the scissors. Back to Sam—"

I heaved a sigh and threw up my hands. "I'm not looking for a man. I like my life the way it is!"

"*Fine.* I have nothing more to say on the subject. Sorry I mentioned it—I just think you're trying to hide from life. You're using your parents as an excuse to hibernate. You'll never catch a man's interest unless you try!"

"Don't forget my scissors!" I called after her retreating back. Sheesh. Why didn't people put back what they borrowed?

I grabbed a piece of paper and stared at it. Nelda didn't understand my situation. No one understood. Mom and Pop needed me. Neither Sam nor anyone else could expect me to leave them alone. Besides which, Sam had never even brought up such a subject, let alone discussed it.

I sniffed. Nelda was wrong. I wasn't *hiding* from life. Using my parents as an excuse to avoid a risk. That was non-sense — so like Nelda.

Before closing time a repentant Nelda stopped by my desk. "Look, I'm sorry I shot off my mouth. I need to learn to mind my own business."

"That's all right." I was in a forgiving mood.

"No, it isn't all right. We're friends and I want the best for you, but sometimes I get carried away. Forgive me?"

I sighed. "Sure. I know you meant well, but I can't see any way the situation can change. I'm happy as I am."

"Okay. Friends?"

"Always." I was lucky to have her. Not everyone wanted to be friends with someone who had very little free time for socializing. Somehow we had managed to forge the bonds of a strong relationship, and my life was brighter because of her.

FOUR

Saturday I took Mom to the store and dry cleaners. Sunday, to church. That was the extent of my weekend. I caught myself staring out the window a lot, daydreaming about Papua New Guinea. I should never have done all that research. I knew as much about the place as Sam did, and missions were starting to sound interesting.

But that didn't concern me as much as the fact that Mom and Pop were acting odd. I caught them whispering back and forth, but they fell silent the moment I entered a room.

"Are the two of you up to something?"

Pop grinned, eyes as innocent as a newborn calf. "What makes you think that?" He'd regained his strength from the recent hospital episode.

"Call it a hunch." A very strong one. "I haven't seen Margaret in a few days. Where's the ole broad been hanging out?"

Mom glanced up from her knitting with a frown. "Johanna."

I sighed. "Has Aunt Margaret called in the past couple of days?"

Pop chucked. "As a matter of fact, she was here yesterday. Wanted to know if you were still interested in Harvey. Wanted to remind you that several women at church were giving him the eye, but you were his first choice."

I choked on the jelly bean I'd just popped in my mouth. "What part of *no* doesn't that woman understand? Tell her I forfeit all rights; the other women need to make their move and he can take his pick."

"Line forms on the right," Pop agreed. "She's correct on one thing, though. You need to get out more. I thought maybe you were showing some interest in this Sam your mother met at the hospital."

"Sam's heart is on missions, not women. He's in Matamoros right now, doing mission work."

Mom tsked. "He won't be gone forever, will he?"

Had she been talking to Nelda? "He'll be back—to leave in January for two months."

"Let's see, he's been gone how long?"

"Seven days." Three hours and forty-three minutes. Not that I was keeping track. I just happened to do a lot of clock watching.

"Well, I'll wager a steak dinner he'll be around to see you the moment he gets back."

"Please, Pop." I dropped another jelly bean in my mouth. "Sam Littleton is a friend and a library patron." Well, maybe a tiny bit more, but that wasn't the point; the point was that between Mom, Pop, and Nelda, I was feeling pressured.

Pop sent Mom the "look." She nodded and bent to her cross-stitch. They were up to something. I'd bet a cow on it.

Monday I came home from work to find them waiting for me in the living room wearing expressions that stood out like a black snake in a bathtub. Something was going on, and I had a hunch I was about to find out what.

Mom grinned. "Honey, could we talk to you a moment?"

I'd had a rough day, meetings and year-end budget problems. The last thing I needed was more hassle. "Can it wait until after dinner?"

"We're having pizza delivered. Harriet, it can wait until Johanna has a chance to catch her breath." Pop returned to his newspaper.

I dumped my book bag and purse on the sofa. What was this all about? "Are you all right?" Was there a new health problem I didn't know about?

"We're fine. We have a little something we need to discuss with you, that's all." Pop reached over and took Mom's hand. "We're here alone all day and the isolation gets boring. We've discussed this at length and our minds are made up."

I looked from one to the other. "About what?"

Mom's chin lifted, her lips firmed. "We don't want any argument from you about this. Our decision is firm — and final."

"What decision?" Why didn't they just come out and say it! The suspense was killing me.

Pop glanced at Mom. "We're moving into assisted living."

I gaped at them. "You're ... what?"

"I said we're moving —"

"I *heard* that! What I didn't hear was why you would even *think* of such a thing. Aren't you happy here?"

Why hadn't they just stuck a stick of dynamite in my ear? It would have been less of a shock. Assisted living? When had this come up?

"Of course we've been happy, but we think it's time we made a change." Mom picked a thread off her blouse. "I know this surprises you."

Well, yeah. Ear. Dynamite. "I don't think this is a good idea—"

"It's settled, sweetie." Pop's voice was kind but firm. "We've taken care of the paperwork; we're moving Saturday."

"*This* Saturday? That's less than a week!" My voice squeaked like an unoiled hinge. "I can't get you packed and moved in that length of time!"

"We'll be limited on what we can take." Mom refused to look me in the eye. "I've already started packing what we need. It won't be that big a job. We're going to love living at The Gardens."

I threw my hands in the air. "I can't *believe* you're doing this." In spite of my best efforts, tears welled up in my eyes. "What about me? What will I do if you leave?"

"You'll get a nice apartment close to work and you will have more time for yourself."

"I don't *want* more time. What's wrong with the way things are now? What will we do with the house?"

"Oh, we'll not be in any hurry to sell. We'll let you get settled before we put the place on the market. Megan said she thought she already had a couple of interested parties. Good neighborhood, you know, ideal starter house for a young couple with small children."

"Megan?" I seemed to be in a wind tunnel. All I could hear was sucking air: mine.

"Megan ... our realtor."

Our realtor? "You've already consulted a realtor."

"Figured it would be easier this way. Saved a lot of haggling." Pop grinned. "Look at it this way. You'll have time to make friends and have fun, which you don't have now, and we'll get to play bingo and visit with people our age."

"I thought you were happy here with me." I could not understand why they would make this decision without consulting me. Surely they didn't really want to move to The Gardens when they could stay in their own home. "You're not telling me everything, are you?"

"Oh, yes, honey. I know you're shocked, but we feel this will be better for all of us in the long run. We'll have access to nursing care twenty-four hours a day. There will be activities and people around us. The way things are now, we just sit home alone most of the time. It does get a trifle boring." She nodded toward Pop. "Clive needs extra care too."

"You've never seemed to mind before. What brought on this sudden change of heart?"

Pop sighed. "It isn't sudden. We've been thinking about it for some time. Just weren't sure how to go about it. Then we got the idea to call The Gardens and have them send someone out to talk to us. A representative came by last week, and we went over our situation with him. We liked what we heard, so we signed up, and here we are."

"Then it's a done deal?"

"Yes, dear. You'll come around to our way of thinking when you've had time to adjust. Best thing we can do. Good for all of us. We'll have a one-bedroom apartment, three hot meals a day, and all the activities folks like us can handle." Pop beamed.

The doorbell chimed and I went to answer. Pizza delivery. Dinner in a box. A far cry from the meal I had planned. I was so upset I devoured three pieces.

Later, I cleaned up pizza boxes and then went to my room and called Nelda. "Guess what I got hit with tonight?"

"What? You got hit? Anyone hurt?"

"Hit *figuratively* speaking. My parents are moving to The Gardens, putting this house on the market. They told me to get an apartment. I can't believe this."

Silence.

"Did you hear me?"

"I heard. I'm having trouble absorbing the shock. Why did they do that?"

"They said they got bored sitting home alone." I could hear the aggravation in my voice. Even now that we had thrashed out all the details and I'd looked over the information from The Gardens, I still could not believe my life was about to turn upside down.

"How do you feel about it?"

"Betrayed. Abandoned. They did this behind my back, informing me after the decision was perpetrated."

"If they *had* told you, what would you have done?"

"Talked them out of it, of course!"

"That's why they didn't tell you. Don't make such a fuss about it. They're adults; if it's what they want, go along with them."

"You don't understand. This arrangement will never work out. They'll want to come home, and if we sell the house they'll have no home to come back to. They have not thought this through."

"I'll bet they have. Pop is one smart dude. He knows what he's doing."

Not this time. This time he'd made a serious miscalculation.

FIVE

◎◎◎

A catastrophic mistake.

Moving day and I still wasn't in sync with Mom and Pop's sudden mental collapse. They were out of their blooming minds! I'd been born in this house, lived here all my life. Overnight my nice, safe, comfortable world had taken a nosedive.

Mom called from her bedroom. "I can't take all these picture albums with me. If you don't want them, we'll send some home with your cousin Mack."

"What would Mack want with them?" Those albums went all the way back to Mom's childhood. Most of those people were dead. Neither Mack nor I would know 90 percent of those people.

Mom's voice floated back. "He won't want them, but Margaret will. You know her. She'll take anything that's free."

Well, yes, Aunt Margaret, Mack's mother (and how *did* that woman ever raise a sweet boy like him?) was a pack rat. One trait we had in common. I saved everything. Box tops, pieces of string. Everything.

I hated that about myself, but I hung on to stuff until forced to part with it. In my top drawer I even had headbands I'd worn in grade school. Even so, Aunt Margaret could have the surplus photo albums; Mom had doubles of everything. "Fine with me."

I was headed for an apartment—monthly rent, just like all those divorced men and women trying to live on half an income. I was beginning to realize how lucky I'd had it. No rent, no utilities. I *had* bought groceries and taken care of the cooking, cleaning, and caregiving. But Mom and Pop provided the home. Now I'd be on my own with large chunks of free time and nothing to fill the empty hours. Itty Bitty leaned against my foot, sensitive to my emotions. I stooped and ran my fingers through his short, silky white hair.

Now it would be just the two of us. I'd have to find an apartment that allowed animals; Itty would be home alone all day and he wouldn't like it.

Pop called from the living room, "Johanna, you want these encyclopedias? If you don't, we'll put them in the sale."

"Sale?" I squawked. "What sale?"

"The auction." He sounded matter-of-fact, as if we were discussing the weather instead of my entire lifetime now going into cardboard boxes.

I set the copper teakettle I'd been holding on the stove top and walked into the living room. "We're having a sale?"

He stuffed a wrapped vase into a carton. "We can take a limited number of things with us. You won't have room for all of this junk in your apartment. Best to get rid of it."

I didn't *have* an apartment. I didn't want one either. "Junk? Since when did our personal possessions become junk?"

"Since we don't need them anymore. Possessions are fine as long as you need them, but when you don't need them they turn into burdens."

Maybe he had a point, but I hadn't reached that level of objectivity. To me the things I'd grown up with were memories, mementos, treasures that couldn't be replaced. "Pop ...

events are moving too fast for me. Let's not talk sale or getting rid of the house yet. Give me a little breathing space, okay? You may change your minds, and then what would you do?"

He pulled a copy of C. S. Lewis's *The Screwtape Letters* out of the bookcase. "I want to keep this."

"See? One more reason to keep the house for a while. Determine what we need before we have a sale."

He nodded, and for the briefest of moments I thought I saw mist in his eyes. He cleared his throat and reached for another book. "Honey, we thought about discussing this with you first, but would you have been any more agreeable?"

"I don't like change, Pop." I thought he didn't either. How could he and Mom think they could be happy in assisted living? Most of those folks were trying to escape the tedium of their days.

"No one likes change, Johanna. Your mom and I have fought getting older, but God never intended for life to be the same year after year. We change. We get older. It's life's cycle. No use fighting it; it's coming to every one of us."

Depression settled over me like a burial shroud. "Oh, Pop ... I hate that we're all getting old."

"Ah, honey. Praise God for every year and every grey hair. Some don't live to see their twentieth birthday. Remember the story about how the butterfly's wings grow strong because it has to force its way out of the cocoon?"

Sure, I remembered the story. He'd told it to me when I was a child as we watched a butterfly striving to be born. Pop used nature in creative ways to teach me lessons about life and about God. "A man wanting to be compassionate broke open the cocoon so the butterfly could emerge without the struggle," I recalled.

"And what happened? The butterfly's wings never developed the strength to fly."

I knew where he was heading with this and I wanted no part of it. "I'm not a butterfly." I was a flesh-and-blood human who wanted my life to remain the same.

"No, but you've lived in a cocoon for a long time. Before I die, I want to know you've developed good, strong wings."

"You're going to live for a long time, and I'm terrified to fly. I don't know how."

"Flying isn't hard. We develop our wings through faith, and God does the rest."

I knew he was right, but I was already homesick for my cocoon. "I'll make a list of things that will go into the auction." And I'd take my own sweet time doing it. He might be ready for this move, but that didn't mean I was. A new problem surfaced. "How will you get to church? Are you still riding with me?"

"The Gardens have their own services. On the Sundays I don't feel like getting out, we'll attend there. On good days, they have a bus that will deliver us right to the front door of church. If we run into medical problems, there will be experienced nurses on duty. Don't you slack off on church, though, just because we're not here to go with you every week."

Of course I'd go to church; I hadn't thought of not going. But I couldn't help wondering, where was God in this upheaval? If he was in my corner, I couldn't feel his presence.

Mom called and Pop wheeled into the bedroom to answer. I returned to the kitchen, fighting tears. Jim and Nelda arrived, Mack on their heels. They'd agreed to help with the move. The Gardens had furnished and unfurnished units; my parents had chosen unfurnished so they could have some of their own things. Pop pointed out the comfortable couch and chairs from the den, their bedroom furniture, and the small table and chairs from the sunroom. Whoever bought the house would get the stove and refrigerator. I shut Itty Bitty in my bedroom to keep him out of the way. He was so small it would be easy to step on him in the rush.

We loaded furniture into Jim's truck. Soon the house looked pretty vacant. Oh, they left enough furniture to fill my apartment, but the semblance of my former life consisted of dust bunnies on wood floors. Mom and Pop rode with Mack, and they were off, leaving Nelda to help me sort and pack the personal items they wanted to take.

"What you gonna do now, girl?" She folded towels and packed them in a cardboard apple box from Save-A-Lot grocery.

I slumped down on the needlepoint-covered footstool that Mom had made years ago. "I have no idea. I'm still reeling. Why would they want to leave their home?"

"Two reasons, I'd guess." Nelda perched on the edge of my favorite chair, left behind.

I fixed her with a cynical look. "You have it all figured out, I suppose?"

"Not all of it, but I'll bet I'm close. One, they wanted to be with people their own age. Assisted living is a good step for people who need someone to look out for them but are still able to have a measure of control over their lives."

I sighed. "*I* looked after them, and they had all the control they needed."

"Needed—that's the key. When parents get older, we tend to make their decisions for them. The children run their lives, make their decisions, tell them they're too old to drive or too senile to keep their own checkbooks. Your folks will do fine. They'll have bingo, games, crafts, and social activities—companionship with others their age. They had to get bored staying home by themselves day after day."

It was true. I did everything for Mom and Pop, including setting their bedtime. "You said two reasons."

"As long as they stayed here, you would never leave and have a life of your own."

"I beg your pardon? I *have* a life of my own. You know I never begrudged the time I spent taking care of them."

"I know that." She got up and stretched. "Muscles getting stiff from sitting. Look, Jo, they've set you free."

"Booted me out of the nest, is more like it." And I resented it. No one had asked *me* if I was happy with the changes.

"High time too. A forty-year-old baby bird *needs* to be kicked out. You gotta learn to fly before arthritis sets in your wings."

I pitched a cushion at her. Butterflies and birds. What brought on all this advice about flying?

She caught the pillow and turned it over to read the embroidered motto out loud. " 'You can either agree with me or be wrong.' "

Monday afternoon, I went to my office and booted up the computer. Nelda dropped by, wearing her coat, high-heeled brown leather boots, and one of those narrow, fuzzy neck scarves that were so popular right now. Looking good.

"You plan to spend the night here?"

I swiveled to face her. With Mom and Pop gone I was adrift. "I dread going home to an empty house." I wasn't being fair to Itty, I knew. He kept me company, but I missed Mom and Pop. Without them to care for, my life seemed to have lost meaning.

"How are things at The Gardens?"

"Marvelous." I sounded bitter, but I didn't care. "I dropped by last night, and all Mom and Pop could talk about is how busy they are going to be with bingo and bead making. I may have to make an appointment to see them. Mom called this morning to say that tonight they are having a sing-along, and it might be better if I didn't visit."

Nelda laughed. "Good for her. You need to stop being such a mother hen."

Birds, butterflies, and now a mother hen. I might be short on sympathy, but I had an abundance of insects and fowls coming my way.

Foul. Now that was an appropriate word for my mood.

"Come on, Jo. Shut down the computer. If you don't have anything else to do, come home with me. Jim's always glad to see you."

"No, thanks. I need to stop by the grocery store and pick up a few things." I pushed my glasses back up on my nose, scraping the small mole where the nose pads rested. "Drats."

"What?"

I pulled off the glasses and rubbed the mole. "This thing is a nuisance. It's growing and getting to be an eyesore." Had Sam noticed it?

"So? Get it removed. Nothing to it."

"It isn't your nose."

"That's right, it isn't. But if it *were* me, I'd want the icky thing removed."

She was right; the mole was ugly and needed to come off. "I'll call my doctor tomorrow."

"There you go. We women got to keep ourselves looking good for the men. How long since your last salon appointment?"

I touched my hair. "Why? Do I need one?"

Nelda appraised my mass of graying locks pulled back by a headband. "Oh, yeah. Need a little maintenance."

"Not for a man."

"No, no, not for a man."

I picked up my purse and coat and we left together. Our feet echoed in the tiled library corridor.

"Sam's due back from Mexico before long, isn't he?"

I knew what she was hinting at, but I wasn't taking the bait. "Is he? I wouldn't know." There had been so much going on I'd almost forgotten Sam — well, okay, not forgotten. I knew he was due home soon but wasn't sure when. Even so, I wasn't going to have the mole removed and get a salon appointment because of his anticipated return.

I hadn't totally lost my mind.

Wednesday morning the mole was history. The incision left a dime-sized red spot on my nose. I wouldn't be able to wear my glasses for a few days, and someone — I think Nelda again — suggested I look into contacts. Contacts. Me? The idea was ludicrous, but after not seeing a blessed thing the rest of the day I decided maybe contacts were better than a Seeing Eye dog. Thursday night after work, Nelda drove me to the optometrist. My social life was picking up in ways I had never imagined.

The receptionist was a frequent visitor at the library and greeted me like an old friend. "Johanna, so good to see you. Dr. Heuple is ready for you."

I followed her back to an empty room and climbed into the chair, ready for the eye exam. Dr. Heuple, dark hair looking a lot grayer than I remembered, came in and sat down on a small stool beside me. "So, Johanna. How long has it been since your last exam?"

He thumbed through a manila folder, which I assumed held my records. Not much point in evading the truth. I sighed. "Awhile."

Dr. Heuple looked at me over the rims of his eyeglasses. "Six years to be exact."

"Is that what my record shows?"

"Yes, but I hoped it might be wrong."

"No, I'm afraid that's the truth." I operated on the "if it ain't broke, don't fix it" method. I could still see; therefore I didn't need new glasses.

We went through the usual test, and I summoned enough courage to ask. "I ... what do you think about disposable contacts?"

"Contacts?" The doctor glanced up from the chart he was writing on. "I think they're great—been trying to get you into them for years."

"Do you think I could wear them?" I knew a lot of people who couldn't. Runny, red-eyed, miserable-looking people.

"Sure. Some can put them in and use them right away; others take a little time getting used to them."

I had to get used to them? Didn't people realize I didn't like things I had to get used to? I wanted things I was *already* used to.

Before I could say Jack Sprat, I was wearing contacts. The doctor worked with me a few minutes until I was able to put them in on my own. He wanted me back in a week. At that time, he would order my prescription. I paid my bill and stepped outside the office, seeing clearer than I'd ever seen.

Ah, the miracles of the modern-day world. Amazing.

I loved my contacts. I didn't have to keep pushing them up my nose the way I did with the glasses. Besides, I looked better not having to hide behind those big, black frames.

I kept making excuses to go to the restroom at the library so I could sneak a peek at my new image. Had my hair always looked so drab? No style, just sort of ... there. I pursed my lips. Nelda was right. I was long overdue for a trim. Or maybe ... a change. Yes, a change — to go with my new look. Maybe I would call my stylist and see if she could work me in the next day.

I dialed the salon number and asked for Chantel (*Shawntell*, she told me during my first appointment with her). Her voice came on the line. "Hi, Johanna. What's up?"

My mouth opened — then slammed shut. What was I doing? I'd worn my hair like this since I turned twenty. If she hadn't called me by name, I'd have hung up the phone.

"Johanna?"

"Uh ... yes. I was thinking of changing my hairstyle. Could you work me into your schedule?" I knew I was asking the impossible; you didn't just get a Saturday appointment, but I had been going to Chantel for years. Maybe she could fit me in the schedule.

"Hmm. When would you like to come in?"

"Tomorrow." I held my breath.

"Hmm. Tomorrow?"

"Tomorrow."

"Can you be here by eight o'clock in the morning?"

"Eight? Sure."

"Fine. See you then."

She hung up and I released a pent-up breath. What had I done? Well, maybe we could agree on something that wasn't too drastic.

Nelda came in with a new book catalogue. "Think we ought to order these?" She rattled off a few titles.

My mind was on the upcoming change. A new haircut. Contacts. Mole removed.

Sam Littleton wouldn't recognize me—not that it mattered.

Saturday morning I arrived at the salon fifteen minutes ahead of time. Chantel sat me down with a stack of hairstyling magazines with an order to "find what you want" while she finished working on the woman occupying the chair. The cuts in the magazines all looked terrific. Making those styles look good on me seemed a little iffy. Maybe I'd just tell her to trim the ends.

I was trying to work up enough courage to back out when she motioned me to her cubicle. I arranged the magazines in a neat stack and trailed on back.

"So see anything you like?"

"Nothing I thought would work for me."

"Then we'll just wing it." She whipped a cape around my neck, secured it, and tipped me back to lower my head over the basin.

Wing it? This was my hair we were talking about. And why did I keep running into the concept of wings? And flying.

Chantel rattled something off about a perm and an "awesome look." At this stage I was confused and too tired to argue. I just put my fate in her hands. After all, I'd been certain I wouldn't like contacts and I loved them.

"Sure, whatever." Go for it. If I didn't like it, we could always cut it.

Most of the morning clientele were strangers to me, and so I didn't know who the gossip was about. That made it easier to tune out. Gossip made me uncomfortable. Considering all the things God had to say about it in his Word, I figured he wasn't fond of it either.

Chantel rolled, permed, neutralized, and talked, all the while keeping my back to the mirror while she worked. Two hours later, she whirled me around. "Well, what do you think?"

I stared at my reflection, aghast. My hair stuck out from my head in Brillo Pad tresses. *Little Orphan Annie.* I swallowed, wondering how I could go out on the street looking like this.

"Well?"

"I look like I stuck my finger in a light socket."

She frowned. "It's called the spiral effect."

I didn't care. I didn't want it. My earlier complacent thoughts boomeranged back to haunt me. *If I don't like it, we can cut it?* Ha! The curls started flush with my scalp. If we cut it, I'd be bald.

"It's ... bold."

"But nice."

"It may take some getting used to."

"Give yourself time. You'll love it. It's so sassy. All you need to do is shampoo, condition, and air dry. If after a few days you can't live with it, we'll come up with something."

Maybe a bullet? I hurried to my car and jumped in, flipped down my visor, and stared at my image.

Good grief. Sassy? That didn't begin to describe it.

I was looking at a virtual stranger.

SIX
◎◎◎

Unlocking my front door, I entered the house to the sound of scurrying footsteps. Itty Bitty rushed to greet me. He took one look at the new me, yelped, and reversed his hind paws so fast he skidded on the tiled entryway. It took ten minutes to locate him cowering beneath my bed and another five to coax him to come out. He walked a wide berth around me the rest of the day.

Before heading for the shower that evening, I took a long look in my dressing table mirror, turning my head from side to side to experience the full effect. Now that I'd had time to adjust to the change, it didn't look so bad. In fact, I rather liked it. I looked ... chic. Nothing like the drab Johanna—the outdated and behind-the-times mouse. This was the new me. Everyone had been harping for change. Well, change was on the way, and if they didn't like it, they could deal with it.

Sunday morning I hurried into church as the organist played the opening hymn. Mom and Dad were already in their places when I squeezed past them. Mom glanced up when I slid into the pew. "I'm sorry, this seat's taken. Our daughter sits there."

I turned to look at her and her mouth fell open. "My word! What have you done to yourself?"

Now there was a response guaranteed to inspire confidence. "I changed my hairstyle."

"I'll say you did. Put a pink bow in your hair and you'd look like a poodle."

I opened my hymnal and concentrated on the words. *A poodle.* How insulting. "I think it's very chic."

Mom gave Dad *the look.*

A woman in front of her turned around and frowned, and Mom dropped her voice to a whisper. "Are you going through a midlife crisis or something?"

Not. "Can't I change my hair without throwing everyone into a snit?"

"Well ... if it suits you, it suits me. Where are your glasses?"

"I'm wearing contacts."

Mom's jaw dropped a second time.

"I have to. I had the mole removed."

"What mole?"

"The one ... you know. The one where my nose pad fits." I showed her lest she doubt my claims.

"I didn't know you had a mole."

"Well, I did, but I don't now." My chin lifted. *My hair, my contacts, and my icky mole.* If they could move to assisted living, I could come up with a few bombshells of my own.

After church I asked if they wanted to go out to eat. Providing Mom could bring herself to sit at the table with my new look. She shook her head. "I'm sorry, Johanna, maybe next week. We've been invited to go with a group from The Gardens. They're trying out a new restaurant every week, and this time it's that new Chinese place."

Chinese. I waited for my invitation; it didn't come. They were taking this cutting the apron strings serious.

Sunday afternoon and I had nothing to do and no one to do it with. I took Itty Bitty for a drive, which he enjoyed and I didn't.

I hoped Mom and Dad were happy. *Some*body should be.

Monday morning Nelda was speechless. She stared at me, mouth open and eyes wide. "Yowser. Were you electrocuted?"

"I took your suggestion and saw my stylist."

She circled me, eyes appraising. "I like it. Sassy."

"Mom thinks I look like a poodle."

She snorted. "That's funny."

"You favor the canine look?"

"Shake it off. People will get used to it, and the style knocks ten years off you. Tell you what. Come shopping with me tomorrow night and we'll go to Dillard's and get a makeover."

I started to say no, then caught myself. At this point what did I have to lose? "Sure. Sounds like fun."

I dealt with comments all day Monday at work. Some liked the new hairstyle, some didn't, and some pleaded the fifth. I was never so glad to see a day end. After work, Nelda and I went for the makeover—as though I hadn't done enough. Sam hadn't called or stopped by the library. Though I didn't even know if he had returned yet, I had his reason for not calling me all figured out. He'd had time away, time to think. And he'd realized he wasn't interested in a plain librarian. So I wasn't so plain anymore; I was still a woman who didn't share his mission passions.

A woman who looked like a poodle.

The woman behind the cosmetics bar wore a white smock and thick layers of makeup. She greeted us with open arms.

"Just let me get things together. This is going to be so much fun."

While she was arranging her samples, Nelda nudged me. "Wait until she finishes with us. We're going to be knockouts."

I bet.

The clerk returned and started on me. I wasn't comfortable with someone messing with my face, but I forced myself to relax. She smeared on foundation, and then she started on my eyes. "Don't blink."

I sat frozen in place, terrified to move a muscle while she worked. She tilted the mirror to where I could see. A complete stranger stared back at me. The woman in the mirror had smooth, perfect skin, cheeks touched with blush. The eyebrows were more defined, the eyes shaded with dark blue in the creases, lighter shade on the lids. The eyelashes were long and sweeping. Deep rose lips curved in a smile.

"Well?"

I blinked. "So who is it?"

Nelda laughed. "Girl, you are going to knock Sam Littleton's socks right off."

I gave her a dirty look.

The total bill was staggering — a month's rent plus — but I paid without a whimper. Where had that woman in the mirror been all my life?

Nelda was next, and the results were just as dramatic. We walked out of the department store clutching our purchases, feeling like a pair of Cinderellas. Nelda swayed her hips. "You see the way people are staring at us?"

"Do we look good, or what?"

"This calls for a celebration. How about a double-decker rocky road ice cream cone?"

"How about a salad with no-fat dressing?"

She sighed. "Party pooper."

We stopped at the food court and ordered salads. Nelda speared a piece of lettuce. "You know what? I can't wait for Sam to get back and see what he thinks of the new you."

"He should be back by now. But he won't bother to come to the library again." Regret hit me hard. Why had I gotten my hopes up? I was old enough to know a dalliance when I met one.

"Don't you believe it, girlfriend. He'll hit the door as soon as he gets home, and that man is in for a shock."

I hoped she was right. Not about the shock, but about the door. And him hitting it. Regardless, I hadn't made the changes for him. I hadn't.

I *had* not.

Later I sat in front of my mirror, face washed clean of the makeup and looking more like Johanna. Little packets and containers littered the top of my dressing table. Beauty in a bottle. A new Johanna was unfolding. Maybe she'd been there all along, hidden beneath responsibilities and inhibitions. Was this the real me? Somehow I didn't think so, although now that everyone had gotten used to the way I looked, they were quick to praise the new and improved me.

But what did God think? Did he care how I looked? Did he approve this new emphasis on appearance? I didn't know the answer, and I wasn't sure I wanted to.

All I knew was that the new me seemed sort of phony.

⁂

Thanksgiving Day I ate dinner at The Gardens and played spinner dominoes all afternoon. Sam was not back—or at least he hadn't called. The following Thursday morning I glanced up from the return desk and froze when he breezed through the doorway and headed in my direction. He looked good. Thinner, tanned, a little tired, but confident. Had he grown in his faith even more in the time he'd been gone?

He stopped in front of the counter, peering past my shoulder to my office. "Is Miss Holland in?"

"Sam?"

He scanned the area, turned to look away, then looked back. He frowned. "Johanna?"

I nodded.

He clutched his heart, staggered, pretending to study the new me. I never dreamed the man could be so theatric.

SEVEN

Doctor Sam Littleton stared at me as if I'd grown antlers. He flashed an even white grin, his face tanned as brown as a berry. "Sorry, you took me by surprise."

"I had my hair styled." I touched the spiral mound enhanced with molding putty. Did he like it, or was he (like me) searching for a plausible comment? The style looked great on a twenty-year-old, but on me? I still had my doubts.

He sobered, courteous as always. "It ... looks ... well, I think change is always good."

Generic compliment—never good. "Did you have a nice trip?" *Nice? What's with the* nice? *Johanna, get off it.* I managed a more savoir faire comment. "I trust your trip was successful?" I tilted my head, blinking back at him through the thick Revlon eyelashes I'd added to my morning makeup routine.

"It was good, Johanna. I wanted to be back for Thanksgiving, but we had plane delays for a couple of days." He broke into a smile. "We had three people accept Christ and baptized nine in the Rio Frio. I want to tell you all about it. Are you free for dinner tonight?"

My savoir faire remained intact. "Tonight?" I pretended to review my social calendar. When it came up empty (as I suspected it would, seeing as I had no social life), I replied, "I think I could join you tonight." I noticed he was focused on my eyelashes and hope surged. He liked the new look—the hair, the makeup, the contacts.

I'd even managed to shed a couple of pounds the last two weeks. With Mom and Pop gone, I didn't want to cook.

"What's a good time for you?"

I blinked, still unaccustomed to looking through six inches of thick black mascaraed femininity. *Johanna, you are flirting with this man.*

Johanna, I don't care.

"Six thirty." That would allow me time to go home and change into one of my new dresses and matching shoes (a Nelda thing). I gave him my address and he left, promising to meet me later.

Nelda materialized at my elbow with the subtlety of an elephant at a Tupperware party. "See? I told you he'd be back. What did he say about the new you?"

"He was speechless."

She smacked her hand on the counter. "I *knew* it. So dazzled he couldn't find the words to express his appreciation."

I preened on the inside. Smugness is a terrible thing in the hands of the wrong person. A squiggle of discomfort that was becoming all too familiar hit me. Was this trim and toned woman with corkscrew curls and sophisticated makeup me? Did I recognize myself anymore?

Would the real Johanna Holland stand up?

Nelda shrugged. "He'll like it even more when he gets used to it. Takes a man awhile to adjust. Most of them don't like change."

Well, *now* she tells me. Why had I undergone this transformation if not to impress this man? I could kid myself all day long and say the mole needed to come off, the glasses were annoying, and my hair needed change, but deep down I knew why I had gone to all the trouble, not to mention the expense, of a makeover. I could sum it up in two words.

Sam Littleton.

I turned to look at Nelda—friend, confidant, fashion coordinator. Her jaw plunged.

"What?" She was focused on my right eye. I blinked, giving her the full effect of the lashes. "What?"

Her eyes motioned to my false lash as she gathered an armload of books and disappeared.

I blinked. Good grief, the thing was half off! I managed to get it restuck without raising too many brows.

Sighing, I returned to work. Nelda could waste more time yakking than a bunch of utility men digging a hole.

I left work fifteen minutes early and drove straight home. Itty met me at the door. He'd gotten used to the way I looked by now, but I kept any sudden moves to a minimum. The so-called new me had traumatized the poor thing.

I filled his food dish and put out fresh water. "Guess what, pup? I'm dining out with a handsome man. What do you think about that?"

He sat down and cocked his head. His eyes were so bright and alert I expected him to talk someday. He was smarter than most people. I'd been taking him to The Gardens to see Mom and Pop, and half the residents adored him. The other half hadn't seen him yet. He missed my parents. His days now were long and uneventful. I had yet to look for an apartment. I knew I couldn't delay much longer, but too much change too fast was hard on both of us.

I hurried to dress, wanting to be ready when Sam arrived. I showered and then pulled my new gray and white pinstripe suit out of the closet. I spent thirty minutes on my makeup, determined to be subtle but perfect. Or at least strive for eyelash stability. I remembered the halcyon days when I didn't worry about my looks, just slapped on a little foundation and took off. Now I agonized over every stroke of the lip brush, every feathery touch of shadow. Blend, stroke, layer, line, curl, pat, powder.

I needed to get a life.

The doorbell rang before I had time to wonder if Sam would show up. Great to look at and prompt too. Be still, my heart. I opened the door and turned speechless at the sheer wonder of him. Tall, broad-shouldered, dark silver-streaked hair combed back from his forehead, smiling lips curved beneath a silky mustache. He had a dimple in one cheek. How had I missed that? The man was gorgeous in his gray dress pants, charcoal herringbone jacket, and a black turtleneck. How had he managed to stay single all these years after Belinda's death?

He had reservations at the Seafood Center, a favorite haunt. I ate there because Mom and Pop didn't care for seafood and I didn't mind going by myself. Our hostess showed us to a table by the window. I stared at the well-appointed table and wondered how I, Johanna Holland, had been so blessed. I was having dinner with one of the nicest men in town. My cup was running over.

We ordered seafood platters, with an excellent variety of delectable shellfish. Sam held my hand while he said the blessing. I listened as he asked God to take care of me, and I was overcome by his humble sincerity. Over dessert he talked

about his recent trip, and every word was like a hammer blow
to my heart.

This man was in love with his work—with the people of
Mexico. And Papua New Guinea. People everywhere. Especially those outside the US.

"Have you ever been to Mexico?"

"No." I'd been out of the state only on rare occasions.

"We'll go together sometime—"

"Oh, I don't fly—"

"Then we'll drive. Just past the last intersection in
Brownsville on the US side there's an intersection called Boca
Chica. Then there's a tollbooth. Then we cross a bridge over
the Rio Grande and get to the border, complete with guards,
razor-sharp barbed wire fencing, and security dogs. The
guards may pull us over or they may not. They're looking
for the obvious—drugs and weapons—but more than that,
they're looking for anything we might bring into the country
to sell."

"To sell?"

"Anything that threatens their economy. There are speed
bumps every few yards and a muffler shop on the other side."
He flashed a grin. "Convenient, huh? Now we're in the large
city: Matamoros: Wal-Mart, HEB Markets, Pex-Mex gas
stations, and Super D's—similar to our convenience stores.
The smell of the open sewers is terrible. They call them black
lagoons. There are taco vendors, and schoolchildren dressed in
blue and white uniforms wave as we go by. Soon the landscape
will begin to change, to look like what you would imagine
in Mexico. As we travel deeper and deeper into the country-
side, we begin to leave the flatland and sagebrush, and after
hours, there it is, a deep fertile land lying between mountains.
Pure Mexican culture, our town. The Rio Frio snakes through

the valley. It's beautiful, Johanna. The sugarcane fields, the tropical river. I want to show you my Mexico; I want you to experience the beauty and the fulfillment of working with its people. Then I want you to know Papua New Guinea and its people, the beauty of the land and their culture."

Oh, if only I wanted the same.

My heart ached as I listened. Sam was so excited, so dedicated. But this was a part of his life I couldn't share. At that moment it became crystal clear: if I continued to see this man, I was inviting disaster. He would fulfill his calling, and I would be left behind. It reminded me of an old B-grade Western where the cowboy was in love with his horse and the heroine was left in the dust. Except my cowboy was in love with God.

How could a mortal woman compete with the Almighty?

Despite my realization, I didn't pull away. In fact, that dinner shifted our relationship. I continued to see Sam almost every night, in addition to the hours he spent in the library. In January his work would take him to Papua New Guinea for a month; he had read every book we had about that area of the world. Now he was rereading our entire collection in case he'd overlooked anything. He'd also added missionaries' biographies to his list.

By now I'd started apartment hunting, and Sam came along to cheer me on. I couldn't find a thing I liked. He teased me and said my heart wasn't in the project. Of course he was right.

One afternoon on the way back to the car, I asked why he'd retired so young from his medical practice. His age had never come up in conversation, but he was too young for Social Security—way too young.

"When Belinda died I lost heart for life for a while. Then the Lord began to work on me, and since I was alone, I knew I could do more for mankind than live my life in a sterile operating room."

So like Sam. The Lord had indeed begun a good work in this man and would see it to completion.

If only I knew what God was working within me.

Trees had shed their foliage and shrubs had taken on their bare, wintry look. Almost every morning frost coated the hard ground.

I stamped the last book in Sam's pile and added it to the stack. Instead of gathering them up and leaving, he bent toward me. "How about dinner and a movie?"

I smiled. "I haven't gone to a movie in years." Mom, Pop, and I rented movies to watch in the comfort of our home. Since they'd moved out, I had overdosed on tear-jerking, star-crossed romance flicks until I'd gotten tired of my self-imposed pity party.

"All the more reason to try something new."

Sam kept trying to get me to break out of my shell, as if a new look demanded a new lifestyle.

"What movie did you have in mind?"

He mentioned one I'd heard patrons discussing, and I agreed to go. Nelda assured me I'd like it, and I knew our taste was similar.

I couldn't say why I continued to feed the relationship with Sam. I knew it was hopeless. Come January Sam would be off to Papua New Guinea, and who knew when he'd be back? I didn't want a long-distance relationship; I continued to tell myself I didn't want a relationship at all. But I knew I was fooling no one, not even myself.

With each passing day I was falling more deeply "involved" with Sam.

I dressed with care that evening. The movie was a documentary, a general audience rating. It wasn't a romantic evening on the town, but for some reason I decided to be a little more daring than usual. Instead of more conservative attire, I wore something that was more Nelda than Johanna, a leopard-print skirt and matching shawl with a black scoop-necked top and gold hoop earrings so big you could throw a basketball through them. I gelled my hair, scrunched it into spirals the way Chantel had taught me, and applied makeup and false lashes. One touch remained. I climbed onto my three-inch spiked-heel shoes Nelda and the sales clerk had insisted were so me. I was sure the footwear added a whole new perspective to how people saw me. The shoes were so high I feared they might give me a nosebleed.

Or a panic attack. I was afraid of heights.

I hobbled out to the living room to await my prince. Itty took one look at me—and ran.

———— ❧ ————

The theater was crowded. While Sam purchased our tickets I stood in the lobby enjoying the Christmas decorations: twinkling lights and a big sleigh holding Santa and toys, pulled by a blinking-nosed Rudolph. I followed him (balanced on the three-inch spikes) to the refreshment counter.

"Want something to drink? Popcorn? Candy?"

I nodded. "Diet soda, thank you."

We made our way through the crowd and found seats halfway down. The theater was filling up. We had time to take a few bites of popcorn before the lights dimmed and the screen came to life.

I settled back and tried to relax. The date was going well. I looked good. Life was good.

* * *

Later Sam held my hand as we worked our way through the crowd. We stepped outside, which left me a bit disoriented, like moving from one world to another. Rain came down, not a downpour, but a decent shower. Sam paused beneath the canvas awning. "You wait here while I get the car."

I started to protest and then stopped, knowing I could never run across the parking lot in these shoes. I couldn't walk—forget run. Puddles filled low places. There was a sullen grumble of thunder and a flash of lightning. The rain fell in earnest.

When Sam's BMW braked in front of the theater, I hurried toward the car. Rain pelted me, increasing in velocity. My left foot slipped off my new platform shoe, twisting my ankle and throwing me off balance. My arms pivoted like a windmill in a hurricane, trying to find something to hold to. My ankle gave and I sat down on the rain-soaked curb, water soaking through my new leopard-print skirt. Pain ripped my ankle.

Sam bolted from the car and hurried around the hood to help me to my feet. I leaned against him, feeling the blood drain from my face. His voice came from a distance. "Johanna? Are you hurt?"

Yes! I was crippled for *life*. "My ankle," I gasped. "I can't put any weight on it." Plus I was going to black out any second. A gust of wind-driven rain lashed my face, startling me back to consciousness. *God telling me to get a grip?*

Sam knelt and gently manipulated the foot and ankle. When I yelped he shook his head. "I think it's just a nasty sprain, but we'll need X-rays to make certain nothing's broken." His eyes focused on the inappropriate footwear, but he refrained from sharing his thoughts. Thank heaven. He helped me into the car and drove to the emergency room.

I hopped into the hospital, leaning on his arm, still wearing my killer shoes. It was either that or go barefoot. I hadn't gone barefoot in public since my teen years. The reception desk was a couple of miles from the door, or so it seemed when one is trying to reach it by hopping on one foot and dragging the other.

I apologized to Sam. "I'm sorry. I should have worn sensible shoes."

He smiled. Though gracious as ever, his expression left little doubt that he agreed. I caught a peek of myself in a lobby mirror. My hair had swelled to monstrous proportions. Primal Headhunter came to mind. Black mascara ran down both cheeks. I was certain either one or both fake lashes were out of kilter by now. My eyes were so dry they squeaked, and I'd left my contact case at home.

I filled out the required form and Sam carried the information back to the receptionist. She reacted the way all women acted when confronted with his startling Tom Selleck looks. She drooled.

I wanted to throw a magazine at her.

After a thirty-minute wait, I was ushered into a cubicle. Dr. Walker was short, with a stocky body, white hair, and an overworked expression. I remembered him from a couple of visits he had made to the library. He glanced at my shoes. "Ah. A woman with a death wish."

For a moment I thought about taking offense, but he was right. As soon as I got home these invitations to disaster were going in the trash, and I was going back to sensible shoes. I didn't need this kind of humiliation.

After poking and prodding my ankle, he announced (like Sam) that I had a bad sprain. He wrapped the injury and gave me a prescription for pain pills. I hobbled out, barefoot now, unable to get my shoe back on and not feeling up to wearing a three-inch high shoe on one foot with nothing on the other. Sam leaned over the desk, talking to the receptionist, drinking coffee from a white foam cup.

We stopped by an all-night pharmacy on the way home. While we waited, Sam suggested a pair of crutches. I cringed at the thought but purchased them anyway. By now my pride had gone down the drain. With Sam I was either falling on the floor in the library hallway, sliding beneath my car, or falling off curbs. He had to suspect I was clumsy.

He helped me into the house, and I slumped down in a chair, crutches propped within reach. Itty whimpered and hid behind a chair. I was turning my dog into a neurotic mess. He seemed to hate change as much as I did.

"Are you going to be all right here alone?" Sam's concern warmed my heart. "I'll call Nelda and see if she can come over and stay the night with you."

"It's just a sprain. I'm going to take a pain pill, and I'm sure I won't know a thing until morning."

Sam sent me a questioning look, but after he was assured I'd be fine, he said good night and left. I hobbled over to the door to lock it. After making sure everything was secure, I made my way to the bathroom, where I spent a good two minutes staring at my reflection in the mirror.

My hair was frizzled and bushed out like a banshee. The dark mascara circles made me look like a clown, and my new leopard skirt was a damp, wrinkled mess. Sam had been kind and helpful, but I'd detected a certain touch of reserve. I wasn't sure he favored my new look. But I *was* sure I didn't care for it. I looked like a train wreck with no survivors.

The next day I hobbled into work on crutches. Nelda watched me thump my way across the wooden floor. "My goodness." Her hands came to her hips. "That was one rough date."

I struggled into my chair, out of breath, my armpits aching from the stupid crutches. "I twisted my ankle when I fell off those platform shoes you made me buy."

One brow rose. "Now why didn't I realize this had to be my fault?"

"Those shoes are *dangerous*. The emergency room doctor said so."

Nelda sniffed. "What does he know about fashion? Just because you had a little incident? Could have happened to anyone. Why blame the shoes?"

I fixed her with a cold look. "Because the shoes were the reason I fell. They aren't safe."

"But they're stylish. Girl, you looked smokin'."

I didn't doubt one bit that my foot was "smokin'" when I hobbled into the emergency room. And so was I — for buying the ridiculous things. "They're an accident looking for a place to happen. I'm pitching them in the trash."

"Fine." Nelda blew it off, but I could see I'd offended her fashion maharishi. "They're your feet. Wear what you like. I'll work the desk today. You stay in the office."

The hours dragged by. The pain medicine left me feeling woozy and out of it. Sam called to check on me, but he didn't come around. My heart leaped when I saw the BMW parked in front of my house when I got home. I parked and maneuvered my way out of the driver's seat to find him standing beside me. I'd been so engrossed in getting my balance on the crutches I hadn't seen him approach.

He lent a hand to steady me. "Easy now."

When we reached the house, he followed me up the walk and waited until I'd unlocked the door and invited him in. Itty bounded to meet us, bypassing me for Sam. He bent and scooped up the wiggling little bundle of short white hair. The Maltese's black button nose quivered; his mouth dropped open, tongue pink and lolling, as Sam scratched behind the dog's ears.

I dropped down in the nearest chair and Sam sat across from me. We sat for a moment in silence. Sam looked as uncertain as I felt. He cleared his throat as if he'd just made a decision. "Shall we have takeout tonight or should I cook for us?"

That is the moment I made my second serious mistake: I allowed the relationship to shift to a different level. We were now talking like a couple.

"Takeout."

"Takeout it is. I vote for Chinese."

I did too.

Right there, right then, on a darkening mid-December afternoon, our relationship turned a dangerous corner. We liked the same things—basically. We were both willing to change. If he'd suggested Thai food I would have agreed to please him. I was sure the change would lead to disaster, but I was powerless to stop it.

Not unlike a hapless driver of an out-of-control car, watching the headlights of an approaching semi.

EIGHT
◎◎◎

I continued to sow a failed crop, dating Sam, aware the ever-growing relationship would never work. But somewhere in my heart I hoped for a miracle. Sam would change. I would change. I was sure of it.

And I was wrong. Nobody changed.

Christmas arrived, and Sam spent the morning with Belinda's parents, then we joined Mom and Pop for late-afternoon church services at The Gardens. We stayed for the evening meal, then headed to my house to exchange gifts. I oohed and aahed over my favorite perfume; he loved the silver cuff links I'd bought for him.

Like a Norwegian freighter, Sam plowed on with his plans to leave for Papua New Guinea. His departure was down to days now. I continued my work at the library and my half-hearted apartment search. Mom and Pop were thriving in their new atmosphere, a fact I resented. I smarted off a lot the few times I was invited to have dinner at their table.

I eyed my dinner plate the Thursday night after Christmas, replete with garnish. "It must be nice to have three hot meals a day." I now existed on Very Cherry yogurt and packaged peanut butter crackers.

"Johanna—" Pop reached for a pat of butter—"I brought you into this world, and I can just as easily take you out."

Pop had never lifted his voice to me, let alone a hand, but I knew I was crossing the line with my persistent resentment. What could I say? I still had bruises from being kicked out of the nest.

On New Year's Eve, Sam and I had a dinner date, and I sensed something different about him. Sort of a suppressed excitement tempered by anxiety. There had been a quiet edginess between us all evening. I think he was feeling his imminent departure as much as I. After dinner, he pushed his dish aside and rested his folded arms on the table.

"We need to talk."

Yes. Be still my heart. He sounded so serious. Could it be ... Was he about to mention marriage? Nothing had been mentioned, but we could feel the connection between us — the unspoken longing. Was it possible?

Was he going to give up mission work for me?

I didn't know whether to feel glad or culpable. What about God? Would he be mad at me? *Why, of course not, Johanna.* Was he mad at the hundreds of thousands of disobedient children he smote?

I shook my head. Of *course* he was! And if he still smote people, I was edging to the front of the line.

Still I was geared up to give Sam at the least an "I'll think about it" when he held up a warning hand. "Don't interrupt until I'm finished, okay?"

I eyed him. Somehow he didn't look like a man on the verge of proposing. Well then, what was on his mind? Oh dear ... breakup. He was going to break off the relationship!

He reached for my hands, expression sober. Soft candlelight splayed across the white cloth. His eyes searched mine, and I realized whatever he had in mind was of utmost importance.

"I want you to come on the mission trip with me."

I stared at him, stunned into silence. He couldn't be serious. I knew love was blind, but even Sam should see how preposterous that was.

"You ... but ... I ..." The idea startled me so that I couldn't put a coherent sentence together.

"Not for the entire mission. I'm not sure how long I will stay, maybe a couple of months."

I swallowed. "How long would you want me to stay?" *Johanna! Stop! Don't consider it!*

"Three weeks — a month. Stay a month — long enough for you to see if you take to the mission field. I know you've never considered mission work, but the trip will allow you a chance to experience the village, its people. What do you think?"

There was more to it than just seeing the country, and I knew it. This trip would give me a chance to see if I could live Sam's life. The tacit, improbable thought seesawed back and forth between us. I sat staring at my hands, which were quivering.

He managed a smile. "You may speak now."

I could? I couldn't think of a single word to say. Then reality kicked in and I cleared my throat. "Sam, I appreciate what you're trying to do, but it won't work. I've seen the pictures and heard the stories. I couldn't live like that — not even for a little while." No indoor plumbing. Flies. Snakes, bugs, disease.

His hold tightened on my hand. "I don't expect an answer tonight. All I'm asking is that you think it over. But don't think too long, because you'd have to get your passport and visa before you leave, and we're already pushing the paperwork deadline."

What *was* it with people in my life not understanding a simple *no*? I shook my head. We didn't have the same calling, no matter how much I wished we did.

Sam's voice came as if from a tunnel. "An extra sixty dollars will expedite the passport process, and I'm a doctor. I can administer the required inoculations." His straightforward gaze silenced my protests. "I know this is frightening to you. Don't say yes or no. All I'm asking is that you think it over. Promise me you'll do that."

Oh, I could promise all right, not that it would do any good. I couldn't leave everything familiar and go to some faraway land because I had fallen in love with this man. "All right, I'll think about it."

What? Someone other than me must have said that!

I stared back at Sam, resolve weakening. Two weeks ... that wasn't a lifetime commitment. Maybe I could think of it as an adventure, one that I could end whenever I wanted. I smiled. "I do have several weeks' vacation —"

"That's my girl." He squeezed both my hands. "But remember, we're short of time and there is a lot to do." His gaze softened. "When I lost Belinda I never thought I would find anyone that would fill my heart and life as you have, Johanna. I'm in love with you, you do know that."

Words failed me. I nodded. Though we'd never voiced our feelings, our love had become obvious. I didn't need bells and whistles; what I'd found in Sam I had never dared to hope I would find in anyone. I adored him. He was twelve years my senior, but we were soul mates. That much I couldn't deny.

Doubt reared its ugly head.

What about Mom and Pop? Even though I no longer lived with them, I couldn't go sailing off to another continent and leave them in Saginaw with Aunt Margaret. And Itty Bitty. I couldn't go away and leave him. Sam didn't seem to understand my responsibilities . . .

That night I didn't drop off to sleep as usual. I lay awake, watching the digital clock turn the hours, wondering how I'd gotten so involved with a man I could no longer dismiss from my mind. God worked in mysterious ways, but this perplexing situation had me scrambling for answers. Before the night was over I was down on my knees, begging for guidance.

Before work the next morning I dropped by Mom and Pop's, planning to discuss Sam's invitation. I was certain I knew what they would think of me traipsing halfway around the world with a man I'd known only a few months, but I needed support.

Too bad my parents had turned senile overnight.

"Excellent!" Pop clapped his hands. "Good idea. Go for it."

"Are you out of your mind! Go schlepping off to Papua New Guinea for a month with a man I just met? I can't believe you said that."

"You know the man. He's a good, solid person. We trust your judgment, honey. We're doing fine here, and if we have a problem we can always call Margaret."

Margaret was as old as dirt. How could they expect her to help? "You mean to tell me you don't care if I leave—" I snapped my fingers—"just like that! I'll be gone for two, maybe three weeks! I'll spend that time living in a mud hut with uncivilized natives and bugs and rodents!" *Why* would my parents encourage me to do such a thing?

Mom smiled. "Sounds like fun."

So said the woman who thought she was roughing it when she went two days without air-conditioning last summer during the power outage. "You don't mean that."

"I do mean it. New experiences are broadening." She tilted her chin, the gesture daring me to contradict her. "It would do you a world of good, Johanna, to see how the other half of the world lives."

"Look, honey." Pop shifted in his leather recliner. "Sam's a dedicated, God-fearing man, and he loves you. Serving God on the mission field is an honor few of us ever get an opportunity to do. Who knows? You may find your purpose in life."

"You don't think I'm already living it?"

"I think you should listen when an opportunity arises. The good Lord may be trying to tell you something."

"Just how do you know so much about Sam?" I asked, suspicious now.

Pop shrugged. "He mentioned that he was in love with you when he called New Year's Day. That's all I need to know."

I groaned. "Tell me this wasn't *your* idea."

He didn't answer one way or the other. "Trust in God, Daughter. He won't put you into a situation without giving you the wherewithal to handle it."

I made a *poof* sound. "You don't know that."

"I know more than you think."

"I know what we should do." Mom put her handwork aside. "Let's pray about it."

"Good idea." Pop reached for our hands.

Before I could protest he started to speak to God about my problem. I was all in favor of prayer, but had I been set up? If there was a chance God was in on this, did I want to know? However, there was something sobering about hearing my parents pray for me. There were tears in my eyes by the time Pop finished asking God to look after me, to grant me wisdom and peace.

Goodness knew *some*body needed to.

Sam phoned that night. "How's the woman I love?"

"Other than being in love and confused, I'm thinking." That was as far as I could commit at this point. That and the admission that late that afternoon I had written a fifty-dollar check and applied for a passport. The step wasn't binding. It never hurt to have a passport. I might decide to go to England sometime.

Well, I might!

"Honey, I'm not trying to pressure you into anything, but I want you to come with me. You know that, but it's your decision."

I choked back tears. "I'll give you an answer soon, Sam. I promise." When I hung up, I dropped to my knees and gave in to the tears, pleading with God for a solution. What I wanted was for him to release Sam from this calling. Unfortunately, I didn't expect that to happen.

Nelda marched into my office January 2, hot as a camel's saddle. "Just what do you think you're doing?" She jabbed a scarlet-tipped forefinger in my direction. "You have been *avoiding* me, girlfriend. I am not happy."

"That's supposed to concern me?"

"Honey, when Nelda's not happy, ain't nobody allowed to be happy. Spit it out. Did he ask you to marry him?"

I lifted a dispassionate shoulder; I loved to yank her chain. "He who?"

"Don't make me hurt you, girl."

"What on earth would make you think that Sam Littleton would ask me to marry him?"

She crossed her arms and eyed me, as mean as a snake with shingles.

"Mr. Littleton asked me to accompany him on his upcoming mission trip to Papua New Guinea."

When she stopped laughing and pulled herself together, she took a deep breath. "You know, that's not as wild as it sounds."

"It's outright hair-raising. Can you picture me living in a hut?"

"Maybe. You've changed a lot—you're not as prim and uptight as you used to be."

"I beg your pardon? I am not prim. How insulting. Just because I don't swing from rafters and scratch fleas—"

"Girl, you were as stiff as an unopened package of spaghetti."

"I am not!"

"Maybe not now, but you used to be. You've loosened up. Look, Jo, you've got a lot of vacation time coming, and the new library board of directors has decided we either use it or lose it. You can spare a few weeks' vacation. Go with him. What's it going to hurt? I hear the southern Pacific is beautiful."

"Oh, Nelda." I couldn't hold back any longer. "I'm terrified. What if I get over there and hate every moment of it—and I will! He'll see the real Johanna—shallow, spoiled, the fortitude of a slug."

"Girl, where is your *spirit*? God can take care of you in Papua New Guinea same as he can here."

"You haven't heard the stories. The village is so primal." I shuddered. "I don't—maybe I'd stare!" I shook my head, falling silent.

"One month, Johanna. You can do anything for that length of time and you might love it. Where's your zest for life? Neither one of us is getting any younger. Live! Experience life while you can."

"What about the food? I'm not sure I can eat strange things—and if that means I'm spoiled, then yes, I am." I would *not* eat bugs. Or reptiles or any other gross thing like I saw on *Survivor*.

"One day at a time, girl. One day at a time."

I wanted to stay home. I wanted Sam to enjoy his retirement and serve God, but why couldn't he volunteer for medical clinics in Saginaw? I wanted him in the States. Let someone else work the mission field. Most of all, I wanted my safe, secure, boring life back.

I didn't think I had the chance of a snowball in August of getting what I wanted.

The passport did it. When the thing arrived in the mail a week later, I sat for a long time, holding it and thinking about what it represented. To my surprise, intrigue overshadowed my doubts. What would it be like to travel so far away? To witness the things Sam had talked about? Meet the people he spoke about with such warmth and dedication; behold the beautiful scenery he loved so much?

How would I make myself get on the plane?

Later that evening I summoned enough nerve to pick up the phone. I had kept Sam waiting long enough. I dove into dark waters, headfirst.

I, Johanna Holland, was going to the end of the earth.

***

January 15th arrived long before I was ready. The past few days had been utter chaos. I'd made list upon list, trying to ready myself for the upcoming adventure. Nelda and Jim promised to look after Mom and Pop and to assume Itty's care while I was gone. I was going to miss that pup. Sam had updated my inoculations. Nelda and Jim drove us to the airport to see us off.

Jim hugged me. "You're going to be fine, Johanna. Have faith."

I hugged him. He was solid, dependable, and symbolic of all I was leaving behind. He released me and reached to shake Sam's hand. I walked into Nelda's waiting arms.

"Keep trusting, girl. I'll be praying."

I managed a faint smile. "Then my worries are over."

"Got that straight." She gave me the thumbs-up. "Monday morning faith — not!"

They announced our flight, and we boarded the regional jet in Saginaw to fly to O'Hare and then begin the long flight with a thirteen-hour time difference from Chicago to Papua New Guinea. My insides were pulp. I had been up half the night popping antacid like M&Ms.

I stowed my carry-on bag beneath the seat in front of me and fastened my seat belt. My nerves hummed like a high wire. If Sam hadn't been seated between me and the aisle, I might have bolted and chased Jim and Nelda down for a ride home. The fear of disappointing Sam kept me seated. I had flown once in my life, the year the librarian's convention was in Los Angeles. California was too far to drive, but for the prior twenty consecutive years, thank goodness, the conventions were held in states where I either took the bus or drove.

The flight attendant stood in front of us, giving a demonstration. "In the unlikely event of a water landing, your seat cushion will serve as a flotation device."

I didn't want to hear about emergencies, imaginable or otherwise. A picture of me clinging to the flimsy seat while a school of hungry sharks circled me consumed my thoughts. My stomach heaved and my eyes located the paper bag tucked in the seat pocket in front of me. Maybe I wouldn't need it, but I located it just the same.

Staring out the small window, I thought about all I was leaving behind, the safety, the people I loved ...

My eyes narrowed. The same people, come to think of it, who had worked very hard to convince me to make this journey to the unknown. Maybe I wasn't as loved as I'd imagined.

Sam reached over and took my hand. "Relax. It'll be fine."

I memorized every instruction, every nuance, and repeated them over and over in my mind. In the improbable event of loss of pressure or a water landing (translation: if the plane went down), I was to reach out and grasp the dangling yellow oxygen mask, place it over my nose, and tighten the strap, then *calmly* (she kept emphasizing that word) rip off the back of my seat and clutch it to my pounding chest. I could do that—faster than you can slap a tick.

An overweight businessman wearing a blue shirt with underarm sweat stains loomed over me still trying to force a bulging backpack into the overhead bin. Sitting next to the window, a young woman with earphones kept beat with the music, slapping her hands on her jeans. Perspiration rolled from my temples; the plane's interior was hot.

I glanced at Sam, this man I loved more than life itself. Who was this person? And why was I putting my future in his hands?

The flight attendant was still talking about the possible perils. I tried to focus but noted very few of our fellow travelers were listening. If we did encounter disaster, I doubted calm would reign. We'd have no idea what to do. I decided to pray the entire trip. If I kept God's attention long enough, he'd be alert to any strange happenings.

The plane taxied down the runway, then took off with a rush of engines. I'd prepared myself for the mighty thrust that sent us airborne. The hushed *whoosh*, the sense of lifting, lifting. We were in the air! The ground and the runway rushed beneath us. *Heaven help us, we are flying.* My eyes skimmed the packed cabin. Most of us were overweight. What if our combined pounds brought us spiraling to the ground? Would it help if I held my breath?

The flight to O'Hare was fast and (thank you, God) uneventful. We changed planes and after a short delay took off for Papua New Guinea. I watched the United States, my country, slip away beneath us. I'd really done it. I'd burned my bridges. The pilot would never turn around and take me back to the airport.

Sam leaned his seat back and encouraged me to do the same. He took my hand, holding it, his presence calming my jitters. "Let me tell you something about Papua New Guinea."

I knew he was hoping to distract me, and that was fine with me. I needed a little distraction.

"One of the primary languages spoken is Kairiru."

"That's a language? Sounds more like something to drink."

He chuckled. "The word *Kairiru* comes from a lake in the extinct volcanic crater at the top of the mountain."

"There are volcanoes in Papua New Guinea?"

"Extinct, Johanna. Legend has it that the lake is named after a powerful supernatural being that created the lake and still lives there."

"Supernatural being? Like what?"

"Oh, it's supposed to have a body like a huge snake and the head of a thick-bearded man. It came to the volcano after an argument with its brother."

Huge and *snake* were not two words I wanted to hear in the same sentence. A snake with the head of a man? "Where does the brother live?"

"Nowhere. It's folklore." He brought my hand to his mouth and pressed it to his lips. "Nothing for you to be concerned about." He shifted position, stretching his long legs in the cramped aisle. "Most modern Papua New Guineans have gone to high school and beyond."

"Do they speak English?"

"Many do, although our village is archaic and remote. We've established the barest communication."

How would I be able to connect with these people? I didn't want to fail Sam. I knew as much about the landscape by this time as he did, but I was ill-equipped to serve the Lord in a strange land.

I looked up to find Sam's eyes on me. The smile lines made me think he knew what I was thinking. His grip on my hand tightened. "God will meet your needs, Johanna. You can teach love and preach love, but the true message of love is never completed until you give love. You're about to do that, and God's about to work a miracle in your life."

How I prayed that was true and not just Sam's desire. God promised to provide the need, but not always the desire — that much I did believe.

"The missionaries I'll be staying with. They speak English, don't they?"

"They do. You'll be staying with Eva and Frank Millet. Their home is St. Louis. They've been serving in Papua New Guinea for twelve years now."

"So long." My time there would be minuscule compared to twelve years. The time spent there would be a mere blink in my lifetime. I resolved to cease complaining and do whatever I could to serve where I was needed.

Sam talked throughout the long flight as the plane left American soil and soared over the Pacific Ocean. He kept my mind off flying by telling me stories, some funny and some sad, about the natives and the missionaries. Under his spell I relaxed somewhat and started to feel better about the visit.

"We won't stay with the same family?"

"No, there isn't room. I'll be staying next door with Bud and Mary Laske. They've been working with the villagers for four years."

Four years? Even that sounded like a long time to me. Four years was a commitment — and I could see a problem. Everyone on this trip would be a dedicated, called missionary. Everyone except me. I was the imposter, the outsider, the one who was there because I couldn't think of any way to get out of it. God knew this wasn't a serious commitment for me.

How did he feel about that?

He was an all-wise, all-knowing God, right? Then he knew I wouldn't be worth a stuffed fig as a missionary, and that's why he hadn't called me to the field. The admission took a lot of pressure off. I'd enjoy the journey—treat it like a vacation. The days would pass, and at the end of my visit I'd be winging my way back home and Sam would understand, more than I could ever make him understand with words, that I was not suited for his life.

What if that doesn't happen?

A chill raced through me and I leaned back in my seat, willing tense muscles to relax. My fears were imaginary ones. I was open to a miracle.

The plane shifted hard, jolting me into an upright position. What was that? A quick glance around me revealed most of the other passengers remained unperturbed, as if they hadn't noticed the blip. An older woman seated across the aisle looked up for a second, then returned to her book. Since I'd flown once, maybe I was attaching too much importance to the unexpected movement, though it had been rather nerve-wracking. I leaned back and closed my eyes, willing myself to relax.

The aircraft bounced. No one could mistake it the third time. There was a scattering of startled cries. I jerked upright, darting frightened glances in all directions. The flight attendants looked calm enough, but that was part of their jobs. Paragraph four, page one in the training manual: *"Never scream out loud. There is a strong chance you will throw the passengers into a panic."*

I gripped the seat back in front of me. Never mind that we were cruising at thirty-six thousand feet. I wanted off.

"Johanna, are you aware that more people are killed by mules a year than air crashes?"

"I stay away from mules too."

The pilot's voice came over the intercom. "Ladies and gentlemen, we are experiencing a small problem."

Understatement of the year! Call it what it was! Impending death! Spiraling to the ground in a blazing trail of smoke! For an instant I thought I heard harp music. I squeezed Sam's hand, thanking God that this man was here beside me. If plummeting from the air in a doomed airplane was to be the outcome of this improbable relationship, then I was so thankful that Sam was by my side — even though it was his fault I was here in the first place.

It struck me that I was being selfish. Sam, given a choice, wasn't into death pacts. No doubt he'd as soon live, with or without me.

The pilot continued. "We have what's called an engine cough. I'm going by the manual, and we've been cleared for an emergency landing, but often when a plane is taken to a different altitude the problem will correct itself. I'm going to change altitude and see what happens. I'll stay in touch."

You do that. Close touch. At least changing altitude might give us a shorter distance to plummet.

Oh, *why* hadn't I listened to my intuition and stayed home?

NINE

◉◉◉

I gripped the armrests so tight my knuckles looked like hard white knobs. I fixed my eyes outside on the wing, looking for a flare or a trail of black smoke. Bits of the flight attendant's safety speech came back to haunt me. Why hadn't I taken notes? I ran through the basic points. Seat cushion became a flotation device. Check. I didn't want to think of the implications of that. Oxygen mask will descend. Check. At least we can breathe on our way down. Barf bag? Check. Judging from the way my stomach churned, I'd need that soon.

Sam leafed through his research material, giving me cause to have serious doubts about his sanity. Didn't he realize we had an emergency going on? What good would all that research do him while he was floating in the ocean holding on to the back of his seat, surrounded by big fish with sharp teeth, all of which considered him part of the food chain?

No doubt his calm demeanor was the result of faith. He trusted that God was in control of the situation; I, on the other hand, thought God might need a little advice. *Do something!*

Oh, if I only had Sam's strength, his faith. My own conviction, tentative and unsure, had taken flight with the first thump. I'd never tried to grow spiritually. I'd been content with my life and failed to seek out the real purpose of my being on earth. It was so clear. One is not put on this planet to trip through the daffodils and sing "The Hills Are Alive with the Sound of Music."

I wasn't alone in my soul-searching; others were tight-lipped. A young mother clutched her small child to her chest, lips moving in what I took to be a silent prayer.

After what seemed an eternity, the ride smoothed out and the pilot's voice came back over the intercom. "Good news, folks. The problem seems to be solved."

A collective sigh, like the rushing of a mighty wind, filled the cabin. I relaxed and dabbed the cold sweat from my upper lip. Sam glanced over. "Too hot in here?"

"Temperature's fine." What a great time to be asking. I'd just had a total meltdown right here beside him, and he hadn't noticed. *Men.*

He indicated the research material. "I've read the notes you took for me. They're very engrossing."

"You didn't notice we had a problem with the plane?"

He frowned. "Nothing serious—the pilot was going by the manual."

We had to find a better way to communicate. When I needed him, I wanted him to be present in both mind and body. Not engrossed in a bunch of notes.

Hours passed. The flight attendants pushed a cart down the aisle, taking orders for snacks and drinks. I ate dinner and had a bag of peanuts and a Coke for dessert. Then, while Sam was immersed in study, I slept. The pilot's voice woke me again. My eyes jerked open, but I relaxed when I realized the pilot was announcing our arrival in Port Moresby, the capital of Papua New Guinea.

I'd be grateful the flight was over if I weren't so sure what awaited me was probably even worse.

I sat up, pulling myself together, still dazed from my long sleep. I lifted my shoulders, rotating them to ease muscle stiffness, and the plane jolted again. I grabbed at Sam's arm, knocking his glasses askew in the process. His book flew into the aisle. He looked at me, eyes wide, and heat filled my face. But I didn't turn loose of his arm.

The pilot's voice came over the intercom. "Sorry about that, folks. That last jolt had nothing to do with the engines. We're in our landing pattern and we happened to get caught in another jet's wake."

We were *that* close to another plane? If this flight ever ended and we were on the ground, I was going to walk back to Saginaw. A daunting task, since an ocean stretched between Papua New Guinea and the USA, and to my knowledge, Jesus and Peter were the only ones — man, woman, or child — who ever walked on water. But I was tempted to give it a shot.

The seat belt light flashed on and Sam grinned. "We're here. Get ready for the experience of your life."

I tried, but there was no way I could share his anticipation.

The plane landed with a gentle bounce. I gathered my belongings and prepared to meet what lurked on the other side of the plane door. We taxied to a stop. I heard the click of seat belts. Passengers began to stand and step out into the aisle. Sam stood and motioned me out in front of him.

The airport was crowded and noisy. People were talking in different languages, most of which I couldn't understand. We found our luggage and lined up to go through customs. The official was thorough, running his hands through the contents of my suitcase with practiced ease. We showed our passports and were allowed to move on.

Sam put our cases on a cart and I followed him out the door into blazing sunshine. A driver met us and helped load our possessions into the trunk of the cab. Heat was already building. The air reeked of exhaust fumes and hot pavement. We drove away from the airport. Traffic in Papua New Guinea moved on the left. I'd read that travel on highways outside of major towns could be hazardous. Crime was rampant in the city, and motor vehicle accidents were common causes of serious injury. Several trucks passed with passengers standing or sitting in the beds. Was it any wonder that drivers and passengers are advised to wear seat belts?

Generally, the roads appeared to be in poor repair, and I saw at least three vehicles with flat tires. Potholes and debris littered the roadways. I suspected that during the rainy season landslides were a problem on some stretches of the Highlands Highway. I spotted a criminal roadblock ahead. Signs advising visitors to consult with local authorities or the US Embassy before traveling on the Highlands Highway were clearly evident.

So all my fear about dealing with living here for weeks was for naught. We'd be attacked and murdered long before we reached our destination.

I was surprised to see Port Moresby was modern, yet different. Exotic. The trees and flowers were strange varieties I didn't recognize. Most of the natives I saw would have looked at home in any major American city, but a smattering of individuals wore exotic clothing. The buildings themselves had a subtle, foreign look about them, although I'd have been hard pressed to describe what made them different.

The driver and Sam conversed with each other, but since I couldn't understand what they were saying, I didn't take part

in the exchange. Papua New Guinea wasn't anything like I'd
expected. I'd expected something more archaic. Several of the
shops we passed looked intriguing. Too bad there was no time
to browse. We stopped in front of a hotel.

Sam's smile was warm. "We'll spend the night here and
travel to the village in the morning."

I filled with curiosity when I got out of the car to look
around.

Sam and the driver transported our luggage inside to the
desk. Our reservations were in order, and soon we each had a
room key. A bellhop, wearing a crisp khaki uniform, showed us
to our rooms and accepted the generous tip Sam handed him.

Sam turned to me. "Rest a bit. We'll have dinner at five
thirty. I'll tap on your door when I'm ready."

I nodded. "I'll be ready." I'd have time to unpack and take
a shower; the long plane ride left me feeling grungy.

I closed my bedroom door, and my eyes took in the fur-
nishings. If I hadn't known better I'd have thought we were
in an American hotel. The bed had crisp white sheets, and the
towels in the private bath were fluffy, white, and soft. I took
a few things out of my suitcase and hung them in the small
closet. Later I stood under the showerhead for a long time,
luxuriating in the hot water and my own coconut-scented
shower gel. After toweling off I slipped on a robe, dried my
hair, and dressed. Around five thirty, Sam tapped on my door.
When I opened it, he looked rested and refreshed.

"You look wonderful, Johanna."

"Thank you." I slipped into the suit jacket and slung the
strap of my brown leather purse over my shoulder. My passport was in the bag, and I didn't intend to leave it behind.

As nice as Papua New Guinea was turning out to be, I still intended to leave in two weeks.

The hostess ushered us into an open dining area. We sat at a round table adorned with an immaculate white cloth. A hurricane lamp with a lighted candle occupied the center of the table. The light cast a soft glow. A large palm tree threw fringed shadows over the courtyard. The result was exotic. Romantic.

Sam ordered for both of us (no bugs, I warned), and when our food came I was relieved to find it recognizable: fish with some kind of light sauce, potatoes, vegetables, all delicious. We finished up with coffee and a coconut-cream pudding, savoring every bite.

Sam spooned up the last bite of his dessert. "Don't get the idea the whole trip will be like this. We forfeit luxury after tomorrow."

I concentrated on a buzzing mosquito, the first I'd spotted tonight. Sam was still talking, and I pulled my attention back to him. "Don't worry. I won't expect to be entertained in this style every night."

"Good, because you won't be. I don't want you to be disappointed." He glanced at his watch. "I know it's early, but we'd better turn in. It's been a long trip, and our car to take us to the airport will be here before dawn in the morning."

Now that he mentioned it, I was tired. It would be nice to linger in the courtyard, but the crisp white sheets on my bed beckoned.

Sam kissed me good night outside the door to my room. "Be ready to leave by five."

"So early?" Sleeping in had been on my list of expectations.

"Tomorrow will be a long day." He brushed a hand over the collar of my suit jacket. "You did pack jeans, didn't you?"

"Several pair, as well as long-sleeved blouses — everything on your list."

"Good. Wear a pair tomorrow. Good sturdy shoes too."

I snapped a salute. "Yes, sir!"

His arms closed around me and I leaned into his comforting presence. The trip was turning out better than I'd expected. His lips lowered to meet mine and I forgot all my apprehensions. I had Sam, and as Nelda and Mom and Pop had reminded me, I had God. How could a girl need anything more?

Four thirty a.m. came way too early. I dragged myself out of bed and stumbled to the bathroom. Even a shower didn't revive me. As ordered, I dressed in jeans and a long-sleeved cotton blouse. By the time I had my hiking boots laced, my stomach was growling. I'd seen the dining room hours posted last night. It wouldn't be open until eight. As well as Sam liked to eat, he'd made plans for a morning meal.

I was ready, suitcases packed and locked, when his knock sounded at the door. We staggered downstairs under the weight of our luggage. A cab waited at the door to take us back to the airport. He handed me a breakfast bar and juice carton. *Bon appetit.*

A small single-engine Cessna, looking like a child's toy compared to the big jets, waited on the tarmac. The cab pulled close and we got out. My heart was beating like a jungle drum. We weren't going to fly in something that small! Sam picked up our suitcases and winked. "I didn't mention this part of the trip."

"Why?" I eyed the tiny cabin, hysteria crowding the back of my throat.

"I knew you wouldn't come."

He had that right.

The pilot, an American, looked like he'd just rolled out of bed. Unshaven and sporting a cowlick in his collar-length hair, he was gruff and appeared rather impatient with my lack of speed. He greeted Sam and then turned to take my hand in a viselike grip. "Call me Mike."

Before I could answer, Mike grabbed the suitcases and stowed them in the plane. The carry-on bags followed. Sam, like the gentleman he was, helped me inside. I eased down into my seat and fastened the safety belt. This wasn't a plane! More like a kiddy ride you'd find at amusement parks.

We sounded like an angry gnat taking off. *Buzzzzzz. Pftttbuzzzzzz. Pfft.* Once we were airborne I realized why the earlier turbulence coming over hadn't bothered Sam. The small plane danced and jumped like a puppet on a string, shifting and tilting, sending my nerves into a state of perpetual shock.

Before I had time to adjust to the heinous ride, we were descending to a small landing strip that looked like little more than a mown path.

The plane hit, then bounced along the uneven ground, jarring teeth and eyeballs before it rolled to a stop. I wasn't sure if we landed or crashed. I was still numb from the experience when Mike climbed out of the cockpit, unhooked a latch, and kicked the door open.

"Thing sticks," he explained when he met my startled gaze. I had never left a plane in this fashion.

Sam and I climbed out behind Mike and got into a waiting jeep. A dark-skinned native sat at the wheel. Sam said something in the man's native tongue, and he grinned. Once aboard, we took off and I hung on as the jeep bounced across potholed ground, arriving at a rustic landing where a decrepit motorboat sat moored to wooden pillars. We were at some body of water surrounded by thick, tropical vegetation. Overhead, dark clouds formed.

I watched, horrified, as Sam and the pilot carried our luggage to the boat. Sam had left out a *lot* of information. We weren't going to ride in that *thing*! The boat was small and had dozens of dead fish littering the bottom. The stench was unbelievable; I held my nose.

Sam made a few parting remarks to the driver and then turned to me. "Climb aboard."

I gave him a weak smile, feeling like a condemned woman on her way to the guillotine. The boat owner and a second man sauntered toward us, not in any apparent hurry, which suited me fine. Sam greeted the men with a smile and a handshake. They indulged in a series of hand waving and facial expressions accompanied by guttural sounds I couldn't begin to interpret. It struck me like a physical blow that I was now in a place where I couldn't understand anyone other than Sam and the missionaries. Four strangers. And Sam.

The two men clambered on board, and Sam held out his hand to me. "Come on, Johanna. It's a safe vessel."

If we hadn't been so far from Saginaw, Michigan, I'd consider hitchhiking home. But one look at the surrounding maze told me just how limited my choices were. I grasped his hand

and stepped into the boat, which lurched beneath my weight, threatening to dump me into the muddy green river flowing past the dock.

"Easy does it." Sam steadied me. I shot him a glance that would have fried bacon, one he pretended to ignore. I had a feeling by the time my "vacation" ended he would rue the day he'd ever suggested I come along. I knew he loved me and I loved him, but would our love be strong enough to meet the challenge we were facing?

I had my doubts.

I sat down without tipping the boat and wiped the sweat from my face. The place was a sauna. My contacts fogged over. Damp clothing clung to my frame, and my hair had frizzed into a little stringy pigtail. It didn't get this hot in Saginaw. It didn't get this hot in hell. The sun bore down like a giant spotlight. I wouldn't have been surprised to see the river come to a boil under the intense heat. Brush and undergrowth lined the banks on either side of the water. Orchids dripped from foliage. Birds I didn't recognize hopped through the brush or flew overhead, their strange cries puncturing the silence. It was all so beautiful and exotic and utterly terrifying.

Hordes of insects feasted on the exposed skin of my face and neck. I slapped, hit, and smacked. Thank goodness Sam insisted I wear long sleeves.

I hunched deeper into my seat, staring wide-eyed at the sights unfolding as the boat skimmed the water. Trees crowded in thick lines. Something large splashed in the river behind us. I swerved to look over my shoulder, half expecting to see a rhino headed our way. All I saw were expanding ripples. Nobody else in the boat seemed worried, so I took a deep breath and tried to relax.

We motored deeper into the dense jungle. The heat and silence were oppressive. An occasional animal cry raised the hairs on the back of my neck. Could I handle weeks of this? *God, please don't let me make a complete fool of myself.* I had a hunch my guardian angel would be working overtime on this journey.

Attempting to look more at ease, I trailed my hand in the water, visualizing a Victorian heroine taking a romantic boat ride on the River Thames. One of the natives said something in a burst of rapid-fire words to Sam, who spun and looked at me.

"What language is he speaking?" I asked.

"Tau Pisin."

"What did he say?"

"He probably wanted you to keep your hands in the boat. The river is full of coral catfish — eel-tailed catfish."

I jerked my hand out of the water so fast I sent a spray of water over the boat's occupants. A minute earlier the thought of being sprayed with dirty river water would have repulsed me. At the moment, I was busy counting fingers. When I was satisfied I had my full quota, I switched my attention to Sam. "What's an eel-tailed catfish?"

"It's a species best to avoid. The spikes in the fish's dorsal fins are sharp, and if one spikes you it will cause intense pain that will last for hours. It could even be fatal."

Well, lovely. *What have you gotten me into, Sam Littleton!*

Sam bent forward. "Relax. We're safe."

After what seemed like hours, Sam pointed ahead to the mouth of an inlet. "There — on the left. The village."

I followed his pointing finger and the bottom dropped out of my stomach. We were approaching an island. The main part of the village lay along a cliff line that dropped thirty to forty feet to a narrow, rocky beach. Irregular terraces were separated by rough walks of volcanic stone. The crude residences were of hand-hewn timbers, with walls of light but strong-looking leaf stalks.

"Saga palms," Sam explained.

Palm leaves thatched the roofs. I recognized the huts from the photographs I'd seen. Even framed by the lush forest, the village looked dismal.

Sitting in a lagoon some fifty to seventy feet from shore, two even more primal structures rose out of the water on stilt-like poles. I turned to Sam, eyes questioning. He nodded. "That's where we'll stay. The Laskes' is the one on the right, the Millets' on the far left."

I looked at the two huts with landings surrounding the structures and swallowed. "The missionaries ... live on the water."

"Yes. It's cooler here, and the villagers don't welcome them to live on shore."

My eyes skimmed the thatched huts. "I'm going to live on water that's filled with spiky catfish."

"Yes, but the fish won't bother you if you don't bother them."

Heaven help me. I was going to eat and sleep in the midst of cranky predators. What other shockers lay in store for me? The first fat raindrops fell, dimpling the water. By the time the boat reached the first hut, a deluge fell from the fast-moving black clouds. One moment, scorching heat; the next, pouring rain.

Welcome to your new life, Johanna.

I was suffering from jet lag, and my biological rhythms were seriously out of sync. I was sunburned, bug-bitten, and drenched to the bone — and utterly convinced we'd passed through some horrific time warp.

Water collected in the bottom of the boat. I squinted, bleary eyed, through my contacts and the blinding downpour. Sam told me we were traveling to a region where the yearly rainfall averaged 120 to 150 inches. Apparently we were getting the full load this morning.

And, just to top it all off, the boat was leaking.

TEN

◎◎◎

The driver cut the outboard and we drifted up to the first hut. If I hadn't been expected to live here I'd have said the setting was picturesque, but the word that came to mind was *hovel*. The boat bumped into one of the stilts and came to a stop. A slender woman with a tangle of brown curls held back by a tortoiseshell clasp stood in the doorway, waving to us. Sam helped me out of the craft, up the ladder, and onto the deck. The boat operator and his native helper unloaded our luggage, and I watched helplessly as they climbed back in the boat and jerked the motor's starter cord. It coughed and sputtered, but then began to idle. Moments later the craft disappeared around the nearest land point.

The rain stopped as abruptly as it had started. Steam rose from the wet deck. The sun was like burning coals on my water-soaked shoulders. I stood there drenched in sweat as I listened to the sound of the fading outboard. I'd cringed at having to ride in the smelly, dirty craft, but suddenly it seemed like my only link to civilization. I gladly would have climbed back in for the return trip. If I'd had anyplace to return to.

There was something unsettling about being on a different continent. Unnerving—if I'd had a single nerve left. I'd never realized what a barrier language could be. I could talk to Sam. The missionaries spoke English, but other than that I wouldn't be able to understand a single thing said to me.

The pretty brown-haired woman approached, smiling. Sam grasped her hand, and I recognized the strong bond between them. I peered down at the catfish-infested water. Could those things jump—like leap onto the landing? Sam introduced me to his friend, who turned out to be Eva Millet, my hostess for the duration of my stay. She was friendly, cheerful, and welcoming.

"We've been expecting you, but travel is so unpredictable here we weren't sure when you would actually arrive."

"Unpredictable?" It hadn't occurred to me before, but how would I leave if an emergency arose? What if Mom or Pop took gravely ill?

"Nothing runs on schedule here." She laughed as if that was no problem. Well, I could point out *lots* of problems, beginning with no cell phone signal, telegraph wire, or e-mail. I knew Sam carried a satellite phone, but was it reliable? How did we stay in touch with the outside world?

"Did you have a nice flight over?"

Sam nodded at Eva. "Great trip." He must have forgotten the coughing engine. "We're tired, of course. I think Johanna is still adjusting to jet lag, but other than that we're ready to get to work."

By now we'd been joined by two men and a second woman, who I assumed were the rest of the missionary team. Sam made the introductions. The tall, broad-shouldered one was Frank Millet, Eva's husband and my host. I guessed the couple to be in their late fifties. They'd been here for twelve years. Living in a hut? On this island? Impossible to grasp such dedication.

The short, rather rotund man with a freckled face and sandy red hair was Bud Laske. Mary, his wife, had the same red hair and vivid blue eyes—Irish eyes, set in with a smudgy finger, as the saying went. They were a perfect fit—right and left shoe—where Sam and I must have looked like two left feet wearing an orange sneaker.

The Laskes lived in a nearby hut that looked identical to the one where we'd unloaded. The two dwellings were connected by a narrow, shaky-looking walkway. What would make someone like Mary, who would shine in any cosmopolitan setting, choose to spend her life in the middle of a killer catfish–infested lagoon?

Maybe she'd had no choice. Maybe missions was her husband's dream and she followed out of devotion to him. Hope surged that I might be with two women who could identify with my doubts, my dilemma. Eva and Mary could tell me the real truth about living on the mission field. They could provide me a reasonable argument for Sam. Not a selfish argument, but a matter-of-fact, logical one.

The Laskes were younger than Frank and Eva, maybe in their forties—too young to be buried in this isolated world. But then, Frank and Eva were too old to be here.

Just what age do you think is the proper age for missionaries?

I didn't know. But it wasn't *my* age, of that I was certain.

"Come inside," Eva invited. "I'll show you where you'll sleep."

I released a silent sigh. At least I'd have private quarters. Sam hefted my suitcase and Frank took the carry-on. I followed Eva as she led the way through the door, which I noticed only had a curtain separating it from the outside. Anything could crawl in the house, any animal or snake. Cheerful thought. I planned to be very careful where I stepped or sat down. Inside, Eva pulled aside a curtain and indicated a narrow space with a cot.

"I think you'll be comfortable here, Johanna."

I looked at her, then back at the cot. Comfortable? In a lumpy, sagging cot, in a curtained-off cubbyhole? The thin piece of material wouldn't shut out noise. My suitcase and carry-on filled the allotted space, barely leaving room to move around the bed.

Eva broke the strained silence. "Let me show you the rest of our home."

I could stand still, turn in a circle, and see it all, but she showed me how the privacy curtains drew around the bed where she and Frank slept.

The kitchen had a propane stove and a table with four chairs. I had no idea how they kept butter, milk, or refrigerated items. Eva seemed inordinately proud of her home. She pulled aside a blanket cordoning off a small area containing a very large jar. I looked at her questioningly.

High color tinted Mary's cheeks. She had been quiet during the tour. "The bathroom."

I stared at her, comprehension slow to dawn. She looked at Eva as if asking for help.

"The restroom." Eva sobered. "When you need to go to the bathroom, you use the jar."

Color drained from my face. "You can't be serious."

"You'll get used to it. When you think of the alternative — going outside every time the need arises — it doesn't seem so bad."

I managed a lame grin. Outside? Here? "Well, no, not if those are the only choices." One week — I'd give this experiment one week, and then I was outta there. Back to the States and civilization.

"Come on, Johanna, we'll give you a tour of the village."

Hard as I tried, I couldn't muster much excitement at Mary's offer.

The men were waiting in a small rowboat moored to the Laskes' poles. Paint was peeling off the ugly craft; it looked to be on its last leg. I peered at the relic thinking about the fish beneath us.

Sam helped me aboard, his smile broad. "Your carriage, madam."

I stepped into the boat, grabbing him by his shoulder as I tried to steady myself. The boat gyrated wildly. Mary and Eva gripped the sides. I had to learn to enter and leave boats more gracefully. Sam squeezed my shoulder and gave me a wink. My heart fluttered and for a moment I hoped that maybe everything would be all right. *I'll adjust to all this.* Given enough time. *I'll have to.*

The men rowed across the small lagoon, their paddles breaking the water with gentle, rhythmic splash-splashes that lulled me. I was so incredibly tired now as the time difference caught up with me.

When the boat bumped the shoreline, the men climbed out and pulled the hull onto the beach. Each woman exited with the help of her spouse. Sam lifted me and set me lightly down. Taking my hand, he started up the incline behind the two couples.

"You said the natives are friendly?" In my mind I pictured missionaries staked to a pole with a pile of burning brush beneath them.

Bud picked up the conversation. "Friendly? They're non-threatening, but we have yet to break the language barrier enough to actually know their feelings. We believe we're making progress, but the forward steps seem very small."

"If you can't speak their language, how do you communicate?" I struggled to keep pace.

"We don't." Frank spoke now. "Our goal is to establish communication, make friends of the villagers, gain their trust, and care for their medical needs. We gesture, draw pictures in the air—you know. Anything to try and connect with them. We understand a few basic words, but nothing more, and we have no idea what they understand about us."

"You mean you've been here all these years and still don't understand a thing they say?" Sam had told me as much but still, seeing reality, I was astounded.

Bud smiled. "In God's time, we will. The villagers won't allow us in their huts, but we understand from others that years before Frank and Eva arrived, a group came through and the villagers understood enough that some have chosen to have statues of Mary in their homes."

We topped the incline and the village spread out before us. We stood looking at the row of huts sitting among saga palms and jungle thicket. At first the village looked empty; then my eye caught movement in the bush. A soft gasp escaped me as scantily clad stunted men with long straws threaded through their noses stepped from the thicket. The men stared at us. They were small in stature—not much over five feet tall. I noticed they wore the same straws in their ears.

Bud lifted a hand in greeting.

The natives' black eyes shifted to Sam and me.

Frank spoke, making motions as he talked. "Hello. We have brought the doctor."

Women balancing small children on their hips began to emerge from the bush, older children trailing at their sides. Suddenly they all smiled, eyes dancing with curiosity.

I heard a sharp intake of breath (mine) and I quickly averted my gaze. The women were *naked* from the waist up.

Bud and Frank stepped forward, and for a few minutes they attempted to communicate with the villagers by hand gestures. The guttural sounds that emerged were indistinguishable, but the villagers seemed happy to see Sam.

Frank and Bud motioned for us to come ahead. My boots turned to concrete, but I took Sam's hand and did what I was told. Every one of the savages' eyes turned toward me.

Inside the village the dwellings were even more primitive than the missionary hut. I was beginning to understand why Eva was so proud of her table, chairs, and chamber pot. There weren't any luxuries here. I stepped around pig droppings, pungent in the hot sunshine. The animals ran freely through the village, rooting around the huts and scampering down the muddy track that served as a street between the houses. A sow with a litter of eight piglets barred our way, daring us to pass. Bud turned to speak softly over his shoulder. "Give them plenty of room. We believe the villagers give spiritual significance to their animals."

The sow grunted and ran in the opposite direction, the pigs squealing and dashing after her.

A couple of mangy dogs fought over a bit of raw meat, snarling and snapping. Grubby children peeped from open doorways. Crying babies added to the din. Other villagers had reverted to daily activities. One large dog was tethered to a tree. The animal lunged, baring long teeth, snarling at us. We gave him wide berth.

The abject poverty overwhelmed me, sapping me of energy. I wanted to cry without understanding why. How could a loving God let anyone live like this?

The five people walking with me called out to the natives, smiling. Men lifted their hands and waved back. Apparently the villagers understood the missionaries were friends.

The women looked worn down, old before their time. I couldn't guess ages; the old looked very old, and the young looked almost as aged. Sam kept hold of my hand and led me into a thatched, open-air structure in the center of the village.

"My clinic."

The hut had bare necessities: tables, three folding chairs, and two metal cabinets that I assumed held Sam's medicines and supplies.

We spent over an hour touring the village, allowing Sam to reestablish contact with the villagers. Some broke into wide grins when they recognized the doctor who had helped them. A man ran up pointing to a severed limb, grinning from ear to ear.

"He was bitten by a poisonous spider last year," Sam explained. "Both Ni-ka and I believed he would not live." Sam reached out to grasp the young man's hand. "But Ni-ka is very strong; he lives!"

The native balled his fists and made a victory sign.

Later a young woman carrying a child approached the doctor. She fell at Sam's feet, bowing her head. Sam gently lifted her to her feet and tenderly smoothed her hair. I watched, curious.

"Her baby was born with a large malignant growth on the side of his head. I arranged to fly her and the child to Port Moresby, where the doctors successfully removed the growth. The child shows no evidence of the cancer now. The mother is very grateful." I looked at the beautiful toddler. He had only a hint of a white scar running along his left temple. He flashed a mouthful of teeth at me.

The woman grabbed Sam's hand and pressed it tightly to her lips. Sam's eyes met mine over the top of the woman's kneeling figure. "One day, I'll be able to tell her of God's unending love, mercy, and compassion. For now, I'm simply someone she can trust."

It wasn't much. But as I stood there, watching him with the woman, I realized it was a start. And for Sam, that was enough.

We ate dinner that evening in the Laskes' hut. Frank busied himself outside, leaving Eva and me to get acquainted. Conversation topics were limited. It seemed a wide chasm separated us. Her lifestyle and mine were worlds apart. She asked me about my work at the library, but there wasn't much to tell.

"Do you have family, Johanna?"

"My parents. They moved into an assisted living facility a couple of months ago."

"Have they adjusted well?"

"Better than I have." Because she was a stranger I opened up to her. "They made the arrangements to move without telling me."

"I assume they had a reason."

"I'm sure they did, but it escaped me. I like things to stay the same."

"Nothing stays the same, Johanna. Life is about change. We get older and wiser. We gain experience in new and different areas. God never meant for us to live in a state of suspended animation."

I switched subjects. "I notice there isn't a door on the huts. Aren't you concerned about animals or snakes coming in?"

"Not really. The huts are built on water, so that eliminates a lot of the problem. And on the few occasions something has gotten in, Frank makes short work of the intruder. You learn to not worry about small things."

Small things. What did a woman — this woman of God — know about small things? She focused on the eternal, not the external. Already I missed Mom and Pop and Nelda with a tangible ache. I missed Itty Bitty. But most of all I missed my clean, comfortable home and my simple, uncluttered life. I'd never take anything for granted again.

Sam and Frank entered the hut. I wiped the moisture in my eyes and turned away. This was Sam's life. Everything I had seen today only drove me farther away from him and the life to which God had called him. He gave me a tentative smile, and I realized he could read my emotions.

"How is my Johanna this evening?"

I pushed my glasses up on my nose. The contacts were in my luggage. I couldn't bring myself to complain in front of Frank and Eva. "The villagers are interesting."

"It grows on you," he promised.

I smiled and nodded, not trusting myself to speak. He patted my shoulder and went outside again with Frank.

Eva and I sat at the kitchen table and drank some sort of a root tea—tasty actually. "How have you managed for twelve years?" I desperately needed to understand why a woman—any woman—would choose this life.

"With difficulty in the beginning, but Frank strongly believed this was where God wanted us to be. Sometimes we want to leave and go home, but then something always happens to show us we're needed here."

"Do you ever see improvement?"

"Sometimes. It's slow." She looked past me, out the door. "The country is really beautiful, and of course, in the cities it's more modern. But the villagers, particularly this village, are very poor. Disease is so common; it robs them of their children. We do anything we can to help. Most are grateful, and those that aren't simply don't yet understand our purpose. Language is the enemy. We struggle with communication because the tribe speaks a mixed dialect, one we've not yet been able to translate."

The men came back into the hut and Mary started to prepare dinner.

"May I help?" I asked as she moved to the propane stove.

"Got it all ready; please, sit down. You're my guest."

Frank and Sam had brought a couple of folding chairs to allow seating space for six. Mary bustled around putting food on the table. I was delighted to see I could identify most of it: some sort of dried bean casserole, fresh pineapple, and papaya. There was thick, hard-crusted bread with a delightful nutty taste.

Mom's neighbor's son had been in the navy, and I remember her telling that when he was in Sri Lanka he ate monkey without knowing it. Thank goodness the villagers gave spiritual significance to animals. No chance of my having to eat monkey.

We gathered around the table and Bud blessed the food. His petitions were simple but powerful as he invoked God's hand on the villagers and asked that the mission team continue to succeed in their pursuits.

Talk was general for the most part. The men spoke about planting crops and the building projects they were working on. Mary and Eva held weekly hygiene classes for the women, something that didn't appear to be working.

"Johanna—" Frank reached for a slice of bread—"you'll have to come with us Saturday."

"What happens on Saturday?"

"Oh, that's when we have fun!" Eva grinned. "We take shiny objects, like mirrors and colorful ribbons, and we tie them on trees and bushes deep in the forest."

I put my fork down. "Whatever for?"

"To entice those living deep in the bush to come out. The natives adore the sparkly trinkets. Granted, we barely get a glance of them, but they're back every week for the goodies, so they know we're here. And when one is sick, they come to the clinic in droves." She smiled at Frank. "The crowds are getting bigger every time Sam comes."

After dinner Eva insisted on cleaning the table. "You two go outside and look around. Johanna would probably be interested in learning more about the place where we live."

I followed Mary outside, thinking I already knew more about this place than I cared to. The board planks of the deck were dry now. The small rowboat bobbed at the piling. Overhead, clouds had started to build.

We rested our arms on the railing, staring into the murky lagoon waters. Mary must have sensed my reservations because her tone gentled. "It's all rather overwhelming, isn't it?"

"Sam tried to prepare me, but I guess one never realizes the conditions until they witness them."

"There's no way to explain its magnetism or its exotic beauty. One has to experience the area to fully understand."

"The village is so dirty. So ... so unsanitary."

"Only to us, who know the difference. The villagers are quite happy and content—or so it would seem. Believe it or not, living conditions are better than they used to be."

"You've been here four years. Why do you stay?"

"It's where we feel God wants us to be."

There was the declaration again, the same one Eva had mentioned. How could anyone be that certain of what God wanted? "You're so lovely, Mary. It would be easy to imagine you having a successful career in New York or LA, wearing the latest fashions, enjoying life."

She laughed. "Thanks for the compliment, but I have no longing for what you call a 'successful career.' If I'm following God's leading in the places where he wants me, that's all the success I need."

"I'm trying hard to understand, but I feel—"

"Confused?" Mary picked a piece of bark off the railing and tossed it in the water. "I had the same doubts when I first arrived. Bud and I almost broke up over what he saw as his calling and my reticence."

"You weren't called to missions?"

"Not to foreign missions. If I'd had my way in the beginning, we would have worked in the States."

"And now?"

"Now I know this is where I'm supposed to be." She turned to meet my gaze. "Don't fight your feelings, Johanna. Relax and see what God has in store for you. It may be entirely different than what you think. Pray about it. If you're truly searching for answers, I can promise you that he won't allow you to drift too far in the wrong direction." A flash of lightning lit the darkened night. Mary glanced up. "Here comes the rain, right on schedule." We stood there watching nature's display until the first fat drops hit the landing.

I excused myself and retired to my curtained alcove. Stretching out on the cot, I tried to pray, but words failed me. I missed Nelda. Her plain common sense and outspoken ways had helped me through many a crisis. I desperately needed her now.

The day had been a blur of sights and smells. I thought about the pig droppings, the lunging dog secured to a tree with a thick vine, the smell of wet earth and vegetation, and the scent of growing tobacco. The hubbub of crying babies, combative animals, pigs grunting. Half-naked men with straws in their noses and young women who looked a hundred years old.

Dear God, can this possibly be what you expect from me?

No answer came. I knew that I loved Sam and wanted to share his life — or did I? I was becoming more and more confused. Suddenly one of Pop's earlier conversations popped into my head. We'd been driving home from church. That morning the pastor had told of a man who'd come up to him at a funeral and, knowing the deceased well, asked the pastor if the man was now in hell, paying for his sins. The pastor replied, "No, if he's in hell, it's because he couldn't pay for his sins."

Was this the fate I wanted for these villagers?

No, I wanted them to know the truth. And I knew that if anyone on earth wanted to know the gospel, God would send those people a messenger. Sam, Frank, Eva, Bud, and Mary were filling that role for these people.

But what about me? Try as I might I could not make my piece of the puzzle fit.

I cried myself to sleep, listening to the deafening clatter of rain on a tin roof.

ELEVEN

S am materialized in the doorway to the hut at dawn the next
morning. The Millets and I were still eating breakfast.

"Johanna, you want to go into the village with me and
the Laskes?"

"Give me a minute and I'll be ready." I shoved my chair
back from the table, sounding more decisive than I was.

I dug out my plastic raincoat and put it on. When I told
Eva good-bye I gave a last lingering look around the warm,
mostly dry hut. (The roof leaked in a couple of places, one of
them over my cot.) Though simple and lacking much comfort, it still looked like a palace compared to the village.

When I stepped out on the deck Mary greeted me with a
wide grin. "Good morning. I knew you wouldn't be put off
by a little rain."

If she only knew how "put off" I was by everything I'd
seen so far. But I was here for Sam, and I wasn't going to
disappoint him. And if they knew, they would be shocked
that not once had I thought about the possibility of disappointing God.

We climbed into the boat that held a good three inches of
accumulated rain. The men bailed with a large plastic bucket
as the rain fell in blinding sheets, obscuring our view of the
village. It looked better from this vantage point.

Even with the plastic raincoat I was already damp. A rain-drop hung off the tip of my nose, refusing to release. I sighed and squeezed rain from the soaked hair plastered to my cheek. Was I mildewed? I must be. I was wet 90 percent of the time, with either sweat or rain. This was *not* the way I wanted Sam to remember me ...

That's all I would be when the experiment was over: a mere memory. I'd already made up my mind to break it off with him when I left. By then he would see the wisdom of going our separate ways. Would the realization tear at him as it did me?

The sounds of a village couple in heated argument drifted to us. A woman's high-pitched squeals contrasted with her opponent's guttural tones. For once I was grateful I couldn't understand a word of their language. From the tone of the argument the discussion threatened to turn into a tropical storm. Even in this remote corner of the world, tension between male and female was obvious. But then, why wouldn't it be? It started in the garden of Eden and escalated from there.

The din of barking dogs grew louder as we approached the shore. Village animals ran wild, prowling about and challeng-ing everything and everyone they met.

Bud brought the boat onto the bank, and Sam jumped out and grasped the mooring rope, fastening the craft to a stout post. The Laskes climbed out and I followed. We slogged up the steep incline in ankle-deep mud, struggling to retain our balance. There was nothing to hold on to — not a twig, not even a tough clump of grass. The bank leading up from the water was shale and volcanic rock.

And mud. Everywhere I looked I saw mud. Eva and Frank informed me we were blessed to have the lagoon. It sheltered our huts from the winds and rough sea. The main part of the village faced an unprotected rocky beach, and even in mild seas, landing or putting a boat or canoe in the water was a test of endurance.

The dogs had ceased barking, retreating to drier quarters. The fighting couple was silent too, giving no indication which of the village hovels housed them.

We stopped at the first hut. A man, lips stained red, his teeth almost rotted away, came out to meet us. A small girl stood at his side. He opened his mouth wide, bowing and scraping his hands in my direction. I caught myself bowing in return. From all appearances he was delighted to see me. I made a note to ask Sam later what caused his disfigurement. Bud talked to him, if you could call it that, using exaggerated facial expressions, loud sounds, and much arm waving. Sam winked at me. Bud had his own method of communicating, but if it worked, who was I to complain?

When we departed, Bud left a bag of jelly beans with the exuberant native, who was pleased.

Next we came to the hut of a man who sat beneath a brushy overhang carving a bamboo comb. I pulled Sam back to lag behind so I could question him. "The other man's mouth? I notice many of the men have lost all their teeth. Is it disease?"

I didn't voice the question foremost in my mind: *Is it contagious?*

"Betel nut." Sam explained. "Men use the betel nut like American men chew tobacco. When mixed with lime the nut is a mild intoxicant and stimulant. It's the coffee, tea, beer, and whiskey of many of the natives of Papua New Guinea. When the ground is dry you'll notice many bright red spittle patterns. It's a way of life for the villagers. When they lose their teeth and are no longer able to chew, they resort to crushing their betel in an elaborately carved handheld mortar bowl. You'll see the men carving the paraphernalia from time to time."

"Why would they want to chew something that destroys their teeth?" Some of the men had ragged stumps in their mouths.

"The nut is addictive."

"They're all addicts?" *Figures.*

"We're all addicted to something, Johanna." Sam shook his head. "There's always something that keeps us from being solely yielded to God."

I started to protest and then closed my mouth. Who was I to criticize someone else's weakness? How did I know when my own frailties would enslave me? In fact, wasn't that what was happening to me at this very moment? Weren't my weaknesses blinding me to the world as Sam saw it?

I took a closer look at the men's stained mouths and stumps of teeth as I walked through the village. The villagers seemed to have no regard for health issues. I couldn't live like that. I did all I could to avoid doctor or dental visits. For one thing, I didn't like them. For another, the cost of insurance and copay was astronomical. I'd worked my way up to a decent salary, and I was cautious with my money. I planned ahead. I'd never allow myself to fall into such an addiction as the betel nut —

Yes, but what about security? Could you be addicted to that?

The thought hit me with the force of a clap of thunder. Even worse thoughts came next: *Could you be a possession addict? Addicted to the things you own, the things you've convinced yourself you couldn't do without?*

The unwanted questions rushed through my mind, like a blazing comet in a dark night sky, startling me with their clarity. Was that the way Sam saw me?

My heart chilled at another realization ...

Was that the way *God* saw me?

I pushed the ugly thought away. I did value my possessions. Who didn't? I'd worked hard to gain them. There was nothing wrong or unbiblical with being thrifty with what God had given me.

Frank Millet joined us, and the villagers crowded around him, calling him something that sounded like *boom*.

Sam explained. "*Bum* means grandfather. It's a sign of great respect." After twelve years, the man had earned, if not clear communication, at least great respect. He deserved a citation.

The rain stopped as suddenly as if someone had turned off a faucet. The sun popped out, turning the village into one gigantic sauna. I didn't know I could sweat so much. I peeled off the plastic raincoat and draped it over my arm. A woman villager reached out to rub the thin, clear plastic between her fingers. I couldn't understand what she was saying, but her intention was obvious. She wanted my raincoat.

I gave her a stern look, trying not to focus on her bare chest. "No."

Her eyes widened. Mary came to my rescue, waving the woman away. The woman shrugged and turned loose of my coat, shooting a disgruntled glance my way.

I thanked Mary for intervening. "How did you make her understand?"

She laughed. "I prayed that she could identify the gesture."

"Well, thank you. I can't give away my raincoat." I glanced at the brightening sky. "Does it rain every hour or so?"

"It seems that way." Mary made no mention of my refusal to give the woman the raincoat. Did she disapprove? I had no doubt she would have given it away, along with anything else the villager wanted. But then, I wasn't Mary. She and the others were working to garner full trust with these natives, but I wasn't. Besides, it rained constantly here: I *needed* the raincoat. That woman was comfortable running around loose as a goose. A little rain wouldn't affect her.

"I don't know how you do this, Mary. You're a saint."

"Far from it. Look around you, Johanna. The villagers' ways are not our ways, but they are warm, accepting. Our ways must be very odd and funny to them, just as theirs are to us. Somehow God's love causes them to sense that maybe they need what we have to offer. In time, others—or who knows, maybe even *we*—will collapse the communication barrier. Until then, we're their friends. We know enough to gain their trust; this is good."

I couldn't keep the scorn from my voice. "Look at these living conditions. It's awful."

"Seen from the eyes of someone who hasn't adjusted to the culture, I suppose it is. But if you think we haven't made a difference here, you're wrong. Remember that Simon Peter said, 'Silver or gold I do not have, but what I have I give you.'"

I knew the verse she quoted. "You're talking about the gospel, aren't you? That's what you have to give."

"Exactly. You're thinking of earthly treasure, and we do try to improve their living conditions, but most of all and in due time, we're here to bring them the hope of eternal life."

At her simplistic faith I fell silent. I glanced at the rain-coat—now a serpent in my hand.

The men had walked ahead. Mary and I continued on until we came upon two men sitting beneath a palm, eating pineapple. One pointed to another man and grinned, revealing teeth stained with betel nut juice. "Taik."

I stared at him, biting my lip.

"Taik, taik," he insisted.

Once again, Mary saved me. "This is one word I comprehend. I believe he is saying that the other man is his brother—sibling of the same sex. I think."

I smiled and nodded, trying to convey I understood. "What would he call his sister?"

"That would be *luk*, and *mam* means father. That, my dear sister, is the full extent of my knowledge of their language. Those are the only words they repeatedly use. It's taken Frank and Bud years to make the connections."

"Years. I would have given up long ago."

Dear, sainted Mary gave me a look that spoke volumes. "Just try, Johanna. That's all anyone could ask."

My face burned. Had Sam brought me here to humiliate me? I didn't have his faith—not to say that I didn't want his faith, but I was trying, and I wasn't getting spiritually stronger. If anything, I realized, I was sanctimonious and weaker. And that realization didn't make me feel any better. What must one do to be sold out to God like Eva, Frank, Mary, and Bud? And Sam. Dear love-of-my-life Sam. Burdened with a worm like me. How could God do that to him? And how could Sam not be resentful?

That night my frustrations boiled over. Sam and I were outside the hut, soaking up the beautiful night. Rain had taken a leave of absence, and the dry evening reminded me of how few we'd had. Out of the blue I blurted my feelings.

"I'm sorry, Sam, but I warned you before we made this trip that it wouldn't work."

He didn't seem startled by my declaration. "You haven't allowed sufficient time to make that decision, Johanna. I was hoping you would give it a week or so before you came to any firm conclusions. Mary and Eva are content here."

"I'm not Mary or Eva. I am Johanna Holland—a self-centered, materialistic, sheltered librarian and only child from Saginaw, Michigan. If God meant me to be a missionary, it's slipped his mind. I'm sorry, Sam. As much as I love you, I would be a detriment to your work."

My breath caught in my throat and hot tears sprang to my eyes. I was sure I looked a fright; my hair was frizzed beyond getting a comb through the tangled mass. My glasses were cumbersome and miserable after getting used to contacts, and they were always fogged over in the high humidity. After two days in this godforsaken land, there wasn't a place on my body that wasn't sunburned. The blistering equatorial sun bore right through clothing. And you could forget false eyelashes in this climate.

My feet hurt from the unaccustomed heavy hiking shoes, and I itched from pesky mosquito bites in places I hadn't known existed. And because of the chamber pot I withheld needed trips until I was prostrate with need. If God didn't work a miracle and change me inside and out, I knew I couldn't be the person Sam deserved.

"I refused to give a village woman my raincoat today. Now how selfish and immature is that? A piece of thin plastic that cost less than five dollars at Wal-Mart, and I was too stingy to give it to her."

Sam reached over and drew me close. "You do a number on yourself, Johanna." He lowered his mouth to my ear, and his whispered words caressed my cheek. "If you were that wretched, do you think I would be in love with you?"

"Oh, Sam." I turned into his arms, determined to do better. But I didn't know how. I only knew I would stay the week. I owed Sam that much.

And I owed God more.

***

A crowd of village children descended on me the following morning, grabbing at my pant legs, grasping my hands. The child I had spotted the day before hovered close, trailing my steps. My first instinct was to shrink away from the contact, but the little urchins with black eyes won me over. Dirty, thin, but endearing, they clung to me, jabbering.

Sam was running the clinic that morning; Bud, Frank, and Mary helped. They suggested that I wander around the camp and hand out candy, which I did. Johnny Appleseed planting orchards. Soul orchards. That's me.

I looked at the children and the lunging dog still tied to the tree. (I hated that particular mutt.) I realized I must look like King Solomon to them — though they'd never heard of the biblical monarch. A digital camera dangled around my neck, and a tape recorder was strapped to my wrist. Back in the hut I had more shoes and clothing in my suitcase than they had ever seen in their entire lives. My garish display of wealth shamed me. Mary and Eva dressed and looked as humble as Amish women.

I distributed the jelly beans, trying to give each child one. The kids' eyes lit up, but the brightest gaze was that of a child the natives called *Poo*. I wasn't going to worry about the candy rotting their teeth. If these children followed their parents' habits with the betel nut, they wouldn't have teeth much beyond age thirty anyway.

As I passed the snarling dog, I acted on impulse and tossed a packet of jelly beans to it. The animal tore into the wrapping and downed the treat so fast it made me blink. The poor thing looked half starved. With a quick glance around, I tossed him another morsel, then walked on.

A half-grown shoat wandered around the side of a building, grunting and rooting. The children ignored him, but I cast a wary look in his direction, cutting a wide path around his general vicinity. The last thing I wanted was to step on one of their spiritual symbols.

I'd never get used to pigs running loose. What stopped them from wandering into the huts? Not one thing that I could see.

The sun beat down on my unprotected head until I was light-headed. I had forgotten my hat, and nobody had reminded me to bring one. No doubt they were getting sick of babysitting me.

The blistering sun didn't seem to affect the others, but I couldn't catch a clear breath in the humidity. Around noon, Sam appeared from the clinic and saw my distress. He suggested we go back to the Millets' hut for lunch. Steam rose from the water and the lagoon vegetation. As soon as we arrived at the landing I clambered out of the boat and hurried inside the hut. A blessed coolness washed over me. Utterly drained, I sank down on one of the kitchen chairs.

Eva turned from the stove. "You're here! Lunch is about ready. How was your visit this morning?"

"Hot." I fanned my flaming face with my hand. Never before had I realized what a wonderful invention air-conditioning was. The man who dreamed it up should be enshrined on Mount Rushmore. He'd done more for the world than some paltry president.

Lunch was fish, and more pineapple and papaya and bread.

"Don't you ever just want a McDonald's Big Mac and fries?"

Eva giggled. "No, but I would give all I own for a plate of General Tso's chicken, all white meat, extra sauce."

We ate with hearty appetites, though Bud kept consulting his watch. "Sam, I think I'm going to check on the landing strip this afternoon. Can you make do with Mary and Frank's help?"

My ears perked up. "The landing strip?"

"Once every two months a small plane brings supplies," Bud explained. "It's our job to keep the strip cleared. The rain and wind last night may have blown limbs and other debris onto the strip. I'll need to check." He looked up. "Johanna, you might come with me and see where the strip is located."

I could get out of here. *Today.*

Mary must have read my thoughts. "The aircraft is for supplies and emergency use." She set a glass of tea on the table.

"Oh." The thought of a plane every two months appeased me. I would be long gone by then. "Okay, I'll go with you, Bud, if Sam doesn't need me."

Sam shook his head. "Go with Bud. You'll enjoy the walk."

Bud and I bypassed the village and followed a narrow path through the jungle. Long vines dangled from trees crowding close to the trail. Vegetation brushed against us, dense foliage loaded with parasites. Bud forged ahead, apparently unconcerned about bugs, snakes, or wild animals — all the fears dominating my thoughts.

We walked for what seemed like miles before we reached a large clearing. I gazed at the overgrown weed patch they called a landing strip and realized it would be a huge undertaking to keep it mowed. The rain and hot sun grew the grass at an alarming rate.

"It needs mowing," Bud conceded. "Too wet to work today — maybe tomorrow morning. Plane won't be here until late next week."

"What do you use to cut the grass?" Probably scythes. Or maybe they tied a goat on the strip to let it eat one patch before moving it to another.

Bud motioned to a small thatched hut sitting off to the side. "Got a little power mower we use. Keep it stored in there and locked up tight so the natives won't get it."

A villager with a power tool. Scary.

"Lucky for us, they're afraid of the machine." Frank came to stand beside me. "If they weren't, I'd expect it to come up missing someday."

"Are you saying the natives steal?"

"Well, let's just say they're naive to the concept of personal possessions."

Great. I made a mental note to lock my suitcase every morning. The villagers could swim the lagoon with ease.

We spent the next hour picking up broken limbs and debris. The heat was overpowering. Wading through the tall grass was like wading through a steam with a giant spotlight shining overhead. After a few minutes I was so groggy and disoriented Bud slid an arm around me. "Why don't you sit in the shade for a while? I keep forgetting you're not used to this climate." He led me to a giant tree, like nothing we grew back home in Saginaw. I slumped down on the ground, eyes closed, feeling as if I'd been rolled in sweat and deep fried. Finally I cooled enough to take stock of my surroundings. The grass here was thick and luxuriant and alive with bugs and insects. A small lizard watched me from under a large leaf; a monstrous black beetle crawled up my pant leg.

I leaped to my feet, stamping my foot.

Bud glanced up from the strip. "Everything okay?"

"Bug!" I shouted, still stamping. "Big one, but I'm fine!"

The beetle lost its grip and fell to the ground, landing on its back, legs scrabbling in the air. I brushed my pant legs, hoping I'd not picked up a bunch of parasites. Ticks! Did they have ticks here? Tick fever. I shuddered. Ants scuttled across my left shoe and up my pant legs. Lots of ants.

Then they started biting. Hard.

I leaped from one foot to the other, swatting the invaders, releasing shrill yelps.

Bud dropped an armload of limbs and rushed toward me. "What in the world? Johanna? What's wrong?"

"Ants! Oh! *Ow!* Help me!"

Bud began to stomp out the pesky critters with his heavy boots. "I should have warned you. You have to be careful where you sit."

"They're biting. Ow!"

"Here—" he grabbed me by the shoulders—"into the brush. Quick."

I dug in my heels, resisting. "I don't want to go in there—"

"You have to get out of those pants now!" He shoved me toward a thick patch of undergrowth. "Go on. Strip!"

Strip! The warmth in my cheeks turned nuclear. This was beyond the call of duty!

I dashed into the brush and unzipped and stepped out of my jeans. Seconds later the blouse came off. I picked up the pants and shook them, hard, sending a shower of ants through the air. I did the same to the blouse.

"You all right?" Bud called.

"This gives new meaning to the phrase 'ants in your pants.'"

He laughed. "You're okay, Johanna. You're going to fit right in, despite your reservations."

I looked around. Now what? Here I stood in my unmentionables. Did Bud have something to cover me?

"Should I come out now?" Surely he'd offer some kind of covering. His shirt, perhaps.

"Come out. I think most of the ants are gone."

I stood for a moment, thinking. He didn't offer his shirt. Maybe underwear was considered overdressed in these parts. The village women wore next to nothing. I couldn't stand there all day. I had to try and fit in for Sam's sake. Biting my lip, I tried to cover my condition as best as I could with hands and arms. Still, I was embarrassed, but Bud had told me to take the pants and blouse off. I stepped out of the brush.

Bud was standing, hands on hips, waiting. He focused on me, and his jaw dropped. Crimson spread across his already flushed features. He spun on his heel, looking the opposite direction.

"What's ... wrong?"

He cleared his throat. "I ... uh ... meant for you to put your clothes back on ... Sorry."

Heat flooded my face and I dove back into the bush.

See, Lord? I huffed when I picked up the jeans, gave them a sharp snap, and dragged them on. *I begged you not to send me here!*

Ants or no ants, we finished at the landing strip and returned to the village. Bud didn't mention the embarrassing incident, and I certainly wasn't going to say anything. The afternoon line in front of the clinic was even longer than the morning line had been. Bud and I approached, threading our way to the front. Sam looked up at me and smiled.

"Are all these people here to see you?" It would take hours—into the night—for Sam to evaluate all of their needs.

"Word spreads fast when the clinic is open." He continued with his work. "Can you hand me one of those cotton swabs?"

I gave him the requested item. A small child sat on the wooden table, his mother holding him. I spent the remainder of the afternoon working beside Sam, a new adventure for me. I experienced firsthand his skills and compassion. The villagers trusted him; you could see it in their eyes. I knew he'd earned their respect.

Yes, indeed. I was proud of my man.

As I'd thought, darkness had fallen by the time the last patient disappeared into the bush. Frank, Bud, Mary, and Eva had left earlier; the older couple was exhausted from the heavy workload. Bud returned after dark to row Sam and me back across the lake.

I took a deep breath. I hated to mention a delicate topic, but the situation was becoming desperate. "I need to ask you something."

Sam turned on the seat to face me. "What is it?"

"With all the heat and humidity, I need a bath."

Oh yes, I needed one. I'd never been this dirty or gone this long without bathing. Ever.

Bud entered the discussion. "You can bathe anytime you like, Johanna, right here in the lagoon."

My mouth opened. I hadn't heard right. "Pardon me?"

"In the lagoon. It's where we bathe."

I spoke slow and distinct. "There are catfish in the lake."

"Sure, but they won't bother you if you leave them alone."

I looked from Bud to Sam. He nodded. "I know you've been warned to keep your hands out of the water, but we bathe in the lagoon and the fish never bother us."

Fish, no. Eel-tailed catfish? He had to be joking. I stiffened. "I am not bathing in a lake infested with dangerous fish."

Bud tried again. "Sam's telling you the truth; they won't bother you. Eva and Mary bathe every night."

"Well, I can't ..." I looked to Sam, my eyes pleading with his in the moonlight. "Sam, I would be terrified."

"You could dip up a bucket full of water and take a sponge bath."

A sponge bath wouldn't cut it. I wanted to stretch out in cool, clean water and soak away layers of thick grime.

Sam was quiet for a moment, then, "I'll see what I can rig up. There are some two-by-fours stacked on the deck. Is it all right if I use them, Bud?"

"Sure. Use whatever you need."

"Well, my carpentry skills are weak," Sam confessed, "but you never know what you can do until you try, right?"

Bud shrugged and kept rowing. "Frank and I will help, but I must warn you we're novices when it comes to carpentry."

I grinned. "You can do it! I'm counting on you."

Sam winked back. "Have I ever let you down, my lady?"

I just shook my head. Of course not. He'd never let me down on anything.

As tired as Sam was, the dear man went right to work on my tub, refusing dinner. I helped, nailing boards together, getting needed items. I had given up on my carpentry skills when he called for me to step around the corner. Right there on the Millets' deck stood a crude wooden frame with a canvas lining.

Eden.

"I've filled it with lake water for tonight, but as soon as it rains you'll have fresh water." He looked so proud of himself my heart was touched.

I stood on tiptoe to kiss him. His beard was scratchy; he smelled of antiseptic. He was my hero. "You are a real miracle worker. I'm blessed to have you."

He sobered. "I'd do anything for you, Johanna. You know that."

Yes, I knew, and that made my plan to defect at the end of the week more contemptible. But love him as I did, I still knew that pretending an enthusiasm that I didn't feel would only lead to deeper problems.

I waited until the others were in bed and asleep before I slipped out of the hut. Dropping my robe, I stepped over the edge of the makeshift tub and lowered myself into the cool water. I hitched the bathing suit top higher; I wasn't taking any chances on someone waking up and coming out on the deck for a breath of fresh air.

Ahhh. *Absolute paradise.*

I stretched out as full length as possible, luxuriating in the sheer bliss of my first bath since coming here. A canopy of stars blazed overhead. They seemed closer, larger, and brighter here. Frogs croaked from the lake, and the village drums were loud tonight. A celebration? I'd seen the drums earlier, hourglass-shaped wooden bodies with taut, stretched monitor lizard skins for the drumhead. The sound was eerie and penetrating, but rather peaceful and soothing. I nestled deeper into the water, leaning my weight against the side facing the lake. What was Nelda doing tonight? And Mom and Pop? Were they under the same moon, the same stars? Hard to believe that thousands of miles separated us. Were they thinking about me? I sensed they were, and I sensed their prayers. Prayers for health and safety, for spiritual wisdom.

With a sigh, I sat up. Time to get clean. Now ... where was the soap?

With a groan I realized I'd left it on the deck, beyond my reach. I stood and started to step out to get it. My foot had other ideas. It slipped, and I leaned hard against the wooden side. With a subdued *crunch* the framework began to collapse. I lost my balance and floundered, grabbing for anything solid … but the whole tub was coming apart. The tub—and I—plunged into the catfish-infested lagoon.

My *eeeeeeeee!* resonated across the continent.

I dropped, the two-by-fours hitting the water around me. The lagoon waters closed over my head as I plunged into the depths. Struggling to overcome panic, I fought my way to the surface.

Sam leaned over the broken railing above, shouting my name. Some weird quirk of my mind made me realize the drums had stopped.

A mighty splash rocked me like a boat, and Sam, still clothed, surfaced beside me. He shook the water from his hair, sending a shower in my direction. "It's okay. Don't panic, Johanna, I'll get you out of here."

He reached out for me and I latched onto him, holding on with a grip born of pure terror. He made an effort to break my hold, but fear sent strength surging through my veins like a shot of steroids.

"Johanna! Let go! Don't fight me!"

"There's something biting my feet!" My scream reached the decibel of a jet plane on takeoff.

He swam around me, staying just out of reach, clearly afraid I'd drag him under. I could swim a little, but I'd forgotten everything I knew about the art. I went under again.

Sam dove for me, grabbing my shoulders and spinning me around. Then he got an arm around my neck and dragged me to the boat. He helped me aboard, and Bud offered me a hand up the ladder to the deck.

I collapsed onto the rough, splintered boards of the wooden platform. Sam climbed out of the water and dropped down beside me, gasping for breath.

I lay staring at him.

What had I ever *seen* in this man? Who was he? He must have satanic power to talk me into coming here. Him and his cobbled-up bathtub! When I finally managed words, they came out in a taut, controlled tone. "You weren't kidding about your lack of carpentry skills, were you?"

He started to answer, but I was already struggling to my feet.

"Johanna." Sam's voice held a note of pleading.

I kept walking, fearing I would break down in tears and say things I would regret come morning. But though I held my silence, there was one thing I knew.

No one — not Sam, the Laskes, or the Millets — could be surprised to know that I *hated this place.*

TWELVE
⊙⊙⊙

Sam had turned silent.

An undeniable cord of tension stretched between the two of us. I suspected he was avoiding me the next morning, but even if he had been inclined to talk, there was no time. Natives formed a long line to the clinic. I tried to help, but there wasn't much a librarian could do. I said as much to Sam, and he touched my arm.

"You can start by folding bandages." He indicated the cabinet filled with rows of blue boxes.

"Okay." I wouldn't be an ounce of help elsewhere, but I could fold gauze. I meandered to the cabinet and took out a couple of boxes and dumped the contents on the table. "You want square? Round? Oblong?"

"Square."

I folded a patch, then looked around. How was I going to cut this material? I glanced at Sam. "Scissors?"

A frown creased his forehead.

"Scissors — I need something to cut with."

In a moment he'd located the tool and handed it to me, then returned to his patients.

"What do you want me to put them in?"

"Anything — doesn't matter."

I began to cut the flimsy fabric. The material was so feathery light I chased it over the table, finally pinning it with my elbow before I managed a ragged cut. I held up the crooked piece—clearly not Chicago-Hope standard, but it would do.

Once I was through both boxes I knew I'd found yet another calling I didn't have: making bandages. The stack of pitiful-looking patches lined the weathered table. Flies buzzed the tent, and I guessed the heat was building to crematorium levels. My stomach churned.

"Are you okay, Johanna?" Sam's voice penetrated my fog.

"Fine. Just … fine." My eyes fell on the bandages and my imagination kicked in. Every injury that came through the clinic was bloody. Soon these bandages would be soaked … in blood …

My head swirled, and I reached out to grip the side of the table. The tent sides waved and changed shapes before my eyes.

"Johanna …"

"I'm *fine*, Sam!" I knew I had snapped at him, but for heaven's sake! I might be perceived as useless, but I could fold gauze! Straightening, I took a deep breath …

My knees promptly buckled and everything went dark.

***

"Johanna?"

Bud's gentle voice penetrated the darkness, and I opened my eyes. "Did I …?"

"Faint?" He nodded. "You did. But that's okay. We've all done it at one time or another."

Bud glanced at Sam, who was working on a patient. "You gave us all a scare. Sam told me I had to sit with you until you came to. He would have done it himself, but—"

I nodded. "The patients need him."

With Bud's help, I stood and went to watch Sam as he worked. The villager on the table had an infected arm, which he held out for Sam's inspection, wincing from the pain. The skin was red and tight, swollen, with a bulbous area protruding like an undersized coconut.

Two stout natives pinned him on the table while Bud went to hold a basin under the man's arm. Sam proceeded to lance the wound. He slashed the shiny scalpel down in one swift, piercing stroke. The villager's body arched; his pain-saturated cry filled our ears and senses.

I recoiled from the stench of decay as Sam worked until the infected area was drained. The patient slumped in his friends' arms while Sam probed the wound with tweezers. He withdrew the instrument, holding it aloft, triumph on his face as he waved it around for all to see the half-inch black thorn.

I was going to be sick.

The natives grinned and nodded. The patient looked immensely relieved. He nodded and offered a weak smile.

I took a deep breath. "You mean that little thorn caused that much infection?"

"This is tropical country, hot and humid. Infection can set in quickly here." Sam grinned. "I'm glad you're back with us, but you still look a little green around the gills. Bud can help me here. Why don't you sit in on the women's meeting?"

"I think I will. Thanks." I knew now why I'd never followed my childhood wish to be a nurse. Bud took over, and I wandered to the open-air meeting.

A sizable group of women gathered near the clinic entrance. They sat on pieces of logs, large rocks, or stood. I noticed none sat on the ground, and I had a good idea why. They didn't want ants in their pants—if they wore any. I leaned against a large tree, the likes of which I'd never seen before, and hoped it wasn't harboring anything that would attach itself to me.

Eva did most of the gesturing, and though the women seemed polite enough, I sensed a certain disinterest in the subject. How many of them cared about personal hygiene? Eva worked with picture boards, showing images of babies, buckets of water, and bars of castile soap the missionaries handed out. Old campfires, animal waste, rotting vegetation, and unwashed bodies made up the pungent essence of everything that bothered me about this village.

I listened as Eva sought to make connection. As a woman pulled her toddler from the dirt and onto her lap, preparing to nurse the child, I decided none of the women were listening. Didn't Eva see their total lack of concern for cleanliness? My eyes wandered around the gathering.

A woman seated across the circle stroked the strip of bright-colored fabric tied at her throat. I squinted, then, eyes wide, peered closer. A scarf. I leaned for a closer look.

That *was* my scarf!

That woman had *my* scarf, the one that two hours ago was lying across the foot of my cot. I wanted to leap across the open area and snatch it away from her. I was stopped from the foolish action by the realization that she was at least three inches taller and twenty pounds heavier than I and could probably sling me into the branches like a rag doll. Yet I couldn't stand by and allow blatant thievery!

I eyed the intruder from beneath lowered brows. She'd been in my space, handling my possessions. The very thought made me seethe. How could Sam find such compassion for these people? Stealing—on top of everything else. It wasn't the loss of a scarf; I found the whole concept of stealing offensive. I eased around the circle and sat down beside the woman. She was preoccupied with fingering the silk, her dark eyes shining. I sat as still as a church mouse, then reached over and snatched the scarf from her neck. My eyes remained on Eva, pretending a rapt interest in the art of lathering soap.

A soft gasp had escaped the villager. She sat motionless, her eyes flicking from the scarf to me. I refused to look at her. The very *nerve* of her slipping into the Laskes' hut and taking what belonged to *me*. Confident that my possession was mine again, I relaxed and watched the lesson.

She tore the scarf from my hands.

Gasping, I ripped it back.

Back and forth the fabric went until I realized our behavior was causing a scene. Others turned to look at us, brows wrinkled. Eva glanced up, sending me a frown. She shook her head, eyes focused on the scarf.

One vicious rip and the silk returned to the thief's hands. I sat quivering with rage. How dare she! How *dare* she! That scarf had cost me a day's pay. I stewed until my blood pressure oozed out of my brain before I stood up and stomped off. When I left the meeting, the villager was immersed in the lesson, my scarf draped around her neck.

I waited for the meeting to end, pacing back and forth, one frustrated thought after another chasing through my mind. Clearly, from Eva's reaction during the meeting, neither she nor Mary would be inclined to help me reclaim my scarf. Fine. I'd accept the loss. But there was something else that bothered me even more. Something I couldn't escape.

At last the meeting ended, and as Eva, Mary, and I walked back to the boat, I asked the question that had been tearing me apart. "Why do you have classes? The women weren't paying attention to you. Why waste the effort?"

Eva's reply was placid. "We plant the seed. Someone else may water it, and still others may reap the harvest. It's not ours to question God's purpose for calling us here. Our job is to do our best to serve him by helping to enrich the villagers' lives where we can."

I had to admit they were doing that. Their zealous dedication made me feel small and unworthy. Each new day here brought home the fact that I was a librarian, not a missionary. I didn't belong. I would never belong. So why fight it? I would tell Sam that I was leaving and let him make the proper arrangements.

We ate a simple lunch prepared by Mary. I was more in the way than anything else. The others talked about their morning's work. Sam had treated a man for dog bite, another for an impacted tooth. I didn't want to know what he'd done for that one. My treacherous mind insisted on picturing him with one knee on the man's chest, wrenching out the painful tooth with a pair of rusty pliers. Surely it hadn't come to that. Then again . . .

I prayed for continuing good health during the remainder of my brief stay.

After lunch Sam pushed his plate aside and stood, looking straight at me. "Would you like to take a walk?"

I didn't. After the ant episode I didn't plan to enter the forest again. But if Sam wanted a walk, I would go. Resigned, I rose from my chair. Was he going to tell me how disappointed he was in my lack of effort to adapt? If so, he had every right to express his dissatisfaction. No one could accuse me of being an overachiever. Sam deserved better.

We got in the boat, and he paddled upstream from the village to a sandy cove so peaceful I could feel tension draining from me. Songbirds chirped and the wind strummed through the branches of the overhanging trees. We got out of the boat, and Sam secured the craft to a narrow sapling growing at the edge of the strip of exposed shoreline. He spread a blanket and we sat down on the beach. I slipped off my shoes and socks, pushing my toes into the warm sand. Sam slipped his arm around my waist and I leaned against him, content for the first time since—well, I couldn't think of the last time I'd felt at peace.

"Look, Johanna." Sam pointed at a cluster of yellow orchids growing in a tree. "See how they cling, with no visible means of support? God created them and put them there for our enjoyment."

"Very nice. I've never seen an orchid that particular shade before."

Leaning closer, he nibbled on the tip of my ear. "Want me to pick one for you?"

I smiled, allowing his affection better access. "No. They're perfect where they are. Let's not disturb them."

"I want you to look at the island. Really look. This is one of the most beautiful places in the world. Look around you. Tell me what you see."

Okay, I'd play his game. "I see trees with long vines hanging from them. I see thick brush, flowers, a large bird—a buzzard, I believe—and catfish-infested water."

"Yes, all of that. Like anywhere you go, this island has danger as well as beauty. Conflicting emotions, as it were. Like you seem to have."

Where on earth did he get that idea? There was no conflict in *my* heart. I didn't like it here, period. I would never like it here.

You don't want *to like it here.*

The insight brought me up short. Sam had only asked that I try. Guilt assailed me. How he must resent me for my lack of spiritual growth.

"Listen." Sam held up a finger. "You might hear a deer's alarm snort. Clouded leopards sneak through the undergrowth. The birds range everywhere — from the huge argus pheasant to dozens of species of babblers and almost as many bulbuls. Look in the water and you'll see a rich assortment of fish. All around us are primates, but that's not all. There are squirrels here too — a wide range of sizes and a great variety of habits, from five-inch-long pygmy squirrels scampering on the ground to giant flying squirrels in the trees."

I looked around us as he talked, seeing, as if for the first time, all he was pointing out. Sam's Papua New Guinea unfolded before me.

I leaned against him. "The people have placed their trust in you. You must be very gratified." I made a conscious decision not to mention the woman and the pilfered scarf. I was trying. Really I was.

"The people in this village have done so. But in the more remote areas, we'll have a more difficult time winning their respect. Did you know that headhunters still exist in the far recesses of the jungle?"

My jaw dropped and I forgot to breathe. Headhunters? Half-naked natives who killed and ate people? Cannibals? The memory of a shrunken head I'd once seen surfaced like scum on a pond. How could Sam sound so calm?

He glanced at me, and his gaze sharpened. "Is something wrong? You look pale."

"Is something *wrong*? You mention headhunters and then ask if something is wrong? I can't believe you, Sam. Aren't you the least bit concerned for our safety?"

"I told you they were in remote areas. You'll never see one."

He had *that* right. I would do everything I could to avoid making personal contact. "How do you know the villagers won't decide to revert back to their old ways and start collecting heads, beginning with ours?" Still (and I get points for this one) I didn't mention the pilfered scarf. But in my mind, the woman's thievery just pointed to the fact that in some ways the villagers were still as primitive as the headhunters.

He laughed. "You're funny, you know that? I'm glad you came with me. Having you here makes it more enjoyable." He bent and stole another kiss.

"I'm glad you find me amusing."

"I find you totally enchanting." He got to his feet and pulled me to mine. "Let's walk."

We picked our way along the rugged shoreline, hand in hand. After the first few minutes I forgot to look over my shoulder for headhunters—imaginary or otherwise. The jungle seen through Sam's eyes was fascinating. I experienced the most delicate, exotic plants and flowers, butterflies, fish, things I hadn't noticed before. His love for the island glistened through his words and expression. He wanted to be here—was proud to put his entire heart and soul into his work.

"You do love this place, don't you?"

He helped me over a fallen log before answering. "It's my world, Johanna. Or at least, I'd like it to be—with you by my side. There are multitudes of doctors back home, and for a while I was content to be one of them. But now I see the discomfort, the human misery, the celebrations of beauty and exotic pleasures, the triumph of the human spirit in the face of so much hopelessness, and I know this is where God wants me. Whether here or elsewhere, what could be a better basis for contentment than for a man — or a woman — to know he is fulfilling a God-determined purpose?"

I shriveled in the face of true dedication. Like Eva and Mary, Sam was confident of God's purpose for his life.

We paused at a grove of pineapples. "You see these plants?"

I smiled. "How could I not see them? They're beautiful." I knew from experience they were delicious too. Mary served the sweet, juicy fruit three times a day.

"This field was planted by missionaries many years ago."

I studied the grove with new appreciation. Here were tangible results of previous missionaries' tenure on the island. They had left behind something of beauty and usefulness. Just as Sam and the others would do for those who came after them.

Further along we discovered papaya and mangoes. Sam peeled a large mango and handed it to me. I bit into the luscious yellow-orange fruit and juice spurted out, running down my chin. The sweet explosion refreshed my dry throat. I'd eaten supermarket mangoes, but they couldn't begin to rival this one — fresh-picked, sun-warmed, and full of rich fruity flavor with a hint of pine aftertaste.

Sam laughed. "I take it you like mangoes."

"Adore them, and according to Mary, this is the way to eat them. She says cutting the fruit from the seed and eating it with a fork changes the taste."

177 / LORI COPELAND

"I've heard her theory, but I don't think a fork could dent this flavor."

No doubt about it, this afternoon would be one of my good memories. Had there been more days like this, maybe I wouldn't be so anxious to leave. I nibbled the last bite of pulp from the flat, fibrous seed. "What do I do with this?"

He grinned. "Toss it into the brush. The next time you come by here you'll find another mango tree. Things grow fast here."

If only my faith would do the same.

We picked our way through an outcrop of volcanic rock. On this island one either climbed or descended the stony escarpments. Sam held tight to my hand, guiding me over the more treacherous places. We paused at the edge of a high cliff, facing the sea now. Here, with the wind blowing through my hair, I didn't know why I was troubled. One could almost hear the voice of God in the breeze.

We stood, listening to waves slap the ragged shoreline. A gentle draft touched my face, filled my spirit. Sam slid his arm around me, and I relaxed against him, feeling more like we were back in the library coffee shop. He bent his head, his lips meeting mine, and I yielded myself to his affection. I loved this man with all of my heart.

Enough to set him free?

I didn't have the answer. This afternoon had calmed me. Maybe I wasn't giving the experiment enough time. I would have gone on forever in my safe, predictable world, but God had intervened. I understood he did that sometimes. Took a person's life and turned it inside out and upside down. He'd rattled my cage and yanked my pitifully short leash all at the same time.

Sam raised his head and gazed into my eyes. "How are you doing, Johanna? Really."

I met his probing eyes, knowing what he wanted to hear, yet incapable of saying the words. "The isolation bothers me. Just like the dirt, the bugs, the mosquitoes. I abhor the leeches, which I've not experienced yet, but I still fear."

Sam turned to stare out at the water. His expression sobered, and I searched for the disappointment I knew he must be feeling. I knew my words had wounded him. He had expected much and I was offering nothing. I thought of the stack of children's books packed away in my luggage. I'd thought I might read them to the children, but I hadn't even unpacked them yet.

Had I made my best effort to minister to these people?

I knew the answer and it shamed me. So far my concern had been for my discomforts, and I'd wailed long and loud about them. *Lord, I'm so sorry. I'll try. Really try. Not for Sam ... but for you.*

It was settled. I would stay on. Sam need never know I had contemplated leaving sooner.

He turned to meet my gaze, mischief twinkling in his eyes. "Have you forgiven me for your bathtub?"

I laughed. "I'm working on it. Are you sure it's safe to bathe in the lake?"

"Ask Eva and Mary to let you go with them the next time. They'll take care of you."

I sighed. "They have so little, but they're so happy." Happier and more contented than most women I knew back home.

"They're dedicated women, confident in their purpose. Frank and Bud are blessed."

179 / LORI COPELAND

Pain filled me and I choked back a sharp response. Frank and Bud were blessed. But not Sam. *He* wasn't blessed with such a woman. Well, not all of us had the conviction that we knew God's will.

But I wanted to. Oh, how I wanted to.

Twilight colored the sky when we rowed toward our huts. Nighttime spread over the village, and I could picture the families gathered, sitting cross-legged on a ribbed floor of split palm or bamboo, or stretching out for a rest with their heads pillowed on the well-worn timber, crunching thick green betel nuts between their teeth. Their ways were not my ways, but fresh from my afternoon in the jungle with Sam and my mental talk with God, I was filled with a sense of peace. I liked the feeling better than the disquiet I'd been harboring.

Sam let the small boat drift. He seemed in no hurry to return to the huts. The jungle embraced us, wrapping us in shadows. The moon, a platinum crescent on the black velvet sky, crept over the line of trees and brushed the lagoon with silver. A sleepy bird twittered from nearby, and from deep in the jungle came the hunting cry of a nocturnal animal. Beauty and danger, the good and the bad, the same all over the world.

Just more obvious here than in Saginaw.

Sam reached for my hand. "Do you see the beauty, Johanna? The good?"

"Yes, I can see it." The shadows hid the dirt and squalor. The moonlight touched everything with a dreamlike glow. Overhead, diamond dust stars twinkled with a radiance I'd never seen anywhere. Everything here was more defined, closer to nature. Closer to God. I had a feeling he was smiling down on the two of us. We drifted hand in hand, saying very little, but I was aware of Sam. So aware I could have closed my eyes and still seen his image printed against my eyelids, imprinted on my mind. Mom and Pop and Nelda—my former life was a vapor.

I lay back and drank in serenity, letting it fill my pores and filter gently to my heart.

And I prayed like I'd never prayed before that it would last.

THIRTEEN

◎◎◎

The village roosters (I had come to think of them as the village idiots) woke me with a wild racket, as if they had a duty to crow the sun out of the eastern horizon long before the earth awoke. The noise wouldn't have been so bad if the animals had sounded off at the same time, but their crowing apparatus was set seconds apart, so some came in a few beats behind the others. One with a shrill screech waited until the others had finished before blaring his morning greeting, starting high and ending on a low, long, drawn-out note.

For a few minutes I lay fantasizing about wringing a few scrawny necks and serving the missionaries my specialty: a pot of homemade chicken and noodles. (Mom, a champion noodle maker, had taught me her secret: add an envelope of chicken gravy to the broth.) I gave up the idea, though. I couldn't kill a gnat, let alone a chicken. Even if I could manage to dispatch the thing, I'd have no idea how to clean it. My chickens came from the supermarket, plucked, cleaned, and ready for the pot. And I didn't destroy someone's grandmother ... or what the villagers believed were sacred.

I stretched and peered at my watch. Five a.m. Light was beginning to filter through the window. Frank and Eva were already in the kitchen. A missionary's day started early and ended late. It would be hard to revert back to my old routine of sleeping until seven when I returned home.

The smell of perking coffee lured me out of bed. Before pulling on my clothes, I gave them a hefty shake to remove any unwanted visitors, like spiders or other insects. Having the huts on stilts eliminated the fear of snakes, but flying insects invaded in hordes.

Once dressed, I reached for my glasses in their usual place on the table beside my bed. My hand encountered empty space. I looked down. What in the . . . ? *Where* were my glasses? I remembered putting them on the stand last night, moments before I went to sleep. Maybe they'd slipped off and fallen on the floor.

Grunting with the effort, I got down on my hands and knees to peer under the cot. No glasses. After five minutes of searching, I gave up. The specs were not in my cubicle. Perhaps I'd left them out in the main part of the hut, but that didn't seem likely.

I stumbled out into the kitchen to face the day, which was more than a tad blurry without my glasses. "Good morning."

"Johanna." Eva turned from the stove. "Did we wake you?"

"No, the roosters took care of that. Have you seen my glasses?"

"No, where did you leave them?"

"Beside my bed, but they're not there now."

She exchanged a knowing look with Frank. "Did you hear anything during the night?"

He sighed. "No, but that doesn't mean anything."

"What are you talking about?" From what I could discern of their expressions they suspected something; I should have guessed what by now, but I hadn't.

"The huts are supposed to be off-limits, but sometimes the villagers break the rules."

Of course! The thief had struck again! "You mean someone was in my room last night?" The thought of a native creeping across the floor in the dark, standing beside my bed, stealing my glasses sent shivers down my spine. But only for a moment. Anger jumped in to displace the shivers.

Stealing my *glasses*? Now they had gone too far. I needed those glasses; the contacts were uncomfortable in the muggy climate. Whoever took those glasses was in serious trouble. My Christian charity extended just so far, and this superseded a saint's limits.

Eva frowned. "Did you look under your bed?"

"I looked everywhere. The glasses are gone."

She glanced at Frank then back at me. "If someone's taken your glasses, they'll show up. The villagers tend to show off their pilfered objects with great pride."

Well, how nice for them. And Eva didn't even sound upset. Of course, she wasn't the one walking around blind. Those villagers were a pack of thieves! They were—

So is this the way you try to do better?

I clamped down on my mental rant. Today was supposed to be the beginning of a new era when I'd do my best to communicate with these people, make an effort to understand their ways. Fine. I could do that. In fact, if I found the crook who stole my glasses, I intended to communicate big-time. And they were going to have no problem understanding me.

Scripture. I needed to read Scripture. Calm down. Gain strength from the Word. Wasn't that what Sam had done?

I pulled the small Bible out of my backpack. I held it between my hands for a moment, then let it fall open. *Okay,*

Lord. Words of encouragement. I need wonderful words of encouragement. I glanced at the top of the page. Jeremiah. Good. I looked down, and a verse seemed to jump out at me: Jeremiah 22:10. With a grateful smile, I read it.

"Do not weep for the dead king or mourn his loss; rather, weep bitterly for him who is exiled, because he will never return nor see his native land again."

I slammed the book shut before I took the message to heart.

We cleaned up after breakfast and walked to the boat. Mary sat on the bench beside me as we crossed the lagoon. "Are you ready to see your little shadow again?"

The little girl they called *Poo* had latched onto me the past couple of days, dogging my every step. Efforts to discourage the child had proven useless.

"What *is* the child's name? It's not actually Poo, is it?" I couldn't imagine anyone, even the villagers, naming a child Poo. The little girl with bushy black hair the size of a basketball and sparkling round, black eyes lived with her grandfather in a hut on the village perimeter. The missionaries had no information regarding the whereabouts of the child's parents or siblings.

"I don't know the child's name," Mary admitted. "Her name sounds like "Poo" when her Bum and others address her. She's an intelligent little girl. Eva feels she might, in time, communicate with the child."

I didn't doubt that. More than in any of the other children I'd recognized certain intelligence in Poo's young eyes.

Mary turned toward the village. "Poo understands more than she admits. In fact, I believe some of the adults understand more than they let on. After all, they've been listening to Frank and Eva for twelve years and Bud and me for the past four. They're bound to have picked up a few words in that length of time."

"Why wouldn't they use them then?"

"A general resistance to change?" Mary shrugged. "Who knows? We'll get a breakthrough someday. We just have to keep plugging away at the communication gap."

Bud guided the boat to a gentle stop, and Sam climbed out and secured it to a large rock, then helped us women out. As soon as my feet touched land, Poo was there. She grasped my sleeve, spouting a stream of garbled words. Sam responded to my upraised eyebrows.

"You don't have to understand the words; just watch the gestures. I'd say she wants to be your friend."

Friend? This child was more nuisance than anything else. I couldn't move without tripping over her. Poo was like a possessive cat, always underfoot, clawing at my sleeve or pant leg. I'd turn around and she would be gone, then a second later she'd be back.

She was making me dizzy with the way she came and went.

Sam reached for my hand and we started up the steep incline. "Want to help in the clinic today?"

"Sure, why not. I'm a born medic." We both smiled.

On the way through the village we passed the scruffy black and white dog still tied to a tree. Sam indicated the menace. "That's a mean one. Even the villagers are afraid of him. Don't get too close."

The dog hunched down, growling low in his throat as we walked past. He lunged toward us. I jumped and clutched Sam's arm. He stepped between me and the snarling animal. The grapevine tied to him held fast, jerking the animal backward. Sam smoothed my hair. "He's secure. He can't hurt you."

I didn't mention that the dog had a fondness for sweets. I'd been feeding the growling monster for several days now, though he still seemed anxious to bite the hand that fed him.

Why would the villagers keep such an animal? The owner was nowhere in sight. I wasn't sure who fed and watered him, but someone must. The villagers didn't need a watchdog, unless ...

I froze.

Headhunters! They kept the dog to alert them of enemies who might prowl through the night seeking unsuspecting victims. My gaze darted to the jungle, visualizing painted warriors peering from the shadows.

Either that, Reason whispered, *or they're simply nuts and don't know what to do with the animal, so they just tie it to a tree and let it bark.*

I let out a sigh. I'd been in that jungle and hadn't seen a single headhunter. Sam was right—the more familiar things became, the less I feared them. No, I would not add headhunters to my list of worries.

A long line had already formed in front of the clinic. Today some of the natives were on crude, homemade stretchers, while others sat on the ground, supporting their heads with both hands. Mothers carried infants, and small children crowded the area, running and yelling. I held to Sam's shirttail as he pushed through the crowd, trying to enter the clinic. The villagers parted, then surged back in a wave of unwashed flesh, all jabbering at once. My stomach roiled, more from anxiety than distaste. One could become claustrophobic in such close contact with all these needy people.

We threaded our way inside the clinic to find it as crowded as the outside. Sam set his case of medical instruments on the low table, pausing to speak to a woman in the front of the line. The woman grasped his hand, her eyes radiating pain. She had a large laceration on her right arm.

According to the wall thermometer the temperature hovered in the upper nineties; the flies were so thick they covered the ground and swarmed in a black cloud inside the clinic. I blinked, fighting my contacts in the heat and humidity.

Sam motioned for the woman to take her seat on the low stool while he examined the cut. After cleansing the wound and applying an antibiotic ointment, he moved to the next patient. The multitude of injuries and illnesses became a dark cloud hovering over me. Sam was so tolerant, so eager to help, but he worked with inadequate supplies and equipment. True, he supplemented with prayer, but it had to be discouraging when he thought of the state-of-the-art medical equipment and medicines he'd left behind.

The wretched dog outside barked, driving me to distraction. He was an ill-tempered beast. "What *is* he barking at?"

"The children like to taunt him." Sam pushed his way through the crowd to the outside. A second later I heard him roar. "You kids *get* away from there and leave that dog alone!"

A sudden hush fell over the villagers, and I didn't blame them. I'd never heard Sam raise his voice before. The villagers might have no idea what he said, but you could see they recognized his angry tone. Clearly, Dr. Littleton was ticked.

And I? I was astonished at how moved I was.

Sam's compassion extended even to something as unlovable and fierce as that dog. But the creature was helpless and needed a champion.

Truly, Sam was a strong, vital witness for his God.

Poo had burrowed her way through the mass of people to stand beside me. I'd stumbled over the half-pint at least a dozen times that morning. Each time she would look up and give a hint of a smile. She liked me — why I didn't know, because all I'd done for her was hand her a few pieces of candy. Still, her adoration shone in her eyes and brightened her smile. I sighed and tried to concentrate on the medical tasks at hand. My anger was so ghastly my head pounded.

Around one o'clock the crowd had thinned enough that we paused for a break. I was eating a mango when I looked up to see Poo's Bum staggering across the muddy stretch of ground, headed for the clinic. Judging from his uneven gait, I decided he'd had more than his allotted share of betel powder this morning.

I watched as he approached. He looked different today — and not just because of his drunken step. He was wearing the usual scanty loincloth, his hair matted and tangled, a straw threaded through a large hole in his nose, but something was different.

The realization hit like a hammer blow.

Glasses.

He was wearing glasses.

I stared, my eyes narrowing. Anger swamped me like a tsunami. So the case of the missing glasses was solved. That wretched old man was wearing *my* glasses!

I forgot Sam and Poo and all my good intentions. Dropping my half-eaten mango, I waited until he reached the door of the clinic, then snatched the glasses off his face. He reared back, outraged shock showing in every line of his scrawny body. Once I had the glasses in my hands I paused to examine them.

I should have run while I had the chance.

The old man grabbed the rims, catching the earpiece. We struggled like a pair of snapping, snarling dogs, though I tried to be gentle and not destroy the valued spectacles. He jabbered in his language and I screeched in mine; it would have been difficult to say which of us made the most noise.

Using one hand to hold the glasses, I used the other to shove him backward, hard. He stumbled, losing his balance but holding firm to the left earpiece. I stared down at my mangled eyewear, overcome with rage. He'd *broken* my earpiece.

I lunged at him, yanking the severed piece from his hand. Ignoring his protestations, I worked to fit the two pieces back together. Well, great. Just *great*! Where would I find an optometrist out here?

About that time Sam came around the corner of the hut, eyes wide. He jumped in to break up the fight and send Bum on his way. I watched the man's normal gait and realized he hadn't been drunk. My prescription was too strong for him.

Sam took the glasses from me, turning them over in his hands. "I take it these belong to you."

"He *stole* them and now they're broken!" I was so mad I could spit. "Now what am I going to do? They're thieves — every last one of them!"

"Calm down, Johanna. What seems wrong to you isn't to them. They see things differently here." He reached for a roll of surgical tape. "Let me see what I can do."

With a surgeon's dexterity Sam soon had the earpiece taped back on my glasses. I had calmed down by the time he finished, but no one could call me happy. I would now wear large black frame glasses adorned with white surgical tape—but so what? This village wasn't exactly a center of fashion.

Sam handed them to me. "See how that works."

I tried them on, and while they sat a little uneven, giving me a cockeyed view of the world, I could see through them—or I would be able to once I removed the contacts. I was still plenty steamed though. Thieves! The whole lot were chronic thieves.

Poo stood beside me, dark eyes clouded. She reached out and patted my leg, but I jerked away. When her eyes darkened, shame flooded my soul. She was a child, for heaven's sake. Drawing a deep breath, I exhaled and reached out to rest my hand on her bare shoulder. Her smile returned and shone like the sun coming out from behind a cloud.

Sam grinned. "She loves you."

"Forgive me if I don't feel warm and fuzzy right now." But I kept my tone light so I wouldn't further upset the child. I gave a reluctant chuckle and admitted, "All right, so I'm not Mother Teresa."

Wild barking split the air. I turned to see that the children were again poking fun at the dog. The animal was going crazy, yipping and bounding in the air. Adult villagers ignored the racket, but the children were laughing and lunging at the dog, twisting away at the last moment to stay out of reach. Then the dog gave a mighty leap—and the vine holding him snapped.

He tumbled end over end, snarling and snapping as he rolled across the bare ground.

Villagers bolted, yelling as they scrambled for safety. I'd never seen a place clear so fast. Men who had been on stretchers, struggling to breathe a moment ago, resurrected and scattered into the vegetation. Women and children scurried like turkeys the week before Thanksgiving.

One native who'd been rolling on the ground, moaning, jumped to his feet and shinned up the side of the clinic wall like he'd been fired from the mouth of a cannon. Now he sat atop the thatched roof, feet drawn up, curled into a fetal position as he stared wide-eyed at the snarling beast.

The village had emptied of natives.

Frank shouted a warning as the dog turned his attention to us, the only fools left in attack range. Frank reached for Eva's hand, pulling her toward the nearest palm. Bud helped Mary up onto a low-hanging limb while the frenzied canine nipped at their heels. Sam grabbed my hand. "Hurry, Johanna! This way!"

The dog bounded from one tree to the other while the missionaries drew their feet higher, clinging to their perches. Sam dragged me across the ground to a low-branched tree. Swinging me up in his arms, he shoved me up and I caught a limb and pulled myself farther into the tree, thankful for my childhood tree-climbing years. The dog hurtled toward Sam. I yelled a warning and Sam leaped straight up, grabbing a limb and swinging himself atop it in one smooth movement.

Until that moment, I had no idea the man was part monkey.

We clung to our lofty perches while the dog strutted from one tree to another, barking out a dare to descend. I was reminded of Goliath and the Israelites, except we had no David to come to our rescue. The dog knew who was in charge. And it wasn't us.

The sun blazed down, filtering through the scant foliage and searing my skin. I leaned my forehead against the rough bark, biting back tears. Every day in this horrible place brought a new disaster. And I had been so good to that dog—jelly beans, sometimes twice a day.

"Don't worry, Johanna," Sam called. "He'll tire of the game before long."

I stared down at our four-legged tormentor. "He doesn't look like he's getting tired. I think he's trying to figure out how to climb trees."

We sat. One hour. Two hours. The dog backed up and took a running leap, snapping at Bud's foot when it dangled just out of reach. Mary screamed and Bud jerked his foot higher. The dog strutted around—king of the hill. Sam tucked his feet up closer and I shifted my position, almost losing my grip on the tree trunk.

Three hours.

The dog had finally decided to lie down, resting his head on his paws.

"Is he asleep?" Sam whispered.

I angled a look first at the beast, then at Sam. "I can't tell."

Sam made a move to descend—and we had our answer. The beast sprang to life. I yelped and clawed at the tree limbs, the rough bark stripping skin off my bare hands. The dog strode back to Frank and Eva's tree. Sam shot me a weak smile. "Think what a funny story this will be when you're back home."

I stared at him. He'd come unhinged. "Hilarious."

"Well, maybe not right now, but you'll be surprised how time will change your perspective."

"Yes, Sam. That will surprise me." I'd had enough. I was tired and frustrated and hungry.

Hungry ... of course! I still had three packets of jelly beans in my backpack. I scanned the ground. The pack was leaning against the base of our tree, and the animal was now sniffing the pack. If the dog didn't eat me alive I had a chance. Why hadn't I thought of the candy earlier?

I glanced at Sam. "Try to distract the mutt. I'm going down."

"You're *what*? Johanna, have you lost your mind?"

"Just try and distract him; throw something at him."

The animal had returned to our tree and dropped to the ground panting, his gaze pinned on us.

"Johanna—"

"Throw something, Sam, or plan to spend the night in this tree."

He broke off a sizable limb and took careful aim. "What if I hit him?"

"Try not to. Just scare him off long enough for me to shinny down."

Sam's throw proved accurate. The stick landed in front of the mutt. He yelped, tucked his tail between his legs, and disappeared around the corner of the clinic. I slid down the trunk and fished in my backpack for the candy, keeping an eye on the clinic. Seconds later the persecutor rounded the corner, ears back, yapping, teeth bared. I pitched a few of the sweets at him, wishing it was laxative instead.

Mean-spirited, yes. But the toughie needed a lesson.

The animal skidded to a halt and started gobbling up the goodies. Then he looked around for more. When he looked up at me I threw two entire bags as far across the clearing as my arm allowed. The dog scrambled after them.

I spun to the trees. "Everyone! Clear out while you can!" I motioned for the villagers to scat!

Natives slid down tree trunks and ran. Sam hurried to help the victim stranded on the clinic roof, supporting him away from the scene. The area cleared in three minutes flat. The patients would have to return the following morning after some brave soul captured the dog and resecured him to the tree.

After devouring the first bag, the beast looked up and then started on the second packet. By then Sam, the missionaries, and I were well on our way to the boat. The six of us were a weary, sunburned, and parched group as our footsteps thundered down the incline to the boat.

Oh, yeah, missions were my thing—lovin' it more every day, Lord.

FOURTEEN

I was up earlier than usual; the thought of a villager prowling the hut cost me a night's sleep. While I waited for Eva and Frank to rise, I decided to secure everything I owned in my suitcases. Sam could excuse the local population's thievery, but I couldn't.

As I rearranged blouses and slacks, refolded and straightened, I came across two large safety pins I'd carried in my luggage since I was the tender age of fourteen. I was always prepared—a throwback from my Girl Scout days. The pins, along with the small pair of scissors I used to cut tags off new clothing, came in handy a few times. Seeing them now gave me a sense of something familiar. A sense I sorely needed.

Once the suitcases were in order, I relocked the luggage and put the key on a silver chain around my neck. *Now* let's see anyone steal my stuff. Tonight I'd lock my glasses in a suitcase too.

I pulled the curtain aside and stepped into the kitchen, where a yawning Eva was ladling coffee into a filter. "Good morning, Eva. Need any help?"

"You can cut the pineapple." She sounded cheerful this morning. "We're having eggs. Poo's Bum delivered them a few minutes ago."

I gaped at her. "He did what?" An egg was believed to be a valued commodity to the villagers, not to be shared with anyone but family.

She shrugged. "I think he meant them for you, but such a treat! There are six. One for each of us, unless you object."

"No, of course not. Let's all enjoy the treat."

She turned and grasped my hand. "Thank you. Luxuries are hard to come by here. We had our own hens at one time, but the villagers . . ."

"Stole them."

She sighed. "We gave up and decided that we could live without eggs."

"Too bad he didn't bring bacon to go with them."

She laughed, returning to the coffee. Frank came in, followed by Bud, Mary, and Sam. Mary busied herself at the stove scrambling eggs. When they were steaming and the toast browned in a skillet, the six of us sat down at the table.

While Sam asked the blessing, I peered at the others around the table. These people seemed so free and so happy, sharing what they had, eating in one hut one day and the other the next. Their smiles warmed me; their spirits challenged me. And, I admitted as I listened to Sam's dear voice, the missionaries were starting to feel like kin. Because of them, there were even times I almost forgot I was in the middle of a jungle, thousands of miles away from all that was familiar.

After the amens, we all dug in. The eggs tasted more delicious than I'd ever remembered them tasting at home. I cleared my throat during a lull in conversation. The missionaries looked at me, and I took a deep breath and plunged ahead. "There's something that bothers me. You live here without comforts most people would consider necessities.

You're surrounded by danger, but you don't appear to feel deprived or afraid. What's your secret?"

Frank smiled. "No secret. We enjoy luxuries as much as anyone, but this is our life's work. We surrender our lives anew every day—" he glanced at his wife, smile widening—"sometimes every hour."

I still didn't understand and it must have showed, because Frank shook his head. "Not everyone is called to the mission field."

"And if not, they shouldn't feel guilty." Bud's tone was gentle. "Mary and I serve where God calls, but Johanna, if you don't feel his call—and I think everyone at this table would understand if you don't—then serve God wherever he puts you. Not where he puts me or Mary or Frank and Eva. Not even where he puts Sam."

I asked the question I couldn't seem to escape. The same one I'd asked the waitress who was giving up her life for missions. "But how do you *know* what God is doing in your life?"

"Honey—" Mary reached over to cover my hand with hers—"my grandmother once told me the way to decide if God is calling you to a particular field was if the thought wouldn't let up. If you have compulsive thoughts to do something, don't analyze them to death; do it. But if you feel no peace about a situation, then *don't do it*. Peace is God's umpire."

I frowned. "I don't follow."

"In some sports, it's the umpire who lets players know if they're doing things right. If they're following the rules. While trust in our God is not a sport, the peace he gives when we are in his will is our umpire, our indication that we're doing it right, fulfilling our purpose. God's will isn't some code we have to break, but rather a marvelous truth to be discovered! I believe what he wants most is our willingness to become what he intends and go where he leads. Often, when we offer a simple heartfelt willingness to serve, he will open the way and provide the power to accomplish the goal — but it won't be one you can predict. I can promise you that much."

I focused on my plate, my cheeks burning. My lack of willingness was so obvious, how could this ever be God's will for me? And yet, Sam's expression suggested he expected me to leap to my feet and exclaim, "Eureka!"

But I couldn't; I still wasn't sure I got it.

"Bum stole my glasses. Doesn't it bother you that he was in this hut prowling around in the middle of the night, touching our things?"

"What things?" Mary laughed. "The nice thing about having nothing is you don't have to worry about losing it."

"I don't believe Bum was the culprit."

I looked at Sam. "If not Bum, then who?" Whoever it was had no business being in here.

"Poo."

I stared at Mary, my mouth gaping. *"Poo?"*

She nodded.

"You mean ..." I opened my mouth, closed it, and then opened it again. "You think the little girl took my glasses?"

"She's fascinated with you. She wanted something of yours."

I had a strong urge to give that little rascal a piece of my mind — one she wouldn't understand, but one she wouldn't soon forget! So *that's* why she clung to me like a tick. The child was looking for something to steal. Well, she'd have a hard time stealing from me again. My fingers went to the chain around my neck, reassuring myself that my luggage contents were safe.

"By the way." Mary stood up and began to clear the table. "Has anyone borrowed the can opener and forgotten to return it?"

There was one can opener for the whole group. We all shook our heads.

"Oh, dear." She paused. "I must have laid it down and someone—maybe Poo—took it."

The women cleaned up the remains of breakfast, scraping the plates off over the edge of the deck and watching as fish snapped up the debris. I salvaged a few scraps, wrapped them in foil, and stuck them in my backpack along with candy treats.

Later we climbed aboard the boat and rowed to the island to begin our morning's work. We expected the clinic to be crowded; Sam would have double the patient load because of yesterday's dog incident.

I spotted Poo waiting at the shore and sighed, not looking forward to another day with her underfoot. Sam helped me out of the boat, and Poo attached herself to me, holding my hand in her hot, sticky little fingers. *What* had she been eating? I didn't want to consider the choices.

Sam suggested I hand out candy in the morning and help in the clinic after lunch. Everywhere I went that morning Poo was underfoot. When she wasn't pursuing me, she stood off at a distance, staring at me. I practically developed a nervous twitch, reaching to straighten my hair, pull my blouse straight, swipe dirt from my cheek. The constant observation was unnerving.

The dog was tied to the tree. When I walked past he remained quiet. His face rested in his paws, eyes straight ahead. I thought he looked depressed. Sneaking a quick look around, I found no one but Poo watching, so I fished the foil out of my pack and approached the tyrant. The dog watched, making no effort to challenge me. I bent closer, my eyes spotting fresh welts on the dog's back. Dried blood encrusted a couple of the wounds.

Someone had beaten him. My hand moved to my queasy stomach.

"It's okay, boy," I whispered. "This will help." I upended the foil and pieces of toast and jelly fell on the ground. The animal sprang to his feet and inhaled the food. When he was through, his eyes turned on me. I fished two packets of jelly beans out of the pack and removed the paper, then dumped the candy on the ground. This way it would last him longer — and cellophane had no nutritional value, which he didn't seem to realize. I stretched my hand out, alert for any sign of aggression, but there was none. I was surprised when he let me stroke his head. I walked on, making a mental note to tell Sam about the abuse. Perhaps he could arrange to have the dog brought to the missionaries' huts. I would see that the animal was fed and watered.

By midmorning, I'd had enough of Poo's scrutiny. She was a child; I was an adult. I did not have to put up with this sort of harassment. I'd do what any take-charge adult would do: I'd lose her. The village men had gathered in a circle in the middle of the village, having what looked to be some sort of a business meeting. I could hear the low rumble of male voices, and I swerved to avoid coming too close, feeling my presence would not be appreciated.

The native male appeared to be quite chauvinistic.

Sam had mentioned that once he and the missionary men had been allowed to sit in on a public discussion. Frank understood enough to surmise the meeting was called for voting purposes: whether to allow Protestant missionaries into the village. Catholicism was strong in the area, and a few huts were thought to contain an unpretentious wooden table with a cross, a small bouquet of flowers, and a colorful replica of Christ or the Virgin Mary—whom the villagers called Satntu Maria or just Maria. From all appearances the villagers weren't comfortable with religious symbols. Instead they practiced the belief that the animals were gods. If missionaries, Catholic or Protestant, were making headway in changing their minds, I'd seen little evidence of it.

Eva and Mary were demonstrating to a group of young women the proper way to care for babies. Such information seemed a moot point, considering the horde of half-wild children running through the village. I paused to listen; Poo leaned against me. Although I knew I was being childish, I was still angry over the theft of my glasses. In my mind the missing can opener made things worse. I claimed no powers of ESP, but I had no doubt what had happened to the utensil. We'd have to open canned goods with a machete if it wasn't found. I used one finger to push my glasses up on my nose. The left earpiece, held with the surgical tape, irked me no end.

A group of women passed me, carrying bulging string sacks containing betel nuts that had fallen to the ground. The men would break the rough brown shells open with heavy bush knives and remove the meat, which they would lay on wooden racks over the fire in a thatched smokehouse. They would tend the fire, replenishing it with the loads of wood the women brought in from the bush. This was a man's world. They ruled in a way and to an extent that few, if any, American women would accept. I could just hear Nelda if Jim ordered her to bring wood while he sat on his dignity and watched.

I shook Poo off, then proceeded on, rounding a corner and then ducking around several more corners to lose my annoying Poo-shadow. I reached the edge of the jungle and followed the worn path. The trail climbed past patches of taro and sweet potatoes grown on the steep mountainside. Bush knives and fire had been used to clear the trees and undergrowth. The larger timbers were used for low erosion barriers.

I'd give the men this much: they worked hard when they worked.

Sago palms grew in profusion. From these trees the villagers made sago powder, thin flour that they mixed with hot water to make glutinous gel globules they garnished with grated coconut, fish, or boiled greens. I had yet to develop a taste for the dish.

Here and there I saw small gardens planted with green onions and pumpkin, which, according to Sam, our own Frank and Eva had introduced.

A thatched hut served as a drying area, filled with bundles of drying tobacco leaves, which thrived in this area. A stand of tall, slender betel-nut palms stood on my left, and on the right women in various stages of undress fished the shoreline or gathered shellfish in buckets. My brows arched, not because I was startled at the women's state of undress, but because I realized I wasn't. Sam had said I'd get used to things here. I'd doubted him, but apparently, at least where the women were concerned, he was right.

While not pretty or even attractive by American standards, the women of the village carried themselves with a
proud stance and seemed happy and eager about their work.

As the trail narrowed and I passed the women, I looked
back to see if Poo was still following. She was.

I strolled along, as if going nowhere in particular, until the
foliage grew denser. Running, I ducked around an outcrop-
ping of rock and slid down a steep incline. At the bottom I
stopped and listened, holding my breath. No sound except the
twittering birds in the bush.

No sign of Poo.

Pleased at how fast I'd evaded her, I wandered deeper into
the bush. Here the foliage was varied in color and texture,
and birds with bright plumage chattered overhead. Sam was
right—once you were clear of the village, the island was a
garden of Eden. My earlier reservations about the jungle had
vanished. Between Sam and Mary and Eva, my eyes were
being opened to the natural beauty of this land.

Now that Poo was no longer underfoot, I let the solitude
saturate my mind. A fallen log beckoned, and I sat down
to rest, ignoring the wet seeping through my jeans. Indis-
criminate rays of sunlight sifted through the canopy of thick
branches overhead. The jungle floor was alive with insects,
but a careful inspection revealed no ants. After a while a sense
of unrest invaded my aura of peace. The others were back in
the village working; I should be there too. But I wasn't ready.
Not yet.

I stared up at the towering trees, at the stray shafts of
sunlight. Here the trees formed a restful canopy. From the
air the leaves must look like flowers. I sat for a moment in
the coolness, admiring a large ceiba tree covered in vivid red

flowers. Hummingbirds and insects swarmed around the tree. Orchids in varying shades and sizes — small and yellow, big and pink — drew my eyes.

Dead leaves littered the jungle floor; the animals blended well, which made them difficult prey. Moths, tree frogs, and katydids were numerous and camouflaged themselves well, looking like leaves — dead or alive.

As I took it all in, I found myself talking to God.

"I know I should be witnessing, working among the villagers, gaining their trust. You created them too, and we're all your children. Or I could be helping Eva and Mary or rolling bandages for the clinic. But, Lord, these people stink. Literally."

If God had wanted me to serve the villagers, either he shouldn't have given me a queasy stomach or he should have given them a bar of soap. I don't know how the others stood without complaint the stench of unwashed bodies and fetid breath.

Something moved overhead, and I shifted my focus to find two monkeys staring down at me. I had to grin. They looked so inquisitive. Something about their attitude reminded me of Poo. Poor little girl. She just wanted to be friends. She didn't know she was so aggravating.

The sun's rays disappeared and cloud cover darkened the jungle. A fine mist started to fall, dampening my hair and clothing. I'd never seen such changeable weather — so different from Saginaw. I got to my feet; it was time to return to the village. Sam would be going to the hut for lunch, and I wanted to be there.

I started working my way back through the thicket, following the thin path. After at least a half an hour of branches slapping my face, I paused. The village was to my left, wasn't it? I'd followed the trail so I couldn't be lost.

Or could I . . . ?

I swallowed back panic. Lost in this jungle? Sam and the others had no idea where I'd gone; I was supposed to be handing out candy bars.

An hour later, I was still walking, still fretting, following a path that seemed to lead to nowhere. Ahead, something blocked my way, like a thick rope. I stopped, my full attention on the foreign object.

Snake! A very large snake.

Every horror story I'd ever heard or read about poisonous snakes raced thorough my mind. What kind was this? Cobra? Fer-de-lance? What kind of snakes made their home in Papua New Guinea? Whatever kind lived here, they came big.

I backed away, holding my breath. As soon as I could no longer see the serpent, I broke into a run, not caring if I followed the path. I only wanted to put distance between me and the reptile.

An hour later I was sure I was no closer to the village, and terror had become my constant companion. Rain pounded now. Hungry, drenched, I fell to my knees.

"Oh, God, let Sam find me!"

But Sam had no idea where to look for me. I'd slipped away from everyone. What a foolish, childish thing to do. Monkeys chattered overhead. They didn't seem so amusing now. Insects skittered across the jungle floor. Darkness seeped around me as the sun sank lower in the branches.

My prayer had dissolved into disjointed sentences, "Help me . . . God, I'm scared . . . help me."

My thoughts darted here and there, like the bugs in their aimless patterns on the ground beneath me. I would die here. Alone. No one would find me, except maybe a headhunter. Would my head be hanging on a pole by this time tomorrow? I ripped my Bible out of my pack and hurriedly let it fall open. *Strength, Lord. I needed strength and assurance.* My gaze fell on the words of Hebrews 9:27: "Man is destined to die once, and after that to face judgment."

I swallowed. How did people gain so much comfort from the Bible?

I closed my eyes. I didn't want to die here, so far from home, from ...

Mom and Pop.

Sam would have to inform them. *Why* had I come out here like this? I sank to the ground, burying my face in my hands.

A caress, light as the brush of an angel wing, touched the top of my head. I opened my eyes to see Poo. Solemn-faced Poo. In her hand she held the Millets' can opener. My fear dissolved, and I broke into tears, latching onto the child like a drowning woman grabbing a life ring. When I recovered enough to think straight, I took the can opener from her. I shook my head.

Poo smiled, took my hand, and led me to a path. Was she rescuing me or leading me deeper into the bush? I'd not been very nice to this child, and no one could blame her if she chose revenge. However, since I had no idea how to escape my self-imposed prison, I had no choice except to trust my life to this strange little girl.

After what seemed forever, I caught a glimpse of the taro and sweet potato fields I'd passed earlier. The little girl led me past the shed of drying tobacco, into the main part of the village. Sam saw me before I saw him. I heard his jubilant shout. "Johanna! Oh, thank God, she's been found!"

I turned loose of Poo's hand and ran to meet him. His arms closed around me, hard and fast. So comforting. I leaned into him, drawing strength from his solid form. Our eyes met and he ran an unsteady hand down the side of my face. "If anything had happened to you ... We've been looking for you all afternoon."

"I'm sorry. It's my fault; I shouldn't have wandered so far into the bush alone."

"No, you shouldn't have." The tender relief in his eyes eased his scolding. "Don't do it again! If you want to go exploring, take me or someone with you. I don't know how you managed to find your way out."

"I didn't. Poo rescued me." And tomorrow I'd go through my luggage and find something nice to give her to show my appreciation. Suddenly I realized I still held the Millets' can opener. Eva would be thrilled to see it. Maybe having it back would make up in some small part for the problems I'd caused.

Before I left, I gave Poo a bear hug. I could see the child's flashing grin long after I got into the boat and the men rowed us to the huts.

Exhausted, I headed straight to my tiny cubicle to strip off my wet clothing and take a sponge bath. When I removed my jeans I found black slick-looking things stuck to my legs.

Leeches! I must have gotten them when I sat on the wet log.

I pulled one off and it turned and attached itself to my finger. I grabbed it with my free hand, stretching the body like a rubber band until it turned loose — then I couldn't get it off my other hand.

I screamed so loud Eva and Mary ran into each other coming to my rescue.

FIFTEEN

◎◎◎

The women pulled the curtain aside, almost knocking me down in the process. I reeled from the impact, dropping down on the cot. There wasn't room enough for three people in my cubicle. There was room for only one—and the leeches.

"What's wrong?" Mary gasped.

I pointed a trembling finger at the slimy bloodsuckers. "Leeches."

Eva clutched her heart, looking faint. "Is that all? I thought you'd seen a snake."

"Snake?" Why would she think a reptile would be in here? I thought the huts were safe. Hadn't someone said so?

Eva smiled. "You screamed so loud I thought Satan had a hold on you."

"This could be him." I pointed to the leeches. "I can't get them off."

"They're not fatal." Mary patted my arm. "Everyone gets them once in a while."

She sounded so matter-of-fact that I calmed down. I sat down and let the ladies have a go at removing them. "I saw a snake this afternoon."

"You did?" Eva used a cloth to grab hold of a parasite and pull it off. "What did it look like?"

I paused, trying to recall the reptile, but so help me I couldn't remember. Fear had fried my brain. I closed my eyes and tried to picture the menace that had scared me into headlong flight. A picture formed, so vivid I shivered like a sapling in a high wind.

"Big, longer than I am tall, tan with black markings, mean and vicious."

Eva pulled off the last leech and dropped it in a can of gasoline. "Sounds like a ball python. You'll find them in the jungle sometimes."

I shuddered. "Thank heaven the huts are built in the water and snakes can't get in."

"Sometimes when we're bathing we'll see a black-banded sea snake."

"In the lagoon?" My heartbeat ratcheted up several notches. I thought catfish were the only hazards.

"A sea snake is rather pretty." She dried her hands on a towel. "Blue with black bands. We don't see them very often, so it's rather thrilling when we do."

Thrilling. Oh, it'd be that all right. So much so I was sure I'd walk on water if I saw one.

Once I was deleeched, the women left me to my bath. At that moment, I'd have given everything I owned for a hot shower, a large fluffy towel to wrap around me, and a blow-dryer for my hair. How could I have taken such luxuries for granted? If I'd had a pen and paper and waxed poetic, I'd have written a paean: "Praise to Indoor Plumbing."

Eva brought warm water from the stove so I could wash my hair. The women were so good to me, trying to ease the culture shock and make me feel at home.

Finally, dressed in clean clothes, my wet hair combed back from my face, I joined the others on deck, hoping I could catch a breeze to dry my hair. Nothing dried well in this humid air. According to the rusted thermometer on the hut wall, the temperature registered 105.

No one mentioned my ordeal, which was nice since it had been a stupid stunt for me to pull. They had no idea I'd been hiding from Poo, and I had no intention of telling them. I should have realized the child knew the bush as well as the back of her hand, so while I thought I'd managed to lose her she'd always been there. I found the knowledge humiliating, but I didn't care. I was thankful for that little girl.

Did God's love work much the same way? Could one of his children ever truly be lost from him?

Eva excused herself to check on dinner. I could smell sweet potatoes roasting, a staple in our diet. The food was nourishing, but monotonous. "I'll see if Mary needs my help."

"I'll come too." I struggled to rise to my feet, but my bones seemed to have melted, leaving me with no structural support.

Mary waved a hand in my direction. "No, sit still. We'll call you when it's ready."

I settled back on the deck. Sam reached over and took my hand. We sat, me praising God for his mercy, and Sam, quiet. I didn't know his thoughts—and realized I hadn't from the moment I got here.

Today's adventure could have been disastrous. Was he angry? Relieved? Regretting that he'd asked me to come? Was he confused, searching for answers? I hoped he found some—and shared them when he did.

He continued to hold my hand as we sat in the peaceful evening, listening to nature, each lost in our thoughts.

Eva called, and we went inside to sit down to sweet potatoes, steamed greens, and baked fish. When we ate a fish meal, greens always accompanied it. Vegetables composed an important part of our diet, so it was a good thing Eva and Mary knew which greens were safe to eat. They had yet to let me forage with them, and I didn't know why. I wanted to do my part.

Talk turned to the hot day, then to missions in China, Africa, and South America. Even our beloved US, an area that Sam never considered, as far as I knew. Yet his comments indicated that he knew there were great mission fields there, hurting, crying for harvest.

Finally talk switched back to the villagers. As I ate and listened to the chatter, an idea formed in the back of my mind. The more I thought about it the more I warmed to it. How hard could it be to communicate with the villagers? After all, I was a librarian, and I did have a stack of children's books in my locked luggage. Before I left I would read the children a story; it would be like story time at the library. The event would be a treat for Poo. Sam would be proud of me.

Eva served dessert: chunks of sun-ripened pineapple and mangoes blended in a fresh tropical salad. I realized I'd miss the delicious fruits once I was back in Saginaw. I laughed when I thought how hard Nelda and I tried to shed pounds, suffering for days to lose an ounce. I'd been here almost a week and a half and my jeans were already looser thanks to healthy meals of fish, fruit, and coarse bread.

After dinner Sam and I returned to the deck, watching evening settle over the jungle. The sky was a sheath of ebony

213 / LORI COPELAND

silk with star-studded sequins. A crescent moon crept over the horizon. He pulled me close, and I snuggled against him, blotting out everything except the enjoyment of sharing an all-too-infrequent privacy.

He kissed the top of my head. "Thank God, you're all right. I'd never forgive myself if anything had happened to you today."

"It wouldn't have been your fault. You didn't know I left the village. I was foolish to wander off and not tell anyone."

He paused, holding me close. "I don't know, Johanna. I want you here with me so much I ache, but other times I feel that you should be at home. This is rugged, uncivilized country, no matter how tropical and beautiful. Maybe I've made a mistake; maybe I shouldn't have asked you to come with me."

"Oh, Sam." I rested my head against his solid shoulder. "I am such a dismal failure. I'm sorry I've disappointed you."

"No, *I've* disappointed *you*. I should have respected your wishes. I know you're not comfortable here. Would you like for me to arrange for your departure?"

I gazed up at him. Did I want that?

No.

In fact, my answer was a rock-solid no. I couldn't believe it. I meant it. *No!* I'd made it well over a week. I could stick it out for the duration of the trip.

His eyes held mine in the moonlight. "I love you. Nothing will change that, Johanna. Somehow we'll work this out, even if it means I change my priorities."

My hand flew up to cover his mouth. "Sam, that's not the answer. If you changed, that would only make me feel worse." I would live under conviction the rest of my life. Sam belonged here. He was doing what he was born to do, what God called him to. "I'm the one searching for a purpose, Sam. Not you."

"It isn't just the mission work." He sat, staring up at the stars. "I don't know how to explain it, but our culture is so blessed, Johanna. We have everything compared to others around the world. Men and women have fought for our nation's freedom and independence; now others are fighting for its soul. Since the beginning, we've been 'one nation, under God.' It's not that we've deserved his blessing—far from it. America is a great and powerful nation, and from those who have been given much, much is expected."

"I agree, and often wonder why God has given us such favor."

Sam smiled. "'That people may see and know, may consider and understand, that the hand of the LORD has done this.'" He turned to look at me. "Isaiah 41:20. That's why I do what I do, Johanna. I want people everywhere to understand that God still reigns. Whether it's here or on the streets of New York or Los Angeles, whether we speak the same language or we struggle to communicate the Word. I'm not a martyr. I love the good life as well as the next person, but this . . . this . . ."

"Compassion," I supplied.

"Compassion." He sighed. "I've a need to serve."

I pressed closer, nestling in his arms. We stared at the stars, neither of us attempting to offer a solution for our problem.

Later he walked me to the hut door. We lingered longer than usual, content in each other's arms. The hour grew late, and I said good night and slipped inside.

I lay on my narrow cot staring at the thatched ceiling, wanting that "compulsion to serve" so much. How could I know God's will? One thing for certain, to know his will I'd have to *read* his Word. Not just thumb through it and play my hit-and-miss game, pointing a finger at a verse to see how God "spoke" to me that day. I had to *read* his Word. Every single word. I was forty years old and had never done that yet. And if someone put a gun to my head I wouldn't be able to recite the books of the Bible. I'd long ago forgotten my Bible school learning.

Genesis, Exodus, Leviticus—that was it. Blank. *Matthew, Mark, Luke, and John.* New Testament—at least part of the New Testament.

Blank—*oh, Acts.* I knew that because as children we would call the book "Axe." The book of Axe.

We weren't funny, just weird.

***

The moment I got up the next morning I reached for my Bible. I spent the hour between dawn and daylight reading Matthew twice. I'd read the fifth chapter many times, but this time I absorbed more of God's encouragement. "Blessed are the peacemakers, for they will be called sons of God." It began to dawn on me that the blessing of peace was what kept the power of God flowing through our lives so that we could bless others.

Later I searched my suitcases for something to give to Poo. I settled on the light Nelda had given me that I'd yet to use. It was on a headband, making a headlight, handy to read by or light a dark path. Poo would be fascinated. A blue and green scarf caught my eye, and I added it to the pile. If Eva was right and Poo wanted something of mine, I'd grant her wish.

The little girl was waiting on the bank. She latched onto my hand as I climbed out of the boat. I slipped the light around her head and switched on the beam. The thingamajig had three settings: low, high, and blinking. I set it on blinking. Poo's eyes lit with astonishment. When I tied the scarf around her waist, she jumped up and down, her headlight blinking. A stream of words poured from her and I didn't understand a single one. But it didn't matter. She was thrilled.

She caught my hand and pressed it to her cheek, emotion overflowing her gaze. I blinked back tears. This little girl loved me. I stooped down and she threw her arms around my neck. I held her frail body close. This little angel of mercy had saved my life, and I was ashamed of the way I'd treated her. She could have left me in the bush to stew in juices of my own foolish making. Instead, she led me to safety.

Hand in hand, we walked to the clinic. Poo's Bum stood in the doorway of his hut, smiling and nodding, staring at the blinking light. Best of all, Sam's expression made me laugh. I had a long way to go, but I was making progress.

That morning, no matter how hard or how often we wiped down the clinic, it didn't help. Dirt resided everywhere; oppressive heat, mosquitoes, and the ceaseless stench of illness would not give way. My hands moved, washing wounds, wrapping bandages. A family worked their way to the front of the line by midmorning, the child carried by his parents. I drew back, appalled by the little boy's gross disfiguration.

"Dear Lord ..." I turned to Sam. "What happened to this child?" The little boy's arms and legs were enlarged to gigantic size.

Sam spoke under his breath. "Elephantiasis."

I'd heard of but never witnessed the condition.

I helped Sam calm the boy's fear. Tears steamed from the child's eyes, but I sensed that he trusted Sam. He was running a high fever; his chest rattled with congestion.

While Sam tried to make the parents understand how to administer the medication, I held the boy close in my arms. He snuggled like any other hurting child. Remorse flooded the depths of my soul. I had turned away, sickened to look at him. Now, stroking his coarse, sweat-dampened hair, I pressed his head close to my chest. We couldn't communicate, but I think he sensed my love. I hope he did; I wanted him to know that I cared.

Later, Sam and I stood in the clinic door and watched the family disappear back into the bush. "What causes that?"

Sam shook his head. "A parasitic infection."

I shivered. "Parasitic?"

"Filarial worms. They're found in most tropical and subtropical regions, and when they get inside the host, their long, threadlike bodies block the body's lymphatic system."

He might as well be speaking Greek. "And the lymphatic system is?"

His smile was understanding. "It's a network of channels, lymph nodes, and organs that helps maintain proper fluid levels in the body by draining lymph from tissue into the bloodstream. The worms are transmitted by a particular species of mosquitoes." Sam rested a palm against the hut's support pole. "The host's limbs can swell so enormous that they resemble an elephant's foreleg in size, texture, and color."

I turned to stare after the little boy and his family. I'd been sure my challenges and problems since coming here were serious. Now I understood—I didn't even know the meaning of the word.

A toothless older woman who had a gaping wound on her right leg watched as I applied ointment and wrapped a bandage. When I was finished, she patted my arm, her mouth cavernous in a wide grin. I smiled, knowing she was trying to thank me. *Lord, why can't I love these people the way Sam and the others do?* The bright spot in the morning was Poo, who danced around the clinic, her headlight blinking, waving her scarf. The little show-off. I grinned.

The hands of my watch crept to noon, then one o'clock. Breakfast was now a distant memory. My stomach growled, the sound evident in the clinic's close confines. Sam, who was examining a young woman with an angry swelling on her jaw-line, looked up at my stomach rumble. I grinned and placed my hand on my stomach. The young woman laughed and I joined in.

Sam lifted a brow. "What was that?"

"An organ recital."

He chuckled. "We'll take a lunch break soon."

I indicated the long line still waiting to see the doctor. "What about them?"

Sam looked from his patients back to me. "They'll wait. They're patient, and they understand hunger."

I shook my head. "Let's finish up before we stop." I wasn't going to have those poor people waiting while I appeased my appetite.

He nodded and went back to work. Poo had assembled quite a mass of admirers with her new trinkets. No other child in the village had anything like them, and Poo knew it. Her social status had climbed several notches, and I had an idea she knew how to make the best of it.

At last the line dwindled, so Sam and I left for lunch. Eva had our meal covered on the table. I leaned back in my chair, exhausted beyond words. Nothing in my sedentary life had prepared me for clinic work.

"Tired?"

I nodded at Sam. "But it's a nice tired."

Midafternoon, the sound of a small plane sent every eye to the sky. Planes were a rarity here. We sometimes saw jets' white streamers crisscrossing overhead, but this plane sounded smaller and lower. Bud pointed to a black dot in the distance. "Over there. It's coming in like the supply plane."

Frank's forehead creased. "Couldn't be. He's not due for another week or two. The landing strip hasn't been mown." Constant rain had prevented maintenance on the strip, and the moisture and humidity had turned it into a hay field.

We dropped what we were doing and raced through the jungle to beat the plane.

At the neglected strip, I stopped to catch my breath, thinking the grass looked as if it had grown another foot. The plane circled once, twice, before dipping down for a landing. Wheels touched the ground, bounced, throwing the light craft up in the air, and then touched down again, the small Piper Cub seesawing a good fifty feet before it came to a halt.

I winced, turning my head and releasing an audible *whoosh*. For a minute it had looked like the plane would skid straight into the tree line. The pilot climbed out, looking mad enough to spit nails. Scarlet suffused his ruddy features, and, if I wasn't mistaken, those were ... yes, sparks shooting out of his saucer-shaped eyes. Well, almost anyway.

He was too far away to make out the angry words spewing from his mouth, but the meanings were quite evident. The man was ticked.

I waded through the waist-high grass, trying to step in Sam's tracks, all too aware a bull python or something worse could be lurking. The tires of the plane had cut deep ruts in the tall wet grass. Frank was trying to calm down the pilot—who turned out to be the same man who'd flown us out here ... what was his name? Oh yes, Mike. He ranted and raved, waving his arms, pointing to the overgrown strip.

I caught a few of Mike's heated words. "... could have been killed! You're supposed to keep it cut ... Son of a—"

I made myself think he'd finished with *biscuit eater*.

Frank tried to explain. "We didn't expect you for a couple of—"

"What did you plan to do? Run out here and cut it when you heard me coming? Do you know how *dangerous* this is?"

"What are you doing here anyway?" Bud stepped in. "You're not due for another two weeks, and no one told us the schedule had changed."

"I can't come at the regular time! I'm having my gallbladder out next week!"

"Sorry." Frank tried to shake the man's hand. "Our prayers will be with—"

Mr. Personality spun on his heel. "Let's get this stuff unloaded so I can get in the air before it rains again."

We pitched in unloading supplies and stacking the boxes and crates at the edge of the landing strip. Mary volunteered to stand watch so the villagers wouldn't help themselves to the bounty.

"We're sorry about the condition of the landing strip." Frank pitched in to help the men unload the craft. "We'll keep it mowed, even if we have to do it in the rain."

"I won't land next time it's like this." Mike glowered. "If that baby isn't as smooth as a new laid egg, I'll keep on going, and your supplies will go back with me."

We'd have to use heavy scythes to cut through the brush. It would be a lot of work, and who knew what lurked in the thick growth. Still, though Mike was far from likable, I had to admit he was right.

The workers emptied the plane, and Mike climbed back into the cockpit, then fought to turn the aircraft. The narrow strip, I'd been told, was bad enough when mowed. Now the closeness of the tree line and the tall grass made maneuvering the plane that much more difficult. We watched as he finally taxied down the runway, praying as the small craft emerged from the thick grass, then rose and banked to the east.

We moved to the cartons where Mary stood guard. Sam began handing boxes to the villagers, motioning for them to carry the items to the landing area so they could be ferried to the missionary huts.

Frank glanced at Bud. "We have to keep the grass cut."

Bud nodded. "We'll get on it the first possible day we can get a mower or machete through the wet grass. If we make Mike mad enough he won't be back, and he's our lifeline to the outside world."

I stared at him. Without the plane we would be stranded? What about the boat that had brought us here? I recalled the small vessel and realized it wouldn't hold enough supplies to last the week.

They'd keep the strip mowed all right. If necessary I'd chew it down. From now on, maintaining that strip was at the top of my priority list.

SIXTEEN
◎◎◎

Almost every night the Laskes' kerosene lamp burned long into the wee hours of the morning as Sam made notes on the villagers' language. He hungered so to reach these people, to give them better lives, while I . . .

I hungered for a cheeseburger. And comfortable shoes instead of thick boots.

I slapped my palm on the clinic cabinet. Why didn't the fire of evangelism burn in my soul? God must be so aggravated with me. I was disgusted with myself, and I didn't want to consider what Sam and the others were feeling.

Bud was helping in the clinic today so I had free time on my hands. After I finished cleaning, I decided I could use some privacy to clear my head. I'd brought a small tablet of writing paper and a ballpoint pen with me this morning, thinking I would jot down some of my conflicting, confusing emotions. Maybe that would be a first step to understanding all that was going on inside me.

Poo had been underfoot all morning. I stopped what I was doing and pointed to Mary, who was gathering children in a circle, preparing to play games. "Go. Over there. Go."

The little girl furrowed her brow.

"Yes, Poo. Go over *there*."

She gazed up at me, eyes wide and mouth half open, like a baby bird wanting to be fed. The scarf I'd given her was tied around her waist, and the blinking light was around her head. Already we'd been through three sets of AAA batteries. She fingered the scarf now, uncertainty clouding her eyes dark. I took her by the arm and led her to the circle, easing her down on the ground with the others. "Poo, *stay*."

I sounded like I was giving a dog command. Stay? The child didn't know what I'd said, but Eva did and she gave me a pointed look. Okay, I wasn't a saint — nobody in the village mistook me for that. But I needed time alone. Privacy was nonexistent. Even in my cubicle with the curtain drawn at night, I could hear Frank and Eva; one of them snored like a pig in the sun.

I backed away, trying to ignore the query in Poo's eyes. She started to get up, and I held out my hands, palms open like a traffic cop. *"Stay."*

She might not have understood my words, but my tone came through loud and clear. She wasn't wanted, and the knowledge wounded her deeply.

Clutching my tablet, I turned and walked off. A glance over my shoulder told me she was obeying, but not willingly. Big tears rolled down her cheek. Great. More self-reproach to deal with.

Poo meant well, and I knew she loved me, but her constant presence had worn me down.

The jungle was quiet and cool compared to the village, where heat beat down on the thatched clinic roof. I didn't venture far, and I kept a close eye out for snakes and other critters. The need for solitude could have driven me to seek a private moment here among the palms, but the bush was the only hope I had for being alone.

Today I was careful, breaking branches on bushes to mark the short trail. After the way I'd treated Poo, she likely wouldn't bother to rescue me again, and I didn't blame her. A fresh twinge of remorse struck me. I used to be a nice person.

As soon as I was out of sight and hearing distance of the village, I inspected the jungle floor for insects and then knelt down. On my knees, I peered up through thick branches with guilt crowding my heart. I couldn't think of the words needed to express my thoughts. After a while I realized it didn't matter because God knew my heart and there wasn't any point in trying to camouflage my feelings with holy, pious talk.

"God, I need help. I don't know what I want, except maybe to go home. I don't fit in here; I'm sure by now we agree on that point. I believe at times I do more harm than good in gaining the villagers' respect. We might not speak the same language, but we share the same emotions, and they know, God. They *know* the others' dedication and love far exceed mine. If you wanted, you could give me a heart the size of this jungle for these people, but you haven't. I'm doing better than I was a week ago—two weeks ago—but there's a huge void to cover before I can begin to match Sam's enthusiasm. Lord, all I see are thieves, half-naked women, and men with betel-stained or missing teeth. Why can't I see the villagers through your eyes, eyes of unconditional love? Your love."

An image came to mind: Poo's Bum—skinny, dried up, and smelling of sweat and rotting garbage. I shuddered. And yet I knew as well as I knew my own name that God loved that man as much as he loved me. Maybe more.

After a while I stood and looked for a dry place to sit. I chose my spot, conscious of leeches. A shaft of sunlight pierced the leafy overhead canopy. A large black beetle raced around my foot, looking for something and having no luck finding it. As long as he stayed in his space and didn't threaten mine, I'd respect his presence. Funny. I had complete control over that bug's life. I could squash him in a moment, deny him life in a split second. Kind of like my life and God's authority ...

The bug and I were trivial. Yes, compared to the bug I was huge. But compared to God? I was nothing. God could squash me as fast as I could end the bug. Sitting there, I couldn't help but wonder ... Did God ponder the option?

I decided to write Mom and Pop a letter instead of sending a postcard I'd purchased in the hotel lobby the morning we left for the village. Goodness knew when I'd be able to send any mail back home, but if nothing else I'd take the cards home with me and give one to Nelda and others in the library. The same went for Mom and Pop's letter, but I needed to talk to someone. To get my thoughts on paper.

Trees grew like a thick wall here, lining the path and small clearing. Overhead, chattering monkeys swung from treetop to treetop. I noticed that I wasn't concerned; I guess I was acclimating to the bush. Maybe God was watching over me, although I couldn't think of a single reason why he should.

I opened my tablet and began to write:

Dear Mom and Pop,
I hope this letter finds you well. I'm fine but it's hot here in the jungle. I spend my days helping Sam in the clinic or handing out candy to the villagers. They have such a sweet tooth.

I paused, pencil poised on the paper. I'd been about to add, "if they have a tooth at all," but thought better of it. I would save specifics for when I got home.

> *I am sorry to report that I've made small inroads into the mission field. I believe my first thought was correct: I am not mission-minded, though I pray that God will give me a heart for these people. I see Sam and the missionaries' dedication and I feel so ashamed that I don't share their love and compassion for the villagers. It is a strange culture. Women are subservient to their husbands, and we — the missionaries — are never allowed to enter their homes. At times their mission seems hopeless, but Sam reminds me nothing is hopeless with God.*
>
> *I've made a special friend, a little girl who we think is named Poo. Odd name, I know, but it's an odd place. Poverty is the norm, and everything is dirty. The village smells are wretched; you know my weak stomach. But there is also great beauty here ...*

I glanced around at the flowers and birds, recalled the clear streams and luscious fruits hanging in large clumps from trees, then bent back to the page and described it all as best I could.

> *Sam calls this place Eden. While I don't quite share the same opinion, I have to admit the beauty, especially the multicolored sunsets, makes me feel closer to God. Sometimes I think God has given me a glimpse of heaven.*
>
> *I miss you all and am looking forward to returning home and to my work at the library. I know you're*

wondering about Sam. I'm wondering too. I love him with all my heart, but sometimes love isn't enough. Sam Littleton is a decent, dedicated man who deserves a woman who will work beside him. Every passing day brings me to the same heartbreaking conclusion: I am not that helpmate. I long to be, but God doesn't appear to have the same plans for me that he's got for Sam. In fact, I'm not convinced he's got a specific plan for me at all. I'm beginning to despair that he's forgotten me or maybe worse, that the library in Saginaw is the extent of my purpose. I don't know. I just don't know.

Tears rolled down my cheeks and I signed my name, praying I wouldn't be as much a disappointment to my parents as I was to both Sam and God.

Games were over when I returned to the village. Eva and Mary had left. The children had scattered around the village. Poo was standing alone in the shade of a hut. She glanced my way but made no effort to join me. I offered her a smile but she refused it, turning her head away. I felt rotten, but since I couldn't speak her language, I had no way to apologize.

The boat was on shore, so if Eva and Mary had gone back to the huts, someone had taken them and returned. I pushed the small craft off the rocks and hopped aboard. I'd never rowed the short distance from the huts to the village — never rowed anywhere — but I could manage the feat. Once seated, I lifted the oars and gave a mighty stroke. I went nowhere. Surprised, I glanced up and realized I'd not pushed off far enough. I looked to see if any of the women who were kneeling at the shoreline washing their clothing had noticed my blunder, then moved to untie the vessel.

Okay, what now? If I didn't make it back into the boat quick enough, it would drift off without me. How would I explain losing the boat if it drifted out to sea? I eyed the situation and decided I could move fast enough to board.

Before I could put the plan into effect a young boy from the village passed, and I yelled at him. He stopped and approached the water, sending me an inquiring look.

I pointed out the situation, the rocky shoreline, and made pushing motions with the open palms of my hands.

He frowned.

I tried again. More motions, more pushing. I even grunted. This time he caught on, and I moved back into the boat. I was half seated when he picked up the front of the boat and shoved. In a desperate effort to stay in the boat I knocked my large-brimmed hat off my head into the water. Horrified, I watched the wind catch it and blow it away from me. I stared at it, sick to my stomach.

Then I heard the splash. The teenager had dived into the water and was now swimming after my escapist hat. When he reached it, he dived, and all I could see were his bare feet. Moments later, he surfaced underneath it, so that it now sat on his head. Grinning like a skunk eating garlic he paddled back to the boat. I blew him a kiss. He handed me the hat and threw me a look that suggested I'd lost my mind. I didn't care; at that moment I loved that kid.

I managed (through the grace of God) to get the boat across the lagoon to the huts. The chore took longer than I'd expected, and I almost tipped twice, but I climbed out of the boat without turning loose of the rope. The boat secured, I straightened and drew a deep breath. It would snow in August in the middle of this jungle before I tried that on my own again.

Eva and Mary weren't in either of the huts. Had I left them back in the village? If so, I'd *have* to make the return trip alone, and I wasn't sure I was capable of the task. It had been all I could do to make it across this time. I had a feeling practice wouldn't make perfect.

I finally spotted the two women sitting on the shore behind the huts in the shade of a large betel palm. The water was shallow here, easily forded. I suspected this was the pathway the villagers used when they visited the huts in search of treasure. The two women had spread a blanket on the ground to protect them from the elements. They appeared so relaxed and so happy I wanted to join them.

I stepped out on the deck and circled to the back of the huts, waving at them. Mary waved back. "Come join us!"

"How?"

"I'll come get you."

I watched as she stepped into the parasite-infested waters and waded the small crossing. When she arrived at the ladder, she held out her hand. "Come, Johanna. Trust me."

I glanced at the waters; I could see fish darting about. I didn't know what kind, and I didn't want to know. I looked at Mary again, and started. For a second—just a second, mind you—it appeared Christ was holding out his hand to me, saying, *Come. Trust.*

"Don't be afraid." Mary smiled. "I'm here."

Biting my lower lip, I lowered myself into the water, feeling the coolness seep over my ankles, then midcalf. I held my breath, not daring to look down but grasping out for her hand. When our fingers touched, I opened my eyes. Hand in hand, we tackled the small distance and waded to shore.

Lowering myself on the blanket, I caught my breath.

"See," Mary teased, "we told you the fish wouldn't bother you."

"But who knows what's down there." I peered into the swirling water.

"Does it matter?" Eva scooped up a handful of water and let it fly.

No. It didn't. The fish had swum around my feet, but not one had threatened me. I think at that moment I started to understand. Faith had to start somewhere, and mine started here, in this dense jungle where there was nobody to trust but God. I still wanted to know what was in that water, but if it didn't bother me, it made no difference.

We lounged in the shade, enjoying the coolness. The fellowship was reminiscent of conversations I had held with Nelda. If she'd been here she'd have us all laughing and joking, and she'd be handing out advice right and left. Might not be good advice, but she'd have some, regardless.

I'd seen Eva and Mary work side by side with their husbands, dedicated to their service, and envied their spirit. Now I longed to be friends with them. They had their Bibles opened and were engaged in a discussion, which I'd interrupted.

Eva smiled. "We're reading from Luke 14:23."

Mary scooted over so I could share her Bible, and Eva continued, "Then the master told his servant, 'Go out to the roads and country lanes and make them come in, so that my house will be full.'"

I listened as the women discussed the passage, and though I added a few comments, I knew we were on a touchy subject.

When Eva closed her Bible, I decided to involve the women in something less serious: girl talk.

"Do you go into Port Moresby very often? How do you keep up with what's going on in the world?"

"We seldom leave the island," Eva admitted. "But we'll go home for a few weeks each year. We always enjoy being with family and old friends."

"What about fashion?" I settled back to fill them in on the latest trends. "Colors are gaudy bright this year, skirts are short and getting shorter, but there are others who favor ankle length—and shoes are going back to spikes. Ankle breakers, I call them."

Mary smiled. She must think I was discussing rocket science. Undoubtedly, fashion was her least concern. "That's interesting. The last time we were home, some of the skirts were almost indecent."

"I know what you mean." We talked and laughed together, and an awareness began to dawn in my mind. These were flesh-and-blood women. Genuine servants of God, yes, but they cared about the same things other women did.

I studied Mary. "You have such beautiful hair." The shiny mass glistened in the sunlight. Thick, dark cherry red, shoulder length ... I found it her most attractive feature. Lagoon water must be good for hair particles. "Why don't I style it for you?"

She didn't appear thrilled at the idea, but I whipped out a comb, which I'd planned to give to Poo until she'd gotten on my nerves. Mary sat as I pulled her hair back from her face, fastening it into a spiky ponytail, using a band from my own hair to hold it in place.

"There, now we have the same hairstyle. People will think we're sisters."

"We are sisters." She angled a look at me. "Sisters in Christ."

It wasn't what I had in mind, but she was right. We were family.

I took a tiny hand mirror, not much bigger than a saltine cracker, out of my pocket and held it up. "Here. See how you like it."

Mary gazed at her image, turning her head from side to side. Smiling, she handed the mirror back to me. "It will take some getting used to, I guess."

One glance at Eva and I knew her thoughts. It looked downright twittish.

"You'd look nice in this year's shell pink."

Mary laughed. "Pink? With my red hair?"

I perked up. "It's such a delicate pink it would enhance your hair color and complexion. Everything is pink this year: pink, pink, pink. Hot pink, shell pink. You can't go wrong with any pink—not this ... year." I was babbling, spouting nonsense.

Mary leaned back. "Shell pink wouldn't stay pretty for long out here."

We all had to chuckle at that. She was right. Pink was not a jungle color with all the dirt and humidity. And sticky hands. Sticky hands everywhere.

"So what do you two do in your leisure time?"

I wanted to bite my tongue. Wasn't the answer obvious? They didn't *have* leisure time. Not much, anyway. This was the first time since I'd arrived they had taken time for themselves, and they'd used it for Bible study.

We struggled on, trying to keep the conversation going through lapses. Finally, we ceased trying, gazing out over the water.

Mary brushed her hair away from her face. "I noticed this afternoon that my crochet hook is missing."

Eva showed more interest than I'd seen from her since I'd joined them. "Oh, yes? I'll bet I know where it is. One of the village women had something shiny in her hand today, and I meant to ask but I got busy and forgot."

Mary laughed. "My own fault; I must have left it out."

"That doesn't bother you?" I was glad for the chance to ask these women about the thefts. I just couldn't fathom that it didn't frustrate them as much as it did me.

"We'd rather they didn't do it, of course—" Eva looped her arms around her knees—"but I suspect that the villagers feel that what's ours is theirs. They don't seem to understand the meaning of personal possessions."

"And sometimes we have to accept what we can't change." Mary pursed her lips. "I don't think they mean to steal—not in our sense. I think they see something pretty and want it and feel we'd want them to have it."

The subject changed directions when Eva mentioned a former village chief, Macu. "He's very old, maybe close to a hundred. I'm sure you've seen him in one of the men's public meetings.

"He's close to death." Eva sounded so sad. "We've ministered to him for years, but I feel his time is near. We haven't been able to present the gospel to him, and it breaks my heart to think about it."

A shout from the village caught our attention. The men were ready to come home and we had the boat. "I'll go get them." Eva pushed to her feet and brushed the back of her slacks free of blanket lint.

I was more than happy to let her man the oars.

While Eva took the boat across to the village, I washed greens for dinner and set them to steam. Mary filleted fish and then put sweet potatoes in the oven to bake.

After dinner, everyone agreed to retire—all except Sam, who planned to study for a while.

I excused myself and went to my own cubicle and lay down on the cot, pulling the mosquito netting around the bed. Eva and Mary had no clue about styles or trends, and they were content, seemingly relieved not to have to worry about such things. As I lay there, thinking back over the conversation, I realized my tastes had begun to change as well.

Shell pink didn't sound half as appealing as it had, say ... a month ago.

SEVENTEEN

I t was too early to get up, but I couldn't take it any longer. A
 downpour had ended just a few minutes ago, and the heat
and humidity were insufferable. I pushed back the netting
and sat up. Anything would be better than lying in a pool
of sweat. The treetops seen through my open window were
motionless; not a hint of a breeze stirred the leaves or offered
relief from the relentless smothering blanket of hot air. I put
on my glasses and pulled the curtain aside. Eva sat at the table,
Bible open in front of her. She looked up when I joined her.

"Too hot to sleep?"

I ran my hand across my forehead, realizing that I was
dripping with sweat. "It's suffocating."

She smiled. "Sometimes you'd give everything you own
for an electric fan. Can you imagine people who go to the
beach so they can lie around in the hot sun and sweat?"

"At the moment, I'd give a king's ransom for an ice cube."
But even as I spoke, I had to admit the reason for my lack of
sleep was as much guilt as heat. Why had I sent Poo away
yesterday? Why did I fight my growing feelings for the little
imp? I needed to make amends. I would take Poo something—maybe my hairbrush. She would love that.

"Eva, could you row me to the village? I'm not that good
with oars yet."

"I'd be happy to take you. Would you like me to give you a rowing lesson?" This woman had to be approaching sainthood; she was always there when I needed her, always willing to help. I'd never seen either Eva or Mary irritated or angry—just a few hard looks sent my way. They were so easygoing and agreeable—maybe they were clones posing as missionaries! Even on my *best* behavior I'd never been this agreeable.

We left the hut as the dark clouds parted and a ray of sun broke across the water. Eva showed me the proper way to get into the boat, cast off, and row. By the time we reached the village, I actually felt confident I could make my way back and forth.

Eva spotted Mary with a group of women under one of the large trees at the edge of the village, so she left me at the shoreline. I watched her make her way up the incline, then went in search of Poo. I found the child sitting under a bush, headlight blinking, and bright scarf around her thin waist. My heart constricted. This child had so little; all she could offer was friendship, and I had rejected her gift.

She glanced up at my approach but didn't run to me. I sat down beside her and put my arm around her shoulders, pulling her close against me.

Eyes wide, she gazed up at me. More than ever I wanted us to understand each other. How do you say "I'm sorry" in sign language? I touched my heart then placed my hand on her shoulder.

Her brows arched.

Okay, that didn't work. Try something else. I took both her hands and held them in mine, smiling down at her.

She returned the gesture.

So far, so good. I slipped the hairbrush from my backpack and began to work the bristles through her hair. She looked startled but must have decided I didn't mean any harm. I pulled the brush through the ends of the child's tangled locks. Wiry, sweat-soaked hair that hadn't been washed in — well, I didn't care to guess.

When I finished, I pressed the brush into her hand and reached in my pocket and pulled out the mirror. I hoped the gifts convinced Poo that we were friends again.

She brought the brush up to her nose and smelled. She smiled. Reaching out, she touched my hand.

I was forgiven.

I got up from the ground and held out my hand to her. She looked up at me, a question forming in her eyes. After a moment she jumped up and grasped my hand, swinging it between us. Together, we walked to the clinic.

This morning's line stretched into the jungle. Word spread farther every day that the doctor was here, and those who could traveled long distances through the bush to seek medical help. Every village had a medicine man, but some villagers were so ill they sought a cure with white man's medicine.

I found Sam bent over a woman's foot, examining a nasty cut on top of the arch. There were so many hazards here that almost everywhere the villagers turned there was something to hurt them or make them sick. How could Sam ever hope to make a change in their lives? Similar to bailing water with a sieve — excruciating work and little in the way of results.

Sam didn't see me at first, so I waited, watching him. Maybe if I tried harder, worked beside him longer, then the Lord would move in my heart.

He looked up, a smile curving his mouth. That smile I loved so much. His eyes moved to Poo and back to me. She held to my hand, eyes shining with her old love of life, the joy I'd taken from her with my insufferable behavior.

"You ladies look like you're having a good day."

"Wonderful! What can we do to help?"

"I need instruments cleaned. Can you handle it?"

"Put me to work."

Sporadic bursts of hard rain had turned the clinic into a blistering swamp. I stood in water a half inch deep. I reached over and used my handkerchief to wipe sweat from Sam's forehead. He looked up and smiled. "Thanks." Flies clung to my arms and buzzed around my face. Swatting was an exercise in futility.

Some of the waiting patients had huge goiters on the sides of their necks. Sam had explained that the mass compressed the person's windpipe and esophagus, which made the natives cough, feel as though food was getting stuck in the upper throat, or wake from sleep struggling for breath. Surgery was the required treatment; Sam would arrange for the worst cases to be transported to Port Moresby, but that could take months. In worst-case scenarios, he operated himself, despite the crude conditions, and prayed for the best.

Every time I looked up more men, women, and children emerged from the bush to join the line to see the doctor. The sights and the stench made me light-headed. Poo hovered as close as she could while still giving me room to maneuver. Every time I looked down she was there, gazing up at me with huge adoring eyes.

I started to hand Sam a needle and dropped it in the dirt. "I'm sorry! My hands are so slick with perspiration I can't hold on to anything." My insides were about to blow from heat. The clinic's interior swam before me.

"Clean it with disinfectant. No harm done."

By late afternoon we finally saw the end of the line. I looked up to find a teenage boy standing in front of me, sporting a nose bone rather than the usual extended straw. How could they force anything through the tender nose cartilage? It made my eyes tear up just thinking about it. Something about that bone looked familiar ...

Oh, my. It wasn't a bone. I was looking at Mary's crochet hook.

My fingers itched to yank it free, but reason won out. I could hear Mary's understated tone: "It's a crochet hook, nothing to go to pieces about." I forced myself to look away, vowing not to react. The hook didn't belong to me. I shouldn't get involved. Feeling rather proud of my objectivity, I handed Sam a bandage to place over a vicious-looking cut on a young girl's foot. Ah—sweet victory. I had to admit control was good. Nice. The hook was a possession, nothing more. Bright fuchsia poked through nose cartilage wasn't my idea of fashion sense, but to each his own.

I chuckled. Yes, I was improving.

Fifteen minutes later two women carrying three small children stood in front of me. Each woman had a large safety pin in her right ear.

I gaped—then looked again. *My pins.* The emergency pins I'd carried in my luggage all these years.

Instant rage struck, so hot I forgot all about my former progress. I moved Poo out of the way and confronted the women. Pushing my glasses on top of my nose, I screwed up my face and let them have it with both barrels.

"Those are *not* your pins!"

The women looked at me, then to each other. One shrugged.

I reached for their ears and they backed away, hands flying up to protect their new ornaments. My fingers curved into claws.

"Those are *my* pins. Give them to me at once!"

They might not understand my words, but we'd see if communication didn't improve when I *ripped* those pins out of their ears!

The women shook their heads, jabbering. One held me back with a self-protective hand, blocking my advance.

Sam grabbed my shoulder. "Johanna! Stop it! What's going on here?"

"Those pins belong to me!"

He glanced at the jabbering women, then grasped my shoulders and whirled me around to face him. "They're just *pins.* Safety pins, Johanna! You can buy them in any Wal-Mart! Why are you making such a fuss? I'll buy you three dozen if it'll make you happy."

I glared up at him, hot, tired, and woozy. I was sick—sick—inside and out. "I don't want pins; I want *those* pins. They belong to me."

"I'll buy you more!"

"I don't want more. I want *my* pins. They picked the lock on my suitcase!"

Then Sam did something so "un-Sam" I was appalled. He picked me up, threw me over his shoulder, and hauled me out of the clinic.

"You put me down!" I screeched. "You hear me? Put me down this minute!" I had not traveled halfway around the world to be manhandled by this—this insensitive baboon!

He dumped me on the ground, and I scrambled to my feet, livid. "How *dare* you manhandle me, Sam Littleton! Who do you think you are?"

"I am someone who is very tired of your attitude. All you care about is a couple of worthless safety pins."

The cold contempt in his voice brought me up short. I straightened, pushing my glasses back in place. "You don't understand." I wasn't sure I understood myself. "I cannot accept theft, Sam, and I don't see how you condone it simply because these people feel they are welcome to anything we own. You can be angry at me all you like. I'll never fit in, no matter how hard I try. I will *never* fit in here."

"Try?" He snorted. "You haven't tried! You can't think of anything or anyone other than yourself."

His words stung. "I *have* tried. I've worked beside you in the heat and dirt and flies. I'd even considered leaving, but I've stayed on — trying. For you. Trying my best to understand what *you* feel. How can you even *suggest* I haven't tried? It's unfair! You care more for these ... these *villagers* than you do me." By now I was weeping like an out-of-control twit. Sam took hold of my shoulders and sat me down on the ground. He crouched beside me, reaching out a gentle finger to adjust my glasses, which had slipped to the bridge of my nose again.

He lowered his voice. "You have never given of yourself. From the moment we got here you've held back, kept aloof, separated yourself. Why? Are you afraid if you let go and accept these people God will call you to serve? Are your fears driving you to be so selfish?"

I gaped at him, speechless. My mouth opened and closed. I was incapable of speech. I *had* tried. I tried my best to share his passion. Why couldn't he see that?

I tightened my lips and balled my hands into fists to keep from swatting him. I would *not* let this man goad me into losing control. Forget that any semblance of self-control had been notably absent from my behavior already—I would not yield to my baser instincts and resort to violence. That's not to say I didn't *want* to. The palms of my hands itched with the need to connect with something. Especially this arrogant, hot-tempered, unjust . . . !

I glared up at him, looking for any sign of repentance, any remorse for the way he'd just spoken to me. Nothing. His hard jawline was as uncompromising as volcanic rock. All right, if that was the way he wanted it, fine. Two could play this game. Throwing him one final glower, I stood, then spun on my heel and marched off.

Dinner that night was as uncomfortable as the garden of Eden after the fall. The missionaries were aware of the "clinic explosion." Sam must have told them, because I sure hadn't mentioned it. Conversation was stilted, to say the least. Not one mention of work accomplished that afternoon. As soon as we finished eating, Sam left, rowing off somewhere to be by himself. Fine.

Frank and Bud sat outside the Laskes' hut conversing in low tones. Eva and Mary went about their work, saying very little, but I sensed their distress. Okay, maybe I *had* made a fool of myself over a couple of insignificant safety pins. Sure I could buy five dozen if I wanted to, but that wasn't the issue.

Well, what is the issue, Johanna? The pins are valueless possessions—nothing more, nothing less. If a pin would send you into orbit, what happens when someone takes something of yours that really matters? Will you revert to the world's standards?

245 / LORI COPELAND

Take back, at any cost, all you have—which the Lord provided in the first place?

The thought stopped me cold. I lay on my cot long after the others had retired and thought about my life, my self-centered instincts, and realized that often I was as barbaric in my ways as the villagers. Mine, mine, mine. If I was ever going to change, it had to start now.

Dawn found me rummaging through my suitcase, looking for the children's books I'd brought. I couldn't imagine why the natives hadn't stolen them, but maybe they had no interest in literature.

Ha, Johanna. Not funny.

Nelda had chosen stories from the library stock, assuring me that children everywhere loved them. Today, the village children would have a story hour they'd never forget. I could play Sam's game; I could be involved with these people.

I removed the lock from the case and threw it out my open window, listening for the splash as it hit the water. If the villagers took everything I had, so be it. I would not have Sam and the others thinking I was a selfish Neanderthal. I might well be, but I wasn't going to give them the satisfaction of proving it. Let the villagers wear my undies on their heads—I wouldn't say another word.

I shook off the sluggishness and headache that refused to go away. Well, no wonder; I'd slept in snatches, too upset by Sam and our argument to rest.

Sam was sitting at the table drinking coffee with Frank and Mary when I parted the curtain. Our eyes connected with cold distance.

"Morning, Johanna."

"Good morning, Doctor." I poured a glass of juice, drank half of it, and pushed it aside. My appetite was gone.

After breakfast the men and Eva and I left for the village. Mary stayed behind to rest. The missionaries talked among themselves, not ignoring me, just giving me room to sit in the bow. Eva tried a couple of times to engage me in small talk, but I remained silent, clutching the book—and my tattered pride—to my chest. I refused to meet Sam's eyes. The moment we landed, I was out of that boat like a gunshot and striding up the incline. The others followed, keeping pace. I didn't need them; there was nothing they could do to help me. This was my moment, and I intended to milk it for all it was worth.

Poo met me with a wide grin. As I walked I began to gather the village children and herd them up the hill. The boys and girls followed, chattering among themselves. I paused beneath a spreading palm. It took some gesturing on my part to get the group seated in a semicircle. Thirty to forty dirty children stared up at me, the quietest I'd ever seen them. One little girl still stood in front of me, so close I couldn't move without tripping over her.

I stared down at her. What on earth could her problem be? Didn't she see what the others were doing? She turned sober eyes on me.

"Ow."

"Ow?" I wracked my brain, trying to convert the word to English.

"Ow," the girl repeated. She looked at me and then looked down at her bare toes.

I followed her gaze and realized I was standing on her foot. "Oh. Sorry." Mark one up for me—*ow* must be a universal expression of pain.

She hobbled over to sit down beside Poo. I took a deep breath and thought about how to begin. For the first time it occurred to me that my temper might have led me to start something I couldn't finish. But I banished the thought. A librarian could relate to children. It's what we do best. I held up the book, a story about a monkey that flies a kite.

I waved my hands, striving for order, which the children ignored. They jabbered among themselves like a flock of magpies, paying no attention to me. I slapped one hand against the book I held to get their attention. "All right, listen up. I'm going to tell you a *story*." I mimicked words coming out of my mouth. I would have to use sign language, show the pictures, and act the story out. I could do that. It would be a matter of engaging them in the tale. My cup of tea.

"Our story today is about a little monkey named George." I enunciated my words and pointed to the picture, but they looked as blank as a clean sheet of paper. Okay. A kite. How to make them understand "kite"?

I clapped my hands and then raised my arms, using both forefingers to draw a kite shape in the air.

Poo stared, forehead furrowed. She raised her arms and copied my movements. The rest of the children sat like lumps of coal, not responding. Except for those who outright scowled.

Okay, skip the part about the monkey's name, and the ball, and move to the bunny house. Remember the KISS approach: Keep It Simple, Stupid. I pushed out my lower lip, concentrating on the problem at hand. *A hut.* They'd understand a hut.

I pointed to the thatched dwellings, outlined a hut in the air. Eureka! They got it. I knelt in front of a pretend door to take out an imagined baby bunny.

That lost them. Their brows curled.

I hopped around the clearing on all fours. That proved to be a total waste of time. Okay. They didn't have bunnies in this part of the world. We'd go fishing.

I showed how George went fishing, using a make-believe rod to throw the hook in the water.

They shrank back, holding their hands in front of them to ward off a blow. Too late I realized they didn't use rods and reels to fish. They actually thought I was going to strike them.

I skipped the majority of the story and went straight to the kite incident. I sketched the kite in the air. This time two children — one of them the girl whose foot I had mashed — copied my motions.

Encouraged, I took the kite by its imaginary tail and placed it on the ground. Then I hunched over, trying to look like a monkey — which wasn't as hard as it might sound, judging from their expressions. Some were doubled up laughing.

I tried not to let their insensitivity bother me; they would come around soon enough. Even so, drastic methods were called for, so I got down on all fours, used one hand to indicate a long tail, and then pointed to the surrounding trees.

Comprehension dawned on a few faces. All right! Now we were getting somewhere!

I got to my feet and stood still for a moment, lower lip caught between my teeth, thinking. Then I bent over, picking up the imaginary kite. Facing them, I raised my arms and drew the kite symbol.

This time several of the group copied my movements. I pretended to reel out a length of string, and holding the pretend kite behind me, I ran across the clearing, looking back as the kite caught the wind, lifting into the sky. The motion was so real I could almost see that kite.

I ran back across the clearing, so wrapped up in acting out the story that I didn't see the twig jutting up from the ground. My right foot connected and down I went, slamming into the hard ground. The breath left my body in a resounding *oof.*

I lay, waiting for the sudden rash of stars to subside before getting to my feet and facing my audience. Judging from the way they were shrieking with laughter, this was the high point of the story.

"The kite climbed higher and higher," I wheezed. "Bill decided to bring it in because he needed to go home."

I pantomimed reeling in a kite. "Oh no, it's caught in a tree! My fine new kite! Bill can't get his kite out of the tree!"

The children watched me, jabbering in that strange language among themselves and laughing, but not at the story.

They were laughing at me.

"George can get the kite." I reached for a low branch. "He will climb the tree! No tree is too high for George!"

I pretended to pull myself up, branch by branch, until I reached the kite. Little by little I untangled it, telling the story as I went. The kite fluttered to the ground, and I became George again, picking up the kite, letting out the string as it went up. I ran back and forth across the clearing acting like this was so much fun!

The pretend kite jerked me off my feet and I rose with it, a difficult feat with my shoes firmly planted on soil. I threw my heart into the pantomime, leaping, looking around me wide-eyed and frightened, ducking at imaginary birds flying through the air with me.

The adult villagers, attracted by my antics, gathered around to watch. I flapped my hands at them. "Shoo. This is for children."

They laughed and stayed where they were.

A chattering overhead caught my attention, and I looked up to see six monkeys sitting in the tree, staring at me like I was the funniest sight they'd ever seen.

I glanced back at the villagers and saw Sam standing with them, grinning and then outright hee-hawing at my bizarre antics. My glasses slid down my nose. My stomach roiled. I pushed the specs back up and looked at the laughing villagers, out-of-control children, chattering monkeys.

And Sam.

Okay. So much for group participation.

I slammed the book shut and faced the crowd. "The end." I did a swift theatrical bow, then turned and, clutching the paperback to my chest, walked away.

Sam had laughed at me. He wasn't my Sam anymore. He'd turned into someone I didn't even know.

Someone I didn't care to know. At all.

EIGHTEEN
⊚⊚⊚

That evening, I sat alone on the wooden platform, watching the sun drop behind the mountain range. A sultry breeze ruffled the water where the Millets and the Laskes were enjoying a dip. I watched the happy couples splashing around in the water, laughing and creating spouts with cupped thumb and fist. Were they brave or just stupid? Fish that could sting you and take your life lived in their pool. Did this not give them a moment's pause? Since my experience with Sam's manufactured bathtub, I'd stuck with sponge baths. Perhaps part of my inability to adjust had something to do with my longing for a private bath with hot and cold running water.

Sam came out of the hut. We had talked little over dinner. When he paused to admire the sunset, I noticed his forearms were still bright red. The dog incident couldn't have been fun for him no matter how temperate he appeared. My skin resembled a chicken that'd been roasted on a spit.

I thought about my performance with the village children today. Though my intentions were honorable, I had made a complete fool of myself. My emotions were a mass of snakes coiled in my stomach.

After this afternoon I was sure Sam had given up on wanting me to stay. A few more temper tantrums and I could forget about our relationship. Period.

I hadn't made him proud of late. Safety pins and drama performances hadn't done much to enhance my standing with either him or the missionaries.

I just have a question, God. Why did you send me all the way here to reinforce what I already knew? Why did you let me fall in love with Sam when you knew there would be problems we couldn't work out? I don't want to question your wisdom, but I'm so confused! I don't know what to do next.

The boards vibrated when footsteps approached. Sam. Part of me wanted to see him and part of me didn't. What did we have to say to each other?

Boards creaked. He paused beside me. "May I sit with you?"

I shrugged, not trusting my voice. He sat down beside me, cross-legged. He'd been around the villagers for so long the position seemed normal to him, like the way he'd bend his head and step over an imaginary threshold every time he entered the hut or clinic. I'd learned the hard way to duck — anyone with height whacked his head on the low beams.

"Have you noticed the sunrises here?" His voice was calm and gentle, showing none of the stress I was experiencing.

I sat for a moment and then nodded. "The sunrise is a sunset backward."

He laughed, and I sensed his relief that we were speaking to each other. Shame engulfed me. Dear Sam, so gentle and compassionate. How could he put up with my temper tantrums and still be so nice?

"Are you feeling better today?"

"Better now, thank you." A headache still bloomed at the back of my neck, and a general malaise stayed with me, but I had less than a week left to stay in this tropical sauna. I could make it. I stared down at the water lapping against the stilts.

"Sam, what's wrong with me? I love God, and serving him is important to me, but I'm in over my head here. I realize you and the others think serving here is a privilege. I'm very fond of Poo, and I know the children are innocent victims, but—" I shook my head.

"It's okay, Johanna. I understand."

How could he? His first wife, Belinda, had worked side by side with him, enthusiastic. Supportive.

And then there was me.

He sat for a moment while I watched a brown bird skimming the surface of the water, gliding in a rhythmic ballet. Finally he released a sigh. "The Bible assures us that we each have different talents. I don't resent the fact that we don't share the same passion. Only that we're not working together to solve the problem."

"How can we? There's no ready solution. You'd never be happy without your work and I ... I don't know *where* I fit."

"There is an answer to every problem."

I lifted a warning hand. "Don't you think there is *something* I should be able to do? If God has given me a gift, I've failed to find it—except caregiving. I thought that was what God wanted of me—to take care of Mom and Pop. But they're doing better than they have in a long time, and I haven't a thing to do with it. Most days I walk around in a spiritual fog. If God's leading me somewhere, don't you think I should have an inkling of where it is? Look at you and the others. You *know* what God expects from you, and you're content knowing you're in his will. Other than the library, I don't know where I belong."

Sam reached over and took my hand, his expression sobering. "You belong with me, Johanna. I've no doubt about that. You make it sound like we all think that everything we do is Spirit-led. The truth is we don't always know what to do. We have our spiritual fogs too. We spend a lot of time in prayer, asking for wisdom and guidance, and sometimes we make mistakes. We're feeling our way through the situation here too—and, yes, we have more patience with our circumstances than you, but we've been here longer and had time to adapt. You haven't allowed yourself enough time to adjust. But none of that is a final indication that you are or are not called to this particular ministry."

Maybe so, but I had a hunch my chances of fitting in wouldn't improve, no matter how long I stayed.

Eva, followed by Mary, grasped the wooden ladder and pulled up out of the water. The women frolicked, spraying us with water when they walked past to their respective huts.

"Don't let us bother you two lovebirds," Mary tossed over her shoulder.

I locked my arms around my knees, staring at the clouds in the west, flushed with gold and crimson and peach. "I wish I had their outlook."

"God has given you many talents. You've been faithful in your church, and to your position at the library. I've heard people talk about how helpful you are, and how you live your faith through your work. Never feel that God isn't using you if you want him to do so. Maybe your place isn't on the mission field, but trust me—he's at work in your life."

"I want to work beside you." I bent over so my head touched my knees. "I love you, Sam. More than life itself, at times, but our situation seems hopeless."

"There is a solution to every problem," he reiterated, his voice firm and sincere. For a split second I almost believed him. "I love you, Johanna. And I'm proud of you."

"You yelled at me." I'd never heard Pop lift his voice to Mom.

"Well—" he chuckled—"I didn't say I didn't get irritated with you. I'm human and sometimes I speak before I think, but I am and will always be proud of your accomplishments."

Tears stung the backs of my sunburned eyelids. I didn't deserve this man. It all poured out then, my frustrations with the living conditions, my homesickness, the way I missed Mom and Pop and Nelda. The dangers I perceived at every turn, my frustration with the villagers and the thefts.

He nodded with each complaint as if he understood, but how could he? He didn't have a selfish bone in his body.

"Is it possible you're too attached to possessions?" The tone of voice was gentle, but the words were a sharp whip across my heart.

"Yes." I'd considered the thought. "But taking care of what is given to you isn't selfish. God expects us to be good stewards."

"Everything we own belongs to God. Possessions, in and of themselves, are worthless. You'll never see a hearse pulling a U-Haul. When we leave this earth, as we will, we take nothing with us."

I clenched my teeth to keep from lashing out at him. Of course everything I owned belonged to God. That was basic Christianity. But back home, we had laws against theft. Here, no one was held accountable. Was that right teaching?

Sam shifted. "You're angry over something you don't own."

"These people don't understand a word you say. What's the purpose? You can't present the gospel. Look at how long the Millets have been here, and they have yet to break the language barrier. Don't you ever feel like giving up?"

"They understand our intentions. They know love when it's shown — and they recognize resentment."

My anger. That's what he meant. "I'm not a bad person, Sam Littleton. I may have my weaknesses, but if I can't get along with these people it's *their* fault. I've always been able to get along with anyone."

"Sure, as long as you're in your own element."

His words gave me pause. That was part of the problem, of course. In my library I could — and did — take charge. But here I had no idea what to do next. There wasn't even a trace left of Johanna Holland, head librarian. Just a very tired, discouraged woman sitting beside the man she loved and must give up, watching the sun sink over the horizon of a hostile, harsh land.

"Johanna, I feel what I do because I care for their souls."

Though there wasn't a trace of criticism in Sam's tone, I reacted. "*I* care for their souls — "

My next words caught in my throat. I couldn't believe I'd almost said them: "... as long as they leave me alone!"

Johanna! How could you have such thoughts?

It was the headache. A miserable nagging at the base of my skull.

"It's not the possessions, Sam. It's this way of life. It's so ... foreign." I was spoiled: the recognition tightened around me like a cobra. Mom and Pop had me late in life — years after they'd given up on Mom ever conceiving. I had been pampered and sheltered and the princess of the Holland clan. Was it any wonder I hated to share?

257 / LORI COPELAND

He sighed, and I realized I wasn't telling him anything he hadn't already figured out. Reaching over, he pulled me close, and I gave way to my emotions. I buried my face against his chest and broke into wrenching sobs. He held me in his arms, a strong, protective shelter from the raging storm inside me.

Finally my tears ceased and I rested in his strength, drained from my emotional meltdown. One look at his stoic features and I knew that his heart was as heavy as mine. Two people in love separated by God's calling. How could this be? God loved us both, and I'd been taught all of my life that he wanted the best for each of us. So why had we met and fallen in love only to struggle with different ambitions in life?

We sat wrapped in silence. Suddenly a slim young man ran down the village slope and waded into the water.

"Something's wrong." Sam released me and got to his feet as the villager swam toward us.

When he was close, he shouted something and Sam lifted a hand in acknowledgment. The swimmer turned and swam back to the shoreline. Sam helped me up.

"What was that all about?"

"There must be some sort of trouble." He hurried to the huts, calling to Bud and Frank. The three men held a hurried conference, then got in the boat and started for the shore. I went inside the Millets' hut to seek Mary and Eva. Drums sounded in the distance.

"What could it be?"

"Unless there's been an accident, I would guess that old Macu, the former village chief, has passed away."

Of course. The village elder had lain near death for days.

"There'll be a *warap*, a large feast." Eva pulled thread through a cross-stitch pattern.

"The custom is interesting," Mary offered. "Unique. I've seen one once—in a neighboring village. The ceremony is given for a prominent leader, and it also serves to commemorate the leader's deceased kin of lesser importance."

"Will we be invited?"

"We hope so." Mary bit off a thread. "There will be invited guests, many from surrounding villages. The natives will come bearing gifts of food that will be dispersed among the villagers here."

"How do they go about distributing the food in a fair manner?" I winced at how materialistic that sounded.

"I'm not sure how it works," Eva admitted. "It seems to me that no one comes out richer or better fed than anyone else. It's a rather odd custom, but the villagers seem to celebrate death."

Mary frowned. "I think the ceremony must confirm or increase a villager's status—strengthen their social ties and mutual obligations. It seems to be a time of coming together and sharing what one has to offer."

So these people I'd dismissed knew something I didn't: the importance of sharing and showing compassion. They had little, and yet they withheld nothing.

The moon came up and crept higher in the sky. We sat in the huts, waiting for the men to return. Eva sighed and got to her feet. "I suppose we might as well go to bed. We don't know what's happened. The men could be gone all night."

Since I lived in her hut, I stood too. "Eva, I've taken the last of my aspirin. Do you have more?"

"Headache still bothering you?"

"It's better, but I want to discourage it from coming back."

I trailed her across the walkway to her hut and waited while she lit the kerosene lamp. "When you first came here, was it Frank's calling you obeyed or yours?"

She moved to the box where she kept sundries. After a moment she lifted her hands to her face and rubbed her eyelids. "I suppose it was Frank's—at first. I'd pledged my life to him, promised to go where he went, make his people my people, the whole bit. And I meant it. If he came here, I wanted to be at his side."

"Have you ever regretted it?"

"Sometimes."

Her answer surprised me. "Really?"

She smiled. "Regardless of what you may think, I am not a saint. I have my frustrations and breaking points, and no, I don't like the stealing and the dirt and the heat and the insects. But I've learned to let go of possessions, and the elements no longer disturb me. We've come to serve the villagers, and if that means handing over a can opener once in a while, then so be it. The important thing is we're building trust for future missionaries. Through them, the gospel will be taught here in this remote place, where one sometimes wonders if God has forgotten these people. But he hasn't! Wherever there is a necessity, he will meet the need."

"But you see so few results."

"Results are not always apparent. And God doesn't grade us on results, but on obedience."

I took my aspirin and retired to my cubicle to prepare for bed. I froze, unable to believe what I was seeing, or rather what I didn't see.

My Nikes.

They were missing.

When had I seen them last? I couldn't recall. Maybe I'd taken them off at the clinic ... So while I was running around flying an imaginary kite, stumbling over my own two feet, somebody was pilfering my overpriced shoes.

I sighed and lay back on the pillow. Well, here's hoping whatever dirty-footed villager had my shoes would enjoy them. I'd soon see them again — on somebody's feet.

So what?

I yawned, closing my eyes, both surprised and pleased to find my anger was much less intense than in the past. I could always buy another pair of shoes. No problem. (Or at least less of a problem than before.)

My relationship with Sam. Now *that* was something worth losing sleep over.

NINETEEN

◎◎◎

As Sam predicted, trouble was brewing. The old chief, Macu, passed away during the evening. The men didn't return until the moon was high in the sky; Sam said they'd remained behind to help with the grieving wife and children.

"The *warap* will take place sometime in the next week. We've been invited to attend."

"That's good." Eva clasped her hands together. "If they've invited us to their feast, it means they're beginning to trust us."

❦

The stolen Nikes surfaced when the clinic opened the next morning. A middle-aged villager, about my height, leaned against the side of the hut, my shoes dangling from his belt like a trophy. My lips firmed as the all-too-familiar burst of temper hit. Then I remembered Sam's accusation that I was too fond of possessions. There wasn't a smidgen of truth to the claim. Still …

Okay, I'd show them all that I didn't care about *things*. Sam might think I was a materialistic, possession-obsessed female, but he couldn't be further from the truth. Things weren't important to me. I ignored the man and my shoes, feeling saintly. It was, after all, a pair of tennis shoes. Plenty more where those came from, and before long I'd be walking through an air-conditioned mall shopping for new ones.

I was so lost in my sainthood that I didn't notice Poo until she yanked my shirttail.

She smiled up at me. "Jo."

My name? She could say my *name*? Overcome with joy, I dropped on one knee so we were facing each other. "Say it again."

She grinned and obliged. "Jo."

"Jo—" I touched my chest—"and Poo." I touched hers.

"Jo ... Poo," she echoed.

Tears stung my lids. What an amazing breakthrough! Others had been here years and failed to make a connection, but I had been here only a short time and this wonderful child loved me enough to transcend language barriers! I wrapped my arms around her, feeling her bones dig into my chest. The children here had so little, no fancy toys, gimmicks, or games; limited clothing, basic medical care, and not always enough food. How could I have begrudged Poo what little of mine she'd taken? She nestled close and I rested my cheek against her forehead. Poo was offering me the most important thing she had to give: her love.

God, let me be worthy of this child's trust.

I straightened up, took her hand, and we sprinted through the village. I started yelling and waving my hands, filled with elation. Villagers turned to stare at our headlong plunge into the clinic. Sam glanced up as I burst into the hut like an elephant with a toothache. "Whoa! What's the hurry?"

"She said it! Poo said my name!"

A soft gasp escaped Mary. She turned from a patient. "What?"

"Poo!" I beamed down at the child—my prodigy. "She said my name! Clear as a glass." I nudged Poo. "Go ahead. Say my name."

The child peered up at me, silent.

"Go ahead—say my name, sweetie." By now Frank, Eva, and Bud had joined us. We stood waiting. Poo stared.

"Now, Poo. Say *Jo*." My ears had *not* deceived me earlier; she'd said my name. Yet now the child appeared to have lost her voice.

After several attempts to make her speak, it was evident I'd either imagined the miracle or miracles were seldom duplicated the same day. I must have looked as disillusioned as the missionaries, who resumed their work. I looked to Sam, tears suspended on my bottom eyelids. "She did—she said *Jo*."

He paused long enough to give me a quick hug. "Kids. They never talk when you want them to."

Was he just patronizing me? I was not losing my mind. The heat hadn't fried my brain. Poo had said *Jo*.

A patient with an injured foot claimed the doctor's attention, so I nudged Poo outside the clinic to play with the other children and then returned to take my place beside Sam. Each time Poo looked in my direction she would smile, and I could hear her voice in my head: "Jo." She'd said it; I'd stake my life on it.

I caught a whiff of unwashed body and turned to face the lout who'd taken my Nikes. By now he was wearing them, and a tight fit they must have been. He cornered me, preened, holding out one foot and then the other and rubbing his fingers together in the age-old gesture for money.

My eyes narrowed to thin slits. The gall of this barbarian! I drew a deep breath, briefly considered slugging him, and then turned aside to concentrate on cleaning instruments. Sam would not have to carry me out of the tent ranting and raging today. I was above hedonism, at least for the moment.

Poo burst into the clinic marching straight to the thief. Her contorted features shot fire. She stamped her foot. *"Mah pfuh, neho! Neho! Neho!"* She jabbed a grubby finger at his feet.

Shrugging, he turned away, but she dogged his steps like a hungry animal. She blocked his way, and when he started to step around her she fell on the ground in front of him, wagging a finger at him. *"Neho! Neho!"*

He stepped over her and she latched onto his right foot, stripping the shoe off. He whirled.

"Mug, pge, dht!"

"Neho. Neho!"

"Ldy jeit llobh!"

A struggle ensued. Poo flew into him and knocked him to the ground. Horrified, we stood and watched the fracas. The villagers stood back, eyes solemn as they watched the brawl.

Poo held her ground. She bit, kicked, and spit. She was on that man like white on rice, as Pop would say. I fought back a grin. That little girl was scrappy; she and Nelda would make quite a pair. Wouldn't it be something if I could take the child home with me —

I started.

Take Poo with me? How could I? She didn't have proper papers. I couldn't just put her on a plane and transport her to another country. The Johanna who had arrived weeks ago would have been horrified at the mere suggestion. The Johanna I was today was actually considering it!

Poo had the thief pinned to the ground in an armlock. The man struggled, his feet pumping air. Finally the man must have cried out his surrender, because Poo released her grip. Getting to her feet, she stripped off the second shoe. Moments later she presented the sneakers to me.

"Thank you." I glanced at the villager limping off to the bush. Though I didn't know their language, of this I was convinced: he'd never live this down.

***

Around noon, excitement broke out a second time. Two men bearing a stretcher came out of the bush. The natives turned and pointed to the man lying prone, eyes closed, face contorted in pain. The villagers started to mill about, restless, their eyes on the sick man. Sam motioned for men to bring the stretcher into the clinic; Bud and Frank hurried to join him.

From all appearances, the man was seriously ill, but I had no idea from what. Sam and the missionaries conversed in low tones, and then Frank rushed off. When he returned he carried the portable satellite phone. The situation must be grave if they were calling for the plane. Frank spoke into the receiver, his tone terse, words clipped. Bud had one hand on the man's shoulder, holding him flat to the stretcher.

Sam came over to stand beside me. "He's got a hot appendix; I'm arranging to have him flown to Port Moresby today."

"You can't operate here?"

He shook his head. "I don't want to risk it. I suspect the appendix has or is about to burst, and he needs more specialized care than I can provide."

"Thank goodness we worked on the strip—but with all this rain the grass is growing faster than we could keep up."

Sam glanced outside the tent at the light falling rain. "Landing will be tricky, but we don't have a choice. A medical emergency will override the pilot's reservations."

"If we're lucky it won't be the same pilot." Frank lifted his hat and scratched his head. "Wasn't he having surgery?"

Sam nodded. "That's what he said."

It seemed forever before we heard the hum of the approaching plane. The natives had carried the man to the landing strip. Half of the villagers had shown up to wait with us.

"They don't think much of the growling machine," Sam observed under his breath. I looked up to see the curious villagers gathered near the edge of the strip, keeping a safe distance.

The plane appeared on the horizon, circled a couple of times, and came in for a landing. The wheels touched the ground and made two grooves through the high grass. Then the right wheel hit on something—probably a rock—and the machine bounced before sliding to a stop yards short of the end of the mown runway.

I released the breath I'd been holding, once again thankful I'd not been a passenger on that plane. A youthful pilot emerged, scratching his head. He stood in the doorway of the craft, staring at the ragged strip.

"You okay, fella?"

He nodded at Frank. "Man. Thought I'd lost it there for a minute."

The stretcher bearers cowered, reluctant to approach the aircraft. The loud single engine was deafening. After several unsuccessful attempts to urge the natives to load the patient,

267 / LORI COPELAND

Frank and Bud seized control. Scooping up the stretcher, they ran with the patient to the plane. The patient stirred, then shot up to a sitting position, fear dominant in his expression.

"It's okay, fella. You'll be fine."

The patient started to abandon the cot. He jabbered and pointed to the plane, his eyes wide. He rolled off the gurney, grasping his side and shouting the same phrase over and over.

The onlookers backed up another two or three steps.

Sam, Frank, and Bud caught the patient and forced him on the stretcher, holding him down by brute force. Struggling, they tightened the strap and loaded him into the aircraft. I covered my ears to blot out his frantic screams. I've never seen any human so terrified.

The pilot got back into the plane, turned it, and taxied down the overgrown strip. It looked touch and go for a few minutes, but he managed to get the craft in the air. Then it banked and headed toward civilization. In my imagination I could hear the patient's screams long after the plane had vanished from sight.

Excitement over, the villagers faded back into the bush or headed toward the village. Bud looked at the hay field we called a landing strip. "We need to cut the strip today, rain or no rain. We'll have to do the worst part by hand. The pilot will be bringing that guy back within twenty-four hours."

Frank glanced up at the overcast sky, where a light mist blanketed the area. "You're right. I doubt any pilot would try to set that plane down again unless we do."

"We'll help clear the strip." Eva stepped up. "Provided Sam can do without us in the clinic."

"I can handle the clinic; the strip is more important."

I took a deep breath. No telling what lurked in the rank vegetation, but the ground had to be maintained.

We set to work. Frank and Bud used scythes, bending and swaying in an ancient rhythm. We women raked the fallen grass in ragged stacks, and one by one the villagers returned to help carry the debris away. By the time twilight covered the area, we'd cleared a third of the strip.

Frank surveyed our work. "We'll go at it again first thing in the morning. We should have it cleared by afternoon."

Like me, the others seemed too tired to eat that night. We sat on the dock, too weary to move. We tried to unwind as we watched fish feeding in the water.

I looked up to see Poo and her grandfather swimming toward us. From Poo's gestures, Eva decided that the child needed to speak to me. I signaled for her to climb the ladder. She stood beside me, dripping lagoon water, peering in my face. She started to babble. From the inflection in her tone, I suspected she was asking a question, but I had no idea what it could be.

Eva joined us. Poo pointed to the sky.

"Yes, *sky*," I interpreted.

Poo shook her head and pointed again, jabbing and jabbing with her little grubby finger.

"Farther beyond." Mary tipped her head. "Farther ... God?"

The answer seemed to satisfy the child. She moved on. She touched her eyes. Twice, little pats beneath the brows.

"Eye?" Sam joined us now.

She patted again. And again.

"See," Bud prompted.

She paused, smiled.

269 / LORI COPELAND

"God. See." I tried to assimilate the message. "God see!"

Concentration furrowed Eva's brow. "Maybe 'Does God see?'"

Poo pointed to the sky—beyond. Touched her eyes twice. Opened her eyes and squinted.

"Oh, brother." Frank shook his head. "Does God need glasses? She doesn't know about God."

"Frank." Mary jabbed his arm. "I'm sure that isn't the question."

The child pointed to the sky, jabbed far beyond. Touched her eyes. Clamped her eyes shut. Groped the air.

"Dark." Sam smiled. "Does God see in the dark?"

For a moment none of us could find our voices. Was the child asking if God could see in the dark? If that was true, how much did she understand about her Creator?

The child knew nothing about the Almighty or his power, unless her grandfather had conveyed earlier missionaries teachings. Had earlier messengers managed to break the communication barrier?

I nodded. "Yes. God sees everything. In daylight or in dark."

The answer appeased the little girl. She and her grandfather left, their bodies gliding back through the dark lagoon waters. I held my breath until the two reached the shore, then I turned to Mary.

"What do you think that was all about?"

She smiled. "Hard to say, but that child had something on her mind. Something she considered important."

"It couldn't be God—they know nothing about God."

"We *assume* they know nothing about the God we serve, but one never knows for certain."

We sat in silence for a few moments and then retired to our respective huts, ready for bed after the strenuous day. In my exhausted state sleep claimed me as soon as my head hit the pillow, despite the nagging headache that had returned to distress me.

The following morning I came out of the hut to find Poo sitting on the landing. Had the child slept here overnight? I stooped and rested my hands on her shoulders. "What are you doing here?"

She went through a series of motions, and I realized she had stood guard over me and my possessions through the night. The thought of this child protecting me humbled my very soul. She smiled and patted my cheek, then walked to the edge of the landing and dove into the water. I shook my head at the depth of her devotion.

I could never deserve it, but I was grateful for it all the same.

TWENTY

◎◎◎

At long last the rain ended and the sun came, drying the ground almost overnight with a hot, scorching wind. The breeze was like standing in front of a giant blow-dryer stuck on high. That night, I lay staring at stars through the narrow window, gasping for relief, my sheets drenched in sweat. Never again would I complain about Michigan winters. A little snow and ice would have been nice. I smiled. Mom and Pop were in their comfortable apartment, and Nelda was in the climate-controlled library. How I envied them!

My dull headache now was constant. Pain radiated from the base of my skull to the top of my forehead. It had worsened during the night, making my sleep fitful and me unable to relax and unwilling to be awake. Every loud noise or sudden moment brought a pang of pain that was pure torture.

I made my way to the table, where thirst-quenching fresh pineapple waited. Most times I would have enjoyed the rich flavor of the fruit, but today I couldn't bring myself to touch it. Keeping food down seemed to be even more of a challenge than getting it down.

Mary looked up from her plate. "What's the matter, Johanna? You're not eating."

"It's the heat." Bud set his cup on the table. "She's still not acclimated to the climate."

"It's this headache. I can't seem to shake it."

Concern creased Sam's forehead. "I've aspirin in my medical bag. I'll get it for you." He got up from the table and left for the Laskes' hut. He returned with the bottle, opened it, and shook out a couple of pills in his hand. "Maybe these will help." He held them out, palm up, and I took them, placing the small white tablets in my mouth and washing them down with a swallow of juice.

He patted my shoulder. "Why don't you rest this morning? Stay in the hut until you're feeling better."

"No, I'll be fine. I promised to help clear the airstrip."

"Ah yes, the strip. The hospital called by satellite phone. The plane will be back sometime today; our man's surgery went well, and since I can assume his care they're sending him back."

He returned to his breakfast, and I watched him. If I had written my description of the perfect man, I would have created Sam, even down to the way his forehead wrinkled when he concentrated — like now. Bud waved his hands, telling some tale about a clash with a villager over a pineapple. It was a funny story, but my head hurt too much to appreciate the humor.

Sam glanced over. "Aspirin starting to work?"

"Not yet, but soon, I'm sure."

After breakfast we rowed across to the village and walked to the airstrip. Bud unlocked the storage shed and handed out the tools, assigning me the power mower. I was thankful for the machine — at least I'd have something to support me. Frank started the mower, and the roar of it pierced my aching head. He adjusted the throttle and then stood back. By now my head was pounding and I was weak and dizzy and more than a little off kilter.

We heard the returning plane late that morning. I turned the mower off, watching the craft land and skid across the grass at the end of the strip. The strip was in better condition than before, but it was still far from ideal. Villagers lined the band of mown grass. The craft idled in and stopped. Then the door opened.

I covered my ears, anticipating a sonic blast of profanity, but none came. The patient emerged, holding his side and breaking into a wide grin when he spotted his audience. His weakened condition didn't dampen his enthusiasm. He paused in the aircraft doorway, looking as confident as a polished political speaker. He motioned to the plane and then to the sky. His voice rose and fell, extolling his adventure in the "growling machine."

His enthusiasm was contagious. The villagers pointed to the sky and then back to the patient. They were laughing and jumping up and down. Broad beams of pleasure covered their nut-brown faces. A grin was all I could muster with my pounding head. We had no way of knowing the specifics of the man's story, but we could tell he was proud of his accomplishment. He had conquered the roaring beast! How many could claim such a victory?

Sam came to stand beside me, hooking his arm around my waist. I leaned into him, meeting his laughing gaze. He felt so good, so solid to my aching body. The strenuous mowing had intensified my headache. "Great story to remember, don't you think?"

I nodded. "Imagine what it must have been for him. Loaded on that plane and taken to a place where they cut him open and sewed him back up again. I gather the trip home wasn't as frightening."

"He seems to be quite the seasoned traveler now." Sam motioned to where the patient was being lifted on a stretcher and carried like royalty back to the village. "He's become an important man."

"He's fortunate you were able to help him." My fingers patted Sam's waist. "I'm very proud of you, Dr. Littleton."

"That's Sam, to you." He winked and stole a brief kiss before he went back to work.

The plane left, but we decided to work awhile longer to try to stay ahead of the unwanted growth. While Bud and Frank manned machetes and sickles, Mary and Eva wielded rakes.

I pushed the mower into the vegetation, pulled it back, and tried again. The rough foliage was almost too thick for the machine to cut without choking out. Little by little I made progress. The men worked ahead, slashing down the taller foliage while I followed behind. Bud worked ahead of me, his strong body bending and rising with the sweep of the scythe. The sun beat down like a hammer. My head ached in earnest until it seemed someone gripped my brain with red-hot pincers.

Sometimes I was so dizzy it was an effort to stay upright. Other times a wave of nausea overcame me; I'd have to stop and grip the mower to remain upright.

Around one o'clock, we broke for lunch. I took one look at the food and my stomach recoiled. For a minute I thought I was going to be ill, but the feeling subsided, leaving me almost too weak to move. I slumped back against the base of a palm and braced myself. Had I *ever* been this nauseated before? I closed my eyes, blocking out the sight of food and flies. The heat rose in waves off the tall grass.

Soft hands removed my glasses. I opened my eyes to see Mary pouring water from her canteen, moistening a handkerchief. She wiped my hot face. To my horror I giggled. I must have been delirious with heat and exhaustion.

Then Sam was kneeling beside me, holding his canteen to my lips, coaxing me to drink. I thought he was at the clinic? The water hit my stomach and bounced, burning my throat and leaving a bitter aftertaste. I pushed the container aside. My head was reeling, the leaves overhead whirling like a giant kaleidoscope. Sam's face swung in and out of focus.

His hand rested on my forehead and his voice came from a long way off. "She's burning up. Let's get her to the clinic."

I blinked, shaking my head to clear it. "It ... must have been something I ate."

Mary wrung out the cloth. "She's eaten nothing. She must be suffering a migraine."

"Head hurts," I murmured. The village *warap* was tonight. Would I be unable to go? I had so looked forward to the festivities.

"Maybe we haven't been cautious enough," Mary fretted. "Maybe one of the canned foods was tainted."

Eva shook her head. "We all ate the same thing. Johanna has eaten nothing unless she got it in the village."

Fog had moved into my head—not a cool, moist fog, but more of a hot, burning vapor that drifted through my consciousness, coming and going. Interspersed were short periods of clarity. I remember thinking I should answer Mary's question, but then I didn't remember what she'd asked.

Sam's voice penetrated the haze. "She's not working out in this heat any longer."

"I'm fine," I managed. "Just let me lie here in the shade for a while and I'll be all right."

The love of my life scooped me into his arms. "You don't know what you're saying."

I'd have been irritated at his high-handed manner if I hadn't been too sick to care.

On general principles I tried to protest, but he was right. The thought of pushing that mower again was intolerable. I couldn't do it. I'd feel better tomorrow.

I was grateful for his strength where mine failed. He carried me to the shoreline, where Poo raced to meet us, her expression anxious. Words poured out of her in an incomprehensible stream. I hadn't a clue what she was saying, but she sounded upset.

Sam helped me into the boat and Poo scrambled in after me. This was a first. To my knowledge she had never been in the missionary boats, preferring to swim across to the huts. Now she sat in front of me, holding my hands and making little crooning sounds. It was surprising how much I understood her even though there was not an ounce of intellectual comprehension. Love is the same in every tongue, and every gesture and sound from this little girl shouted, "I love you." I reached one hand to cup her chin and assure her I returned her love.

When we reached the huts, Sam secured the boat and then helped me out; Poo pattered across the wooden planks behind us. She kept up a constant chatter, but now it sounded more like she was giving orders to Sam or to me. I wasn't sure which. When I reached my cot, I sank down and stretched out. Poo ran to me carrying a wet cloth for my forehead. I smiled at her, but the worried scowl refused to leave her youthful features.

Sam remained at my side. "I'm staying with you this afternoon. I won't risk anything happening while I'm gone."

By now I had roused enough to be coherent. I struggled to gain some control of the situation. "There is no need for that. I'll be fine once I've rested. Poo is here. I'll send for you if I need anything—anything at all." Nausea was so thick in the back of my throat I could taste it, but I didn't want to slow Sam's clinic work. There were so many ill to see. And the strip still needed work ...

The child reached out and patted my shoulder. Sam glanced from the little girl back to me. "I can't risk it. What if Poo doesn't understand what you need?"

"She will—she's in tune with me." I gave the child a weak smile. "If I worsen, I'll send for you. I promise."

He hesitated and I waved my hand toward the door. "Go. Don't be a mother hen. You worry too much."

"I'm afraid I don't worry enough where you're concerned." He bent and placed a kiss on my dry lips. "I'll check back every hour. If you need anything—"

At the moment I didn't have the strength to reassure him again. Moments later he left, issuing one last order that I send Poo for him should I need anything. The child recognized her name and looked from him to me and back again. I took her hand and smiled at her, and she relaxed.

I dropped off to sleep, into a nightmare where I fled from one monster after another, dashing headlong through dark shadows, aware that something terrible was chasing me. I woke, suffocating heat surrounding me. My heart pounded above a raging fever. Sam had left a full canteen beside my cot; I drained it and craved more.

"Poo?"

Though I'd barely managed a whisper, she materialized. I held out the canteen and pointed outside to the water barrel. Her face lit up, and she refilled the container and held my head as I drank in long gulping swigs. I downed the cool liquid, letting it run off my chin, until she jerked the jug away and shook her head, eyes filled with caution. I grabbed for the canteen and shouted at her.

A haze filled my mind; my fevered gaze roamed the hut, and I frowned. Where was I? Why didn't anything look familiar? And why was I here?

My head throbbed, my bones ached, and I was in the "bathroom" every few minutes, sometimes crawling on hands and knees to the jar to avert disaster. Poo helped me off the cot and supported my weight to the makeshift water closet, a steady companion when I crawled.

The child was an angel sent to minister to me.

Sam came every hour, worry etched on his forehead. I felt a needle prick. I didn't know or care why. The afternoon wore on, and I tossed and turned on the cot, unable to get comfortable. My clothing was drenched, as if some maniacal demon stood above me pouring water over my fevered body. I drifted in and out of consciousness.

Once I opened my eyes and saw Poo standing over the cot, tears rolling from the corners of her eyes. I reached out, touched her arm, and murmured something—but even I couldn't recognize the words. I drifted on a troubled sea under a moonless sky, darkness surrounding me like a velvet curtain. I sank down, down, down . . .

Bright light seared my eyelids. The darkness had loosened, giving the impression I was rising, fighting my way upward, away from the black depths that had held me prisoner. My eyes fluttered open to find Sam and Poo standing over me. Poo was sobbing.

Eva and Mary hovered in the background, and I could hear Frank and Bud talking. I wanted to comfort them but I was powerless to move. My voice when it came was barely audible. "What is it? What's wrong with me?"

Sam's voice came to me in a tunnel. "You've very ill, darling. I've sent for the plane."

The plane? I sat bolt upright, memory flooding me. That single-engine menace. That horrible runway. "No! Sam, I'll be fine!"

Hands urged me back to the pillow. Sam's voice soothed me—then everything faded into silence.

TWENTY-ONE
◎◎◎

I came to, fighting to shake off a lethargic stupor. I drifted in and out of consciousness but was able to piece together some of what was going on. By the grave tone of the voices that filtered through my fog, I realized I was ill, very ill. All four of the missionaries, plus Sam and Poo, were crowded into my narrow cubicle. Eva bent at my bedside, sponging my face and arms.

Calm, unflappable Eva wore a grim expression. "Gentlemen, if you will wait outside the curtain. Mary and I will take care of Johanna."

Sam protested, and I almost jumped when Eva snapped, "I *mean* it. You can pray for her as well on the other side of the curtain. Now *move!*"

Eva and Mary began a new form of treatment. They stripped me of soiled clothing and removed the sweat-damped sheets. Then they bathed my heated body with cool water. Mary knelt beside my cot, wiping my face with a damp cloth, coaxing me to drink from the glass she held. She and Mary were so good to me, caring for me as though I were an infant. As they worked, they murmured encouragement. From the other side of the curtain I could hear the men's voices raised in prayer. For me. Johanna Holland. Saginaw, Michigan, librarian. Disgraceful missionary.

Poo stood at the head of my cot, stroking my hair. Eva motioned for her to leave. "Wait in the other room, sweetie."

The child gripped my hand, shook her head. "Jo."

Eva smiled. "You can say her name."

"Let ... her stay." It took great effort for me to speak, but I needed this child. Small caring hands stroked my hair, comforted me.

"If that's what you want." Eva moved away.

I drifted off again. I was in a canoe floating down a gentle river toward a distant shore. A light appeared on the shore and a soft breeze ruffled my hair. I saw a rainbow and hills covered with bright flowers. I could hear the most beautiful music, music so sweet and pure that tears pooled behind my lids. I strained toward it, yearning for what lay just out of reach. I started to float forward out of the canoe. Then something—or someone—took hold of my arm and pulled me back into the vessel. A dark veil dropped between me and the beautiful scene.

"No ... Let me go." The music. It was incredible. I wanted to blend into the sounds, to be a part of whatever or whoever was performing.

I opened my eyes and there was Poo, holding my arm, tears rolling down her dirty cheek.

"Jo. *Jo*."

I reached over—or I think I did—and pulled her face down onto my chest. Later I realized that was the exact moment I understood what Sam said to me on our flight to Papua New Guinea: "You can teach love and preach love, but the true message of love is never completed until you give love." Even in my groggy state I knew I had somehow reached a new plateau of loving.

Poo drew in a deep gulp of air and whispered my name again, "Jo."

"I'm here. It's all right." I didn't know where I found the strength to answer her, but it must have come from God. At that moment it could have come from none other than the Almighty.

I drifted again, slipping into oblivion. The dreams returned. I heard Mary say, as clear as day, "I thought she was gone."

"Poo's love brought her back." Eva's voice penetrated my feverish mind. "God must need Johanna here on earth for a while longer."

"I believe he has great plans for this woman, though convincing her is difficult. She seems to base her worth on her calling. If only she knew she has nothing to prove. God loves her as she is, and her worth is great in his eyes." A cool glass rim touched my parched lips. "Drink, Johanna. You're dehydrated."

I tried to swallow, but darkness claimed me. I sensed the women's concern, but I wasn't worried. I was aware of a presence, a warm, comforting someone or something hovering just beyond the edge of my consciousness. My concern at the moment wasn't for me, but for Mom and Pop. And Sam. Poor Sam. He would always hold himself accountable for my demise.

Your rod and your staff, they comfort me . . . You are with me.

My eyelids drifted opened, and I stared through my window at the sky, orange rather than blue now that the sun was setting. My cot rocked. I heard a splash and then the sound of oars rising and falling. My groping hand touched a hard surface that curved around me like a shell. Not a cot. I was in the cool bottom of the rowboat. Sam sat in the bow, his familiar shape sturdy and reassuring. Funny how I always felt out of harm's way when he was near. Someone, Bud maybe, sat in the back and manned the oars. A lone bird flew overhead. Going home? Did birds have homes? I giggled. Tiny little jungle town houses with two bedrooms, two-car garages. I laughed out loud at the images going through my mind.

Plasma televisions, treadmills to keep their teensy little legs slim and attractive for male birds ... Male birds.

Mail birds.

Do birds get mail? Do they have tiny mailboxes with infinitesimal little stamps—maybe with pictures of people on them?

Sometime later—maybe a few minutes, maybe an hour, maybe a day—I woke and lay staring up at the canopy of branches overhead. I was on something neither hard nor soft, just a surface, like a piece of canvas swaying back and forth in an unsteady rhythm. A stretcher? Someone was carrying me through the jungle. Fear coursed through me and my body started shaking. I struggled to sit up.

"Lay still, Johanna."

Sam? He was with me? Then I was safe. I sank back down and let the rhythmic swaying pacify me. *Sam is with me ... Everything is fine. I love you, Sam. Everything is fine. Honest. I'll be fine ...*

Mail birds? I don't think so.

Do birds build people houses and put out hamburger feeders? Do they sit in microscopic town houses with miniature binoculars and watch people flit in and out of the feeders on snowy days?

I giggled.

A dull roar filled my ears, growing louder by the moment. A bee? Buzzing around my head? No, the sound was too loud, deafening me. I wanted to clap my hands over my ears, but they wouldn't move. Somehow I'd lost control of my faculties, not just my mind but my limbs and my speech.

Oh, wait. It was the airplane. What do you know—the engine *did* sound like a growling beast. I should have been worried but I wasn't.

Do birds have teensy little aircraft? Miniature cockpits and itty-bitty bags of birdseed and sugar and red food-colored water to snack on—Itty Bitty.

I miss that pooch. Is Nelda taking good care of him?

The heat from the plane's engine washed over me in waves. I curled in a fetal position, arms curved around my head. *Shoot. I'm dying. I must be or Bud wouldn't have called for the plane. I don't want to die now. I'm only forty and I still have so much to do. Sam! There's something I need to tell him!*

I summoned the strength to reach out and grasp a hand. Warm, reassuring fingers curled around mine. I adored Sam. I needed him to know that time was imperative. The most important thing in the world—the only thing in the world at this moment. I had to tell Sam how much I loved and needed him.

"Sam?"

"I'm right here, darling. Save your strength—we'll be in Port Moresby soon."

"Sam." I struggled to form the words in my dry mouth. *I love you. I adore you. I would have gone to the ends of the earth with you, no matter how I've acted.* But words wouldn't come. I opened and closed my mouth, holding to those fingers.

I realized Sam was kneeling beside me, his hands clasping both of mine. "Johanna, don't leave me. I love you."

I wanted to tell him it was all right, that I loved him too, we could work this out. His voice lowered, filled with pain.

"I'm sorry I brought you here. I prayed so long and so hard about it, and I thought this was what God wanted, but now I realize it was wrong. This is my fault. If I hadn't insisted you come, you would be home in Michigan."

I heard each word with a bell-like clarity, even over the roar of the engines. He bent low, his mouth pressed against my ear. Wetness. Was he crying? No, Sam didn't cry.

I had to comfort him, had to look into his eyes, those wonderful Tom Selleck eyes, one last time. With tremendous effort, I opened my lids, and what I saw almost broke my heart. There in his expression, mirrored in his eyes, I saw defeat. Pain. Love.

Incredible love.

But there was something more. Something troubling. Signs of wavering conviction. Sam was having doubts about his calling, and I was the reason for those misgivings.

His voice rang in my heart like a death knell. "I don't know, Johanna. If it means losing you, I will give up my work here."

No, God. He doesn't mean it. Please, he doesn't know what he's saying. It's my fault. I'd done this to him! My stubborn determination to have the world's comforts; my quibbling about the villagers; my selfish, rebellious, bullheaded nature. My rock-hard determination to make Saginaw more important to him than the mission field so I could have my old, comfortable life back.

I clung to him. He must *not* give up his work—not for me, not for anyone.

Then they were loading me into the plane, tightening the strap. Sam was no longer beside me. I reached out to touch the plane's window and get his attention — had to talk to him. Hot. The glass was hot. My hand fell back to my side.

My last glimpse of Sam's face haunted me. We weren't going to make it. Our love wasn't part of our destiny. We'd been trying to work *our* will, not God's. This crazy test, this impossible adventure, had proven love couldn't conquer all. I would not, *could* not, allow Sam to give up his work for me. I couldn't die with that on my conscience.

God couldn't do this to me.

The plane turned and bounced. With a thrust of the engine and a surge upward, I was released from the bonds of earth. I closed my eyes. Whatever happened now was in God's hands.

But then ... wasn't it always?

TWENTY-TWO

Clean sheets.

A room with four walls, sparkling glass windows, and a ceiling. What happened to the thatched roof and open window?

Opening first one eye, then the other, I realized I was in a hospital. What was I doing here, and where was Sam?

The door opened, and a slender young woman with dark hair and eyes entered. She was wearing hospital scrubs, but when she smiled a pleasant welcome it went right to my heart. I returned the smile. If I had to wake up in a strange room in a strange place, it was nice that the first person I saw was friendly.

"Good morning. I see you've decided to join the world again." Her voice, soft with a musical lilt, greeted me. "My name is Priscilla."

"Priscilla. Are you American?" My voice sounded rusty as if it hadn't been used in a while.

"I'm from Australia. My husband is here in Port Moresby, so I joined him."

"I'm in Port Moresby?" So I was still in Papua New Guinea. When had I left the village, and why? "What's wrong with me?"

She shook her head. "You've been very ill, but you're better now." She approached the bed, tucking the ends of rumpled sheets into the mattress.

I searched my mind and came up blank. "Sick in what way?"

Frowning, she appeared thoughtful. "Parasite. In here." She tapped the middle of her chest.

"In my heart?"

"Your lung. The doctor will be in soon. He'll tell you more."

"Am I getting better?"

"Oh, much better; God answered prayers."

"Where's Sam?"

The young woman flashed another smile. "The gentleman who has remained by your side from the moment you arrived?"

"That would be Sam. Where is he?"

"Your doctor will be in to explain." She fished in her apron pocket and brought out a small package. "You have mail."

"Mail?" How long had I been here? One look and I saw cards from Mom and Pop, Nelda and Jim, Bud and Mary, Frank and Eva, and Sam. I must have been here quite awhile.

She stuck a thermometer in my ear, clicked it, wrote down the reading, and left the room. I opened and read my cards; the messages of love and caring brought tears to my eyes. Where *was* that doctor? I needed answers. According to the postmarks on the mail I'd been here several weeks.

I sank back against the pillow. Sam had remained by my bedside. Of course he would be here — thoughtful, kind, compassionate. Memories drifted back ... lying in the boat, crossing the lagoon. The stretcher ride through the jungle, the plane ride, and the terrible fever.

A memory surfaced, surprising in its clarity. Sam holding both my hands, his words so clear that for a moment I was certain he spoke them in the silence of this room. *"Maybe I've been wrong, Johanna . . ."*

A shiver raced through me. Would he give up God's work? Turn his back on the village and its people? I couldn't let Sam make that kind of sacrifice for me. If I couldn't adjust to the climate or the rough conditions of the village, it was I who had to sacrifice, not Sam. I had no choice but to leave him and let him continue his work.

The nurse returned carrying a large crystal bowl containing water and floating yellow orchids. She held the gift out for my inspection, and I touched a delicate petal. "They're pretty."

"From the nice man, Sam."

Warmth curled inside at the mention of his name. "Where is he now?"

"He returned to the village; we were to notify him the moment you woke. I'm sure the doctor will take care of it, but first he'll want to examine you. You've been asleep many days."

My gaze moved to the cards, and their poignant messages floated through my mind. *"Praying for you, Mom and Pop."* *"With deepest love, Sam."*

I closed my eyes, sick at heart. Sam must not be told I was awake. He must not be notified when I was recovered enough to go home. I wasn't strong enough to walk away from him and his love face-to-face. Better to run back to Saginaw, leaving him a message not to follow me.

Was I capable of being that altruistic? Yes, for Sam.

The nurse left and I closed my eyes, overcome by exhaustion. Just opening my eyes sapped my strength. Any additional thought was out of the question.

About an hour later a solemn-faced doctor arrived. He studied my chart and then looked up. "You've been gravely ill."

"From what?"

"A lung parasite, one common to the jungle area." He gave me the technical name, but it meant nothing. "Your recovery will be long and frustrating."

"How long have I been here?"

"Almost a month — three and a half weeks, to be precise."

A month. I'd slept almost an entire month. I couldn't believe it.

"When you're improved enough to travel, I'll arrange a medical flight back to the States, where you can be with your family. You'll need support to overcome this illness, but in time you will recover. I'll advise Dr. Littleton that you are awake."

"No."

He paused, one brow lifting. "I promised the doctor that the moment you awoke I would send for him. He is very concerned."

"I am asking you not to." I turned my face to the wall, forcing my words. "I don't want him to know I'm awake. If he calls or visits, tell him there's been no change."

"I can't do that. I won't lie."

"Then arrange to have me flown to the States tomorrow."

"I would not advise that."

"I'll sign any paper you request." I knew he couldn't release me without my assuming full responsibility for my weakened condition. But my mind was made up. I had to leave Sam. I wanted to go home.

He stood silent for a long moment and then nodded. "As you wish, but I refuse to release you for at least two more days."

I prayed that Sam wouldn't come for a visit within that time. *God, you have to help me with this; I'm not strong enough do to it on my own. You know I'm doing it for you and for Sam.* "Prepare the necessary papers, and please notify my parents that I'm coming home. I assume you have their information."

"We do."

I nodded, closing my eyes. I couldn't talk anymore. I was going home. It was over. If Sam was to continue his work — the Lord's work — I had to end this relationship. He was caving. Even with my still-fuzzy mental condition I remembered seeing it in his eyes that day on the landing strip. Hearing it in his voice.

Sam Littleton loved me, and he wouldn't give his heart lightly. Any woman would be lucky to find someone so faithful and steadfast. But that love left him torn between his purpose in life and his feelings for me. How easy it would be to latch onto his weakness, how very easy.

The old Johanna might have done so. The changed one wouldn't. I refused to do that to Sam or to the Lord. Or to myself. God wouldn't bless such a union, and I was in need of a blessing.

I reached for my Bible — someone, maybe the nurse, had left it on my table. When I opened it, my eyes scanned the pages until one particular passage stood out: Psalm 37:24: "Though he stumble, he will not fall, for the LORD upholds him with his hand." Closing my eyes, I wondered how long he could uphold a confused child.

❧

Two days later, I left Papua New Guinea. Thankfully, Sam hadn't come or called, so no one had told him of my recovery or departure. By the time he came to the hospital looking for me, I would be gone. I'd left a long letter to be given to him, explaining my decision to leave without seeing him again. I'd struggled over the words, and phrases came back to haunt me.

"Our love is futile; it's better to forget me." I knew I'd never forget him.

"I'm sorry, but I fear I've mistaken fascination for love. The feelings between us would not be strong enough to build a solid foundation for a lasting marriage." I knew it was a lie and that it would hurt him, but I had no choice. If he knew I loved him, he would never walk away from me. Nor would he let me walk away. He would come after me. I was sure of it.

Now when he got my letter he would know there could be no Johanna *and* Sam.

Only Johanna.

Only Sam.

A sad ending to a near love.

❧

I traveled by ambulance to the airport, watching Papua New Guinea pass by the window. A cloud of depression had settled around me. I'd come with such hope, but now . . .

I'd never come back.

A verse I'd read, Psalm 32:7, filled my mind and heart: "You are my hiding place; you will protect me from trouble and surround me with songs of deliverance." My morning devotional rang in my ears. *But where, O God, is my song? My deliverance?*

It took a few minutes to transfer me from the ambulance to the waiting plane. I had no luggage. Nothing but articles the hospital had provided. Priscilla, my sweet nurse, gave me a snapshot of the two of us together; that's all I had to show for two months in this strange country. I shook my head that I'd once thought my personal things important enough to fight for. Apparently something about a near-death experience changed a person's outlook. About a lot of things.

The flights were uneventful. I slept my way back across the ocean in drugged oblivion. When I landed in Saginaw, Mom, Pop, Nelda, and Jim were waiting behind the yellow line, their expectant, warm, loving faces saying, "Welcome home." Jim was holding an armful of balloons. Nelda waved a white banner that read, "We love you, Johanna." A group of my fellow library employees and some church members had gathered in the terminal. When the attendants unloaded the stretcher into the waiting ambulance, I managed a weak wave.

"Hoo-ha, girlfriend!" Nelda screeched. "We love you!"

⁂

When I opened my eyes again I was settled in a private room in Saginaw's largest hospital—Covenant Heath Care, an expansive complex with two hospital buildings, an emergency center, and a medical office building. Mom's worried face hovered above me.

"Oh, Johanna, I'm so relieved you're home. Now we can care for you."

I was too weak to do anything but grasp her hand and hold on tight—or not so tight, in this instance.

Pop bent to hug me. "Welcome home, Daughter." His eyes shone with unshed tears. "You don't worry; you'll be back to your old self in no time at all."

I tried to smile, but I knew he was wrong. I'd left my heart in a medical clinic in the middle of the jungle, and the chance of me ever again being my old self was nil.

<hr />

The doctor's prediction of a long and frustrating recovery proved all too accurate. Seven weeks after I entered the hospital, Nelda helped me into the van. She had already packed the flowers, balloons, books, and candy I'd accumulated during my hospital stay. I had enough chocolates to start a store. I'd spent the last week writing thank-you notes and trying to ignore the seven earlier letters that had been lying untouched on the bedside table. The address on the envelopes was written in Sam's bold script. I was afraid if I read even one of them my resolve would crumble like a sand castle. What was done was done—and must not be undone. Not if Sam was going to fill his purpose in life.

"What did you eat out there in that jungle?" Nelda peered at me. "You must have lost twenty pounds." She stacked the last of my personal items in the trunk and closed the lid.

"It wasn't the food." I pushed my glasses up on my nose. "Though one could lose weight on the diet—plenty of fresh fish, vegetables, and fruit."

"Yeah, that pineapple sounded delicious, but all we wanted was to get you back in one piece."

Well, other than a broken heart, I supposed I was in one piece.

She slid behind the wheel and looked over at me. "I sure missed you, girl."

"I missed you too."

Her features sobered. "I was the one who encouraged you to go there. If anything had happened to you I'd never have forgiven myself."

I snapped the seat belt in place. "Something did happen. Something profound and unchangeable. I lost Sam."

"You gave him up." Her eyes shifted to Sam's letters tied in a neat bundle in my lap. "You need to open those, Johanna. I don't know what they say, but I can guarantee Sam isn't going to give up on you easily."

"Maybe. Maybe not." I turned to look out on the cold spring day, snowflakes mixed with rain swirling through the air. Late April was always iffy in Saginaw; snow one day, spring the next. Cold. Slush. I couldn't get warm since I'd gotten back.

Nelda slid the transmission into gear and pulled away from the patient loading area. Her words were more of a grumble at the dash than addressed to me. "How would you know how he feels unless you talk to him?"

I wasn't sure about Sam's feelings, but he couldn't argue with my conclusions. So talk was cheap and answers were nonexistent.

At home, Nelda settled me in my recliner, turned up the thermostat, then left to do grocery shopping and retrieve Itty Bitty. I wandered around the half-empty rooms at a loss. After a while, because there was nothing else to do, I took a shower, reveling in the driving needles of hot water and the soft fragrance of sweet pea shower gel. Afterward I dressed in clean pajamas and climbed into bed.

Nelda returned and called up the stairway, that she was putting the perishables in the refrigerator. I heard the click of nails on the hardwood stairway and then Itty Bitty dashed into my room. With one enormous leap he landed on the bed, wiggled his way across the bed covers, and burrowed under my outstretched arm. I hugged him tight, scratching the backs of his ears and roughhousing for a minute. He licked my face clean, lunging to give me kisses over and over.

"I'll be back in the morning!" Nelda shouted up the stairway. "You get a good night's sleep!"

"Thanks, Nelda!"

Itty crawled between the sheets and my arms came around him. He felt good, like home. We lay that way for over an hour. I could hear his even breathing, the tiny doggy snorts. My bed was soft, comfortable ... and unfamiliar. I couldn't sleep.

I got up and went to the kitchen for a cup of hot tea. Dropping a bag into the boiling water, I carried the cup to the den and settled on the couch. I nursed my mug of steaming liquid, thinking of Sam trying to sleep on a narrow cot in a steamy jungle hut. How he would welcome the forty-eight-degree temperature I was trying to ward off. I closed my eyes, picturing the lagoon surrounding the hut. I heard the cry of night birds in the saga palms, saw the moon coming up over the lagoon, surprised to find that memories I once thought dreadful weren't so bad — were even pleasant, almost.

What was not surprising was that I missed Sam so much it was a physical ache. And Poo. I missed her visits, her chaotic chatter. Even those grubby hands and dirty face.

Tears coursed down my cheeks, and for the thousandth time I begged God to send Sam a woman who shared his passion. He deserved more than a Saginaw librarian with Monday morning faith. The village people deserved more. Poo and the village children needed missionaries who cared, whose love overflowed and transcended cultural boundaries. The villagers needed medical care and a chance—a chance that godly men like Sam, Bud, and Frank provided.

During my ruminating my tea had grown cold, but it didn't matter. I'd lost interest in the drink. I rinsed the cup, set it in the sink, and climbed the stairs to my room. I stretched out on the bed and pulled the electric blanket up around my shoulders. Staring into the dark, I thought about this house. I'd have to find an apartment. Mom and Pop would need the sale proceeds to stay at The Gardens.

Sleep claimed me sometime during the night, and I woke to sunshine streaming through my bedroom window and the cheery weatherman's voice promising moderating temperatures. Outside birds sang and traffic moved up the street with an unfamiliar roar. Why did I feel like a visitor in my own home? I pulled on my housecoat and went downstairs to read the paper Nelda had left for me.

I caught up on the news while I ate a breakfast of bacon and eggs, milk, toast, and apple butter.

I wanted mangoes.

According to the flyers, there was a big sale at the mall. I didn't really care, but I'd lost so much weight my clothes hung on me. I needed to make a few cursory purchases.

This house was filled with possessions. Poo would have been bewildered by the bounty. I fantasized about taking her to the mall to buy a dress and maybe sassy slacks and a few colorful ribbons. Wouldn't she be wide-eyed at all the riches? Little Poo, the child who, by my standards, had nothing but who loved with all of her heart.

Late in the afternoon I pulled myself together enough to dress and take a short walk. The doctor had warned it would be another two weeks before he'd release me for work. I wandered into the local grocery, even though I knew Nelda had restocked my pantry. My eyes scanned the bulging shelves, the fresh produce, and the neat packages of meat. Guilt was almost a physical force. Did Americans realize how fortunate they were?

I picked up a few items Nelda had failed to put on her list and pushed my cart to the front of the store and started unloading my purchases.

The checker recognized me. "Johanna! Welcome back. I heard about your ordeal. I'm so sorry." She frowned, then bent closer and lowered her voice. "You look like death warmed over. You're so skinny!"

Not a very tactful observation, but true, judging by what I'd witnessed in my bathroom mirror that morning. My reflection might not stop a clock, but it would give an unwary stranger a moment of alarm.

"I'm much better — lung parasite," I reported as if I were talking about a head cold.

"You were in Papua New Guinea?" She shook her head, eyes wide. "How fascinating. I've never been much more than out of the city limits."

My response was a lame smile.

I stopped by Chinese Wok and ordered General Tso's all-white-meat chicken and ate the whole thing in honor of Eva. The iced Pepsi tasted almost as good as the pineapple juice I'd grown used to. Would Mary and Eva appreciate a cold Pepsi?

Afterward I lost the whole meal in the restaurant bathroom.

Back home, I arranged the cans and bags and boxes in my pantry. Nelda had bought enough food to last two months.

The television programs I'd once enjoyed now seemed shallow and empty. After a while I switched off the set and looked for something to read. One book caught my eye — it was one I'd checked out of the library about Papua New Guinea and had forgotten to return. I stretched out on the couch and opened it. Soon I was lost in the tropical climate, lush vegetation, and beauty of that island nation.

The phone rang and I reached for it, marking my place by inserting one finger between the pages. "Johanna? Just checking on you, dear. Are you all right?"

"Of course, Mom. I'm fine."

"Did you eat dinner?"

"Ummm — not hungry." No need to mention the plate of General Tso's I'd consumed four hours earlier but lost. Apparently it would take awhile to regain my piggish nature.

"Honey, Pop and I were wondering if you'd feel up to coming here tomorrow night. We want to hear all about your trip."

"Not tomorrow, Mom. I have other plans." I didn't, but it was too soon and my wounds too raw to talk about the trip and the villagers ... because someone would ask about Sam, and I couldn't bring myself to talk about him.

"Day after tomorrow, maybe? If you're strong enough, we've invited a few people to hear your story. You can sit; it'll be almost like being at home. Our friends are interested in you and Papua New Guinea and the mission field."

"Let me think about it—oh, sorry, Mom. Someone's at the door." *Fibbing again, Johanna. You're getting good at it.*

"I'm worried about you, dear. Are you sure you're all right? And Sam—"

"I'm fine, Mom. Call you later."

I hung up, lay back on the sofa, and burst into tears. Sam! *God, how can I let him go? If this is your will, can't you make it not hurt so much?*

He could, of course, but apparently he'd decided not to make things any easier for me. I pulled myself off the sofa and moped to the kitchen. I wanted fish, sweet potatoes, and mangoes. I wanted my Sam.

A week passed, then two, and I still couldn't bring myself to leave the house. I suspected I'd drifted into depression. Mom and Pop had started coming over every afternoon, but I resisted all entreaties to visit them.

Nelda refused to let me wallow in pity. She either called or came by every evening. At first she'd been gentle with me, even when I'd hid a couple of days and pretended that I wasn't home. Now she'd gotten to the point of belligerence.

I cringed when I saw her car pull into my drive and she got out carrying a dish I supposed held another casserole.

She knocked and I let her in. "You own anything besides that rancid bathrobe? I'm right sick of seeing it every time I come over." She brushed passed me, carrying the dish to the kitchen.

"Then don't come back." *Rude, Johanna.* But she had it coming. Who did she think she was coming in here insulting my dress? I shut the door.

"If you'd quit babying yourself and get up and get on with your life, I could quit worrying about you." She set the casserole on the kitchen burner with a thump. "Chicken and rice. Got mushrooms, peppers, onions, and rich gravy. Put some flesh on your scrawny bones."

"What happened to the Diet Guru? Did she choke on a carrot stick?"

"She took one look at you and decided there are more important things in life than worrying about weight. Girl, if you stood sideways you'd disappear."

"In case you missed it, I've been *sick.*" Let the sarcasm roll.

"I didn't miss it, but know what I do miss? The Johanna I used to know. Look at you! Glasses held together with surgical tape, hair looking like overcooked spaghetti. Is there some law that says you have to look like you crawled out from under a rock? How long has it been since you washed that robe? I could grow tomatoes on that thing."

I glared at her. I resented what she said, resented her. Resented life. But I knew she was right. Since I'd been back I'd been suspended between two worlds, belonging to neither. No longer sure of myself, I had no desire to face people.

Nelda shifted, her lips firming. "What am I going to do with you? You have to try, girl. You can't mope around here for the rest of your life."

"I can if I want to."

"No, you can't. I love you too much to watch you do this to yourself. Now I'm giving you an order."

"You can't tell me what to do."

"You watch me. We're going shopping and get you some clothes that don't hang on you like feed sacks—"

"I've bought a few things—"

"—and then you're going back to work. I talked to your folks. We think the change would be good for you, provided you don't overdo. And I'll see to that. We need you at the library and you need us. Whatever happened in Papua New Guinea needs to stay in Papua New Guinea. You have a life to live here in Saginaw, and it's time you got down to living it."

"You don't say." I shoved my glasses up on my nose, then crossed my arms.

Nelda knocked my arms free. "I *do* say. You're coming *back* to work tomorrow morning. Be there or I swear, Johanna Holland, I'll come over here and drag your carcass out the front door and throw you in your car."

She would do it too. My heart hammered. "Don't threaten me, Nelda Thomas. I may be weak but I can still whip you in a catfight."

Nelda left, slamming the door closed behind her.

TWENTY-THREE
◎◎◎

Nelda was back the next morning. She rattled off a string of orders the moment I climbed in the passenger's seat.

"All right now, we'll take a long lunch hour today and work over tonight to make up the time. First, we're going to get those eyeglasses fixed. You can't run around with your specs held together by surgical tape. How'd you break them anyway?"

I told her about Bum and how he took my glasses, the fight we'd had, and Sam's intervention. "Sam taped my glasses and I've not had a chance to get them fixed."

"You mean to say the villager came right into the missionary hut and stole your glasses?"

"The tribe seemed to feel that the missionaries want them to have their personal possessions."

She winced. "It gives me the creeps to think of that half-naked native standing there staring at you while you're sleeping."

"He was harmless."

An eyebrow shot up. "Then why did Sam have to drag you two apart while you were getting your glasses back?"

I shrugged. Nelda wouldn't understand. At the time it was happening, *I* hadn't either. Possessions had been much too important to me then. Somewhere along the way I had lost the desire to accumulate stuff.

The library staff welcomed me back with hot donuts and fresh coffee. Smiling faces greeted me throughout the morning, and visitor after visitor stopped by my office to wish me well. So many friends, so many people who cared about me. I hadn't realized what caring meant. Several times during the morning I'd look up the corridor, hoping to see . . . who? Sam? I knew that was improbable. Sam would give me my space; if I wanted to talk to him I could call the satellite phone, but still I held out.

I didn't need to talk with him. I'd adjust to a life without him. Good heavens, I'd known the man less than seven months—that wasn't a lifetime.

It might as well be.

It was true. How could one person get so engrained in another person's heart in such a short time?

At five minutes after twelve, Nelda poked her head in my office doorway. "Ready to go?"

"Go where?"

"Optometrist first, and then to the mall. They're having a big sale and you need clothes." She squinted, sizing me up. "What size do you wear now?"

I bent over a ledger. "Eight."

"Say what?"

"Eight!"

"No way!"

"Way. I bought this suit two days ago. Eight. Read the label yourself." I hadn't worn an eight since I was born.

Her expression softened and a grin crept over her mahogany features. "And it looks good on you, girl. It's nice to have you back. You scared me when they unloaded you off that plane."

"Scared me too." I leaned over and slipped on my old Nikes, remembering the pair the villager had stolen and the way he'd looked hobbling around in shoes too small for him. Odd how everything reminded me of the village and the people there. When I was in Papua New Guinea I hungered for home. Now that I was home I thought of Papua New Guinea. It didn't make sense.

I had the earpiece on my glasses replaced, and then we were off to the mall. I hadn't worn the disposable contacts since I'd been ill — gotten out of the habit. While I hated to admit it, I was enjoying wearing my glasses. My life seemed more normal again.

Nelda paused before the Victoria's Secret window. "Mmm. Would you look at that white negligee and robe? Wouldn't that look good on this ole body?"

"I'll hold your packages while you try it on."

She sighed, eyeing the lacy confection. "I'd love to, but if I did I'd buy the thing and we can't afford it." She stared at the pure frivolity and then shook her head. "No, better not."

"It would look great on you; Jim would appreciate it."

"Get thee behind me, Satan. Don't tempt this weak-willed woman." We walked on.

"I'm hungry. Let's eat at the food court." Other than the Chinese dish, I'd eaten only healthy food since I'd been back. It was time for a junk binge.

"You're getting your appetite back, are you?"

"Pizza sounds good. Seems like every day I get a little stronger. You're right. Getting back to work was the best thing I could do for myself."

"Well … not the *best* thing, but you're right; getting back to a routine will help."

I overcame the temptation to ask what she thought the best thing was, but I knew what she'd say and I didn't want to hear it. Sam was out of my life. Forever.

I smiled. "Look, there's an empty table."

"Grab it, and then we'll decide what to eat. Lunch is on me today."

We savored every bite of the pepperoni pizza we'd ordered. Not a word was mentioned about calories or dieting. When she finished, Nelda blotted her mouth with a napkin. "So, tell me, what *was* it like living in a jungle?"

"Well, it was hot, and there are no modern conveniences. Our huts sat in a lagoon that was full of some kind of catfish that could spike you and cause painful if not fatal injuries. The huts were built on stilts; we had to take a rowboat to the village. The villagers we worked with didn't speak or understand our language, and we were just as ignorant about theirs. The missionaries are working to break the communication barrier, but it is so difficult since the people speak a mixture of *Leiny Kairiru*, *Leiny Tau*, and their own strange dialect. They're in desperate need of medical help and a better quality of life. That's what Sam and — "

Suddenly I heard the excitement, the enthusiasm in my voice. My eyes narrowed. Nelda the Sneak had tricked me into talking about Sam. I should have known. I toyed with a piece of crust, eyeing her, resentment growing.

With a tube of lipstick paused midair, she raised a well-defined brow. "What?"

"What?"

She applied bright red to her lips. "You were saying?"

"I was saying the missionaries work very hard to reach the people and meet their needs. They aren't able to present the gospel because of the language differences."

"Then they're there to do medical clinics?"

"And gain the villagers' trust — pave the way, so to speak, for future missionaries."

Working her lips back and forth, Nelda shook her head. "You got to hand it to those people. Not everyone is called to the mission field."

How many times had I thought or said the same thing? Too many to count. So why was I still wracked with unhappiness and guilt that I didn't share Sam's passion?

Maybe ... maybe in retrospect, I wasn't so bad at it after all. I *had* made one friend — Poo. She'd even said my name. And the village children seemed to like me.

I sighed. "Oh, Nelda, you should have been there. I held story hour one afternoon and it was hilarious. I tried to act out the book *Curious George Flies a Kite*. Of course the children thought I'd lost my mind. I was jumping and hopping and pretending to be a monkey flying a kite." I broke out laughing. "I fell once. They all burst into laughter!"

"They didn't understand a word?"

"I don't think so, but they enjoyed the story anyway. But oh, Nelda, let me tell you about Poo."

"Poo?"

"This darling little village girl — "

"Her name is *not* Poo."

"No — I mean, I don't know. That's what it sounds like when her grandpa talks to her, so that's what we call her. She latched onto me and followed me everywhere I went. It was crazy. Then one day this dog — this mean dog — treed everyone in the village. We sat in palm trees until late afternoon and then . . ."

I went on for the better part of an hour, and the more I talked, the more I missed Sam and the little girl who lived so far away from my world.

When I finally fell silent, Nelda reached over and covered my hand. "You love that kid, don't you?"

Her observation shattered my reserves, my carefully constructed wall. For so long I tried to tell myself that the child didn't matter. Or Sam. But they did. They mattered more than I could say.

"I'm beginning to realize just how much," I whispered. "You know, at first the child was such a pain. Everywhere I went I tripped over her, and then somehow everything changed. She no longer bothered me, and I found myself watching for her every morning. Did I tell you that she and Bum stood guard at the Millets' hut to prevent the villagers from stealing my stuff? Poo has such a capacity to love. No matter how I behaved, she still loved me. Isn't that remarkable?"

"Remarkable." Nelda smiled. "Very few of us ever find unconditional love, except from God. What about Sam?"

Silence hung between us for a moment, then I gave in. "I love him with all my heart, mind, and soul. I wish I didn't. I've prayed to be released from the love I feel for both Sam and Poo; I can't force Sam to choose between God and me, and Poo doesn't belong in our society. She needs to be with her people."

Nelda's features softened. "I'm sorry, Jo. You and Sam seemed so right for each other. You're sure there isn't a way this can be worked out?"

"I'm sure." It would be easier if I didn't wake up every morning from dreams about betel palms and sunrises and sunsets and thatched huts and a very caring and compassionate doctor.

She frowned and consulted her watch. "We need to go."

Emotionally drained, I gathered the napkin and pizza remains and disposed of them in the trash. Just talking about Sam hurt.

That evening I opened the mailbox and fished out a handful of envelopes. One postmark caused my breath to catch in my throat. Another letter from Sam. And I still had all the unopened ones he'd sent while I was in the hospital. I dropped the house keys and purse on the hall table and carried the mail into the den. Holding the envelope for a moment, I realized I was still unprepared to read the contents. Would I be able to absorb the pain? I was certain he'd accepted my decision, but I was just as sure he'd be angry that I had left and refused to answer his earlier messages.

Drawing a deep breath, I slit open the envelope and drew out the single sheet of paper. The note was short and unassuming. He missed me and he was praying about the situation.

I sat there, my eyes burning with unshed tears, wishing I could hold him close, tell him once more that I loved him. But one show of weakness on my part and Sam would be tempted to turn his back on the village and come home to me. I couldn't let that happen.

Then a new thought occurred—one I had never considered. Sam was a dedicated man. *Would* he turn his back on his work, or had he meant something different when he spoke those words the day they loaded me on the plane to Port Moresby?

I concentrated. What had he said? *"I don't know, Johanna—"*

Finally, feeling old and tired, I got up and went to the kitchen to stand at the window and stare out on the cold spring evening. Saginaw was home. Mom and Pop were here, Nelda was here. Why then did I feel so lacking, so misplaced?

The answer was clear. I didn't belong anywhere anymore.

I fell into my old routine without a hitch. Some days it seemed like I'd never been gone. I hadn't answered Sam's note, and my emotions ranged from resentful to shame. I wanted to write him, but what could I say? I'd walked away from a wonderful man who loved me without telling him I was giving him up so he could serve the Lord. I had left without telling him the truth.

I started eating with Mom and Pop at The Gardens once or twice a week. My parents made a big fuss over me; I could see concern mirrored in their expressions.

"Johanna, how would you like some Sara Lee cheesecake?" Mom asked as I walked her back to her apartment Thursday evening. "I bought it just for you. The kitchen staff will be happy to serve you."

She was trying to put some weight on me, but I liked the leaner me. I had more energy and looked better in my clothes. "Maybe later, Mom. Right now I'm stuffed."

"You're not getting anorexia, are you?" Her face puckered.

I laughed. "Not likely. Didn't you notice how I put away the Swiss steak and mashed potatoes and gravy? I'm eating plenty; I just don't want to regain the extra weight—it's too hard to get off later."

"You were never overweight. You just looked healthy."

"And the doctor said I'm healthy now; in fact, he released me this week. I don't have to go back for six months."

"Wonderful!" She focused on a vase of fresh flowers in the hallway, and my internal alarm went off.

"What?"

"Well—you know how we've been after you to tell us all about the trip. Pop and I took the liberty of inviting a few guests this evening in hopes that you'd agree to give a brief talk about Papua New Guinea."

"Oh, Mom. Without asking me? How could you?"

"And if I'd asked, would you have agreed?"

"No." I was stuck; she'd hound me to death until I did it. "Okay, I'll give a talk. Where?"

"In the activities room, anytime you're ready. I think everyone is waiting."

"Real sure of yourself, weren't you?"

"I was counting on you being an obedient daughter."

I laughed and followed her to the activities room, where Pop was entertaining the group with his Rodney Dangerfield routine. His face brightened when I walked in the room. "Here she is, ladies and gentlemen, my beautiful daughter, Johanna."

Beautiful? In my father's eyes, maybe, but I appreciated the lift his words gave me. He motioned to a narrow wooden podium, and I walked over and stood behind it. I adjusted the microphone, cleared my throat. "Good evening. I've been asked to speak to you tonight about my Papua New Guinea experiences."

The assembled group was quiet, attentive, absorbed in the topic as I began my talk. I started with the plane ride over and then progressed to spending the first night at Port Moresby. To my surprise I found myself laughing with everyone else about my escapades.

"The villagers we worked with have a keen sense of pride." I pushed my glasses up on my nose with one finger. "In their transactions, for instance, they don't barter. The goods being traded are not shown or examined, but when the arrangements are made the exchange is expected to be worthy of all promises made by both parties. If a man trades some of his betel nuts for a bundle of tobacco, he expects a certain amount of tobacco. It's a mystery how each seems to know how much tobacco is enough. If he considers the exchange to be inadequate he has no recourse, but you can bet that in the future he will refuse to deal with this particular person and do his business with another trader."

A white-haired, scholarly-looking man wearing gold-framed eyeglasses lifted his hand.

I acknowledged the gesture.

"Then you are saying that the villagers observe a code of honor among themselves?"

"They do." I frowned, reconsidering the question. "Let me say that they're blatant thieves with others, but among themselves they are forthright and honest."

Now that I looked back, I realized how silly it was of me to get so upset over trivial possessions. Had I really had a meltdown over two old safety pins, for goodness' sake? No wonder Sam thought I was mercenary. Stealing *wasn't* right, but now it was clear to me that the villagers meant no ill intent. They saw something they liked and took it, having no idea what such an act meant in our culture.

I talked for over an hour, reliving my weeks on the mission field, sharing about the children there and my illness and long recuperation. I even hung around later, shaking hands and answering questions. The residents seemed fascinated, and I was so glad I could add joy to their faces—take them where they'd never been and would never go.

"Will you be going back to the mission field?" one elderly resident asked.

"No, I won't." I amended the statement. "I'm praying about it."

A little lady holding on to a walker grasped my hand. "We'll be praying for you and Sam and the missionaries."

"Thank you. That means a lot to me." And it did. More than I could explain, even to myself.

<hr />

Later when I unlocked my front door, my mind was still on the talk. Why was I able to relay the villagers' needs when once all I saw was flies, dirt, poverty, and thieves? An idea stirred inside . . .

I might not be able to serve on the mission field, but what would prevent me from telling others about mission work and the people who did serve? Area churches might be willing to adopt the Papua New Guinea village and offer financial help. There were other nursing homes in the area—other seniors who would welcome the break in daily monotony.

My heart pounded and I caught my breath. Was it possible I could be part of Sam's work, even if I couldn't share his life on the field?

The next day I made a quick trip to the mall and did something I'd been thinking about for weeks: purchase gifts for Poo. I had fun choosing books, fragrances, and lip gloss. That last item was a bit over the top, I knew, but young women here loved it. I added some candy and, remembering how she'd liked my necklaces, picked up a couple of those and some hair clasps.

When I got home I packed the items to mail, smiling as I imagined the little girl's excitement when she received her package in the mail. It probably would be the first she'd ever received. She'd enjoy these little offerings so much, riches for a little girl who had nothing. I enclosed a picture of me so she'd know who sent the treats.

Before I dropped off to sleep that night, I spent a long time in prayer. I prayed for the villagers, for Sam, of course, for Bud, Frank, Eva, and Mary, and for Poo.

As the days passed, I mailed a couple more care packages, this time to the village children. Small trinkets—candy, rings, flashlights, and three dozen batteries. On a roll now, I boxed and mailed a few personal items like scented soaps, lotions, and sunscreen to Mary and Eva.

The day I got a thank-you note from Poo—written by Sam—I circled the date on the calendar in red pen. At least he was still speaking to me. Kind of. I answered the note and continued to send packages. Each time, Sam wrote back, and the messages between us grew more personal. The door I had closed when I left was beginning to open again—a little.

I wasn't sure if that was good or bad.

June turned into July, then August. I had started giving a monthly program at the nursing home on foreign missions, and I'd spoken to my church and to Sam's church about the

Papua New Guinea work. I was in the process of becoming an expert on the subject. Slowly, but surely, I realized my attitude toward the people had changed. I no longer saw them as barbarians, but as souls for whom Christ died. God's children in need of salvation, medical help, someone to care.

One day at the library Nelda saw me poring over a missionary's biography. She crossed her arms and grinned. "Well, lookee here. First miracle I've ever witnessed in person."

I glanced up. "What do you mean?"

"Johanna Holland, girl librarian, thinking about becoming a missionary."

"You think that's what I have in mind?"

"Isn't it?"

"No. I've told you; I'm not called to the mission field. I'm interested in the work that missionaries do. And I can't deny that the children are of real interest to me."

"Did I hear right? I remember when you thought missionary work sounded unnatural, that you couldn't understand how *any*one could leave civilization to live in places like Papua New Guinea."

"I know. And it is true, mission fields, most anyway, have horrible living conditions. But there's a lot of beauty to be found too. Like sunsets and sunrises and watching the moon turn the lagoon to silver, listening to the night birds calling from the jungle. The children—the precious little souls—"

"Uh-huh. It doesn't hurt a bit that Sam Littleton's still over there, does it?"

Was the woman reading my thoughts? "That has nothing to do with it." I closed the book with a snap. "God hasn't called me to full-time mission work."

MONDAY MORNING FAITH / 318

"He may have, honey, in a much different way than you think. God's still in business, you know."

Color flooded my cheeks and I measured her words. "That's silly. If he wanted me in Papua New Guinea he'd have kept me there."

I had no intention of admitting it to Nelda, but something *was* happening inside me. Something I didn't understand. I *was* called to the mission field. A miracle? A burning bush complete with booming authoritative voice? No, but there was a softening within. A willingness — no, a *need* to support those who devoted their bodies, souls, and minds to the work in the field.

My calling might not be the same as Sam's, but I was starting to understand — finally — that it was a valid calling all the same.

Sam's letters came on a regular basis now. He mentioned how his days were long and tiring, the clinic was always full, and the work still rewarding. He'd decided to stay on awhile — much longer than he'd first anticipated. I knew why. He didn't want to come back and face me. He asked about my health, and it thrilled me to know he still cared. The essence of the man came through the written word. Always the same, just Sam, gentle, unassuming.

A man of God.

A man I still loved with all my heart and soul.

A man denied to me. I dared not forget that, even for a moment.

Nelda approached my desk one morning. "I guess women are women, no matter where they are."

"I suppose." I frowned. What did my crazy friend have on her mind now?

"Those villagers, the women, they don't need T-shirts and high-heeled shoes, I know. But can we purchase Bibles in their language?"

"No. Their language hasn't been translated yet." Hadn't she been listening to me?

"Oh, right." She stood, hands on her temple. "Well, we should be able to do *some*thing to make their lives better. You know what, girlfriend, I'll bet if we talk to the women at church we could come up with some nice things to send over there. Postage would kill us, but hey, I'm willing."

I smiled and touched my friend's hand. "You know, Nelda, you're a real nice person."

"You just finding that out?" She took my arm. "Come on. Let's visit the ice cream shop. Too bad we can't send thirty quarts of rocky road to Papua New Guinea."

My prayers that night took on a new urgency. God hadn't forgotten the people of the village. He'd sent men like Sam, and Bud, and Frank, women like Eva and Mary to work among them to help make a better life. And he hadn't forgotten me and my problem. He cared about the people in Papua New Guinea as much as he did for me. I couldn't forget that.

My life had evolved since I'd come home. My faith had grown stronger, and yet I was beginning to see my life was like Scripture indicated—a vapor, a brief puff of breath on a cold morning.

And more important, what I did with that vapor was my choice.

I pulled out of the library lot after work Monday evening. Bright sunshine filtered through leaves turning vibrant golds and browns. I'd exited the parking lot every evening at this hour for twenty years. Traffic was usually light, not a car in sight. I pulled out—and suddenly the air filled with the sound of skids, a horn blaring, and squealing brakes. Events happened so fast I didn't have time to think. I caught a brief flash of car lights in my peripheral vision, an angry face, and a man shaking a fist at me. The car swerved, missing the driver's side of my car by a hand's breadth. Stunned, I sat in the middle of the intersection, unable to move. The car had sped on, but fear incapacitated me. I spotted oncoming lights and heard the sound of car horns again. My heartbeat hammered in my ear.

Springing to life, I mashed down on the gas and careened into the left lane. *Dear Father! I could have been killed!* The oncoming vehicle had barely missed me, and at the speed he was traveling, the impact would have been ...

Words from Scripture filled my mind: "Why, you do not even know what will happen tomorrow. What is your life? You are a mist that appears for a little while and then ..."

And then. I smiled. And suddenly I knew with such clarity it took my breath away. I *knew* what my vapor would count for.

"Thank you, God," I whispered. "Sorry I took so long."

TWENTY-FOUR

◎◎◎

So, here I was, Johanna Holland, halfway across the ocean on a 747, on my way back to Papua New Guinea to tell the man I loved that maybe I wasn't called to full-time mission work, but I was called to love him. Maybe I wasn't called to live on foreign soil, but I could keep the home fires burning in Saginaw, Michigan. If marrying Sam meant a long-distance union, I could live with that. I could accompany my husband on shorter mission trips and enjoy my work with the children during those trips. And when we were apart? I could pray for Sam, encourage him, and support him in whatever endeavor he chose to represent God.

I leaned back in my seat, peering over the top of the seat in front of me toward the flight attendant. The one who'd taken my umbrella before I wounded any other passengers. I had to remember to get my umbrella back from her. Too many downpours in the village to go there ill-equipped.

I smiled. Now that I knew the ropes, so to speak, I was more prepared for Sam's world. My revelation might not be the most ideal solution, but sometimes life's challenges had to be met with acceptable compromises. Besides, this whole thing wasn't my idea; it was God's.

Finally, it was crystal clear: I could serve, but Sam was called. There was a difference. Mary and Eva had adapted to their husbands' calling. So could Johanna Holland. Just in a different way.

Part of me knew I should have written and told Sam of my conclusion, but once my mind was made up, I couldn't get back to him and Papua New Guinea fast enough. I'd booked a plane that same night and left the following morning, record time for a Saginaw librarian. But I wasn't getting any younger; next week I'd turn forty-one.

Did the good physician still feel the same about me? His recent letters indicated he did, but I wouldn't know for sure until I stood face-to-face with him. My heart tripped at the thought. What if I had done our relationship irreparable harm? What if our lengthy separation had made Sam reconsider his feelings?

I pulled my Bible from my purse and held it. Gone were the days of random page search — let the pages fall open and hope to glean a message. One Scripture was poignantly clear in my mind at this moment — Proverbs 16:9: "In his heart a man plans his course, but the LORD determines his steps." God would see his plan through in me. And I would willingly — and gratefully — follow.

⁕⊰❊⊱⁕

I stirred, checking my watch. Twelve hours into the flight. My fellow travelers looked as weary as I did. The man I had whacked with the umbrella had a red welt on the side of his face; he'd kept an ice pack on the injury most of the flight. A little girl — maybe three or so — peered around the edge of her seat at me from across the aisle. I winked at her and she grinned. She'd behaved during the flight, playing with the toys and books her mother provided. A lady four rows back hadn't been such a happy flier. The frequent bouts of turbulence had her shouting for the flight attendant. Her husband alternated between holding her hand and supporting the barf bag.

A silver-haired woman one seat up from me and across the aisle watched the spectacle, her face expressionless. Then she glanced at me. Her eyes spoke volumes: tolerance and patience were assets to be employed at times like this. We exchanged raised eyebrows and pursed lips and then settled back for the remainder of the flight.

I glanced at my watch a second time. I'd been so lost in thought, so oblivious to time, that I could scarcely believe we'd be landing soon. Strange. Once again I'd left family and friends in Saginaw, but the closer we got to Papua New Guinea, the more I felt it.

I was coming home.

Shifting my stiff body, I glanced out the window. Far below, lush, tropical islands surrounded by deep blue water began to appear. I started to make out shapes and forms. We were getting close. I couldn't see them, but I knew there would be palms and rustic huts with thatched roofs, pineapples and mangoes, and ocean waves lapping the shore. And brown-faced children with sticky hands and smiling faces.

I chuckled, imagining the look on Sam's face when I reached the village. He would be *stunned* to see me. I tried to imagine his thoughts when I climbed out of that small plane on the jungle airstrip. Oh dear! The *psft-psft* plane. I still had *that* major obstacle to face.

Oh, Sam, if you knew the love it took for me to climb into that death trap!

The little girl who'd been playing peekaboo with me peered over the back of her seat. I could see she wanted to resume our game. At the moment all I wanted to do was savor my victory of making and carrying out my decision.

Had God answered my prayers or Sam's? Maybe both. At any rate, here I was, committed to working this out even if it meant long separations and major concessions.

I leaned back and rested my head on the small pillow. I assured myself that when Sam saw me his face would reflect joy, love, and gratitude to God for allowing us to come together. After all, Sam thanked God for everything, believing every good thing came from his heavenly Father. And so did I.

I would be less than honest if I didn't admit my concerns still outnumbered my conviction, but I knew my purpose—my "calling"—was to uphold Sam. It had taken me almost a year to understand, but now the conviction was rock solid.

Even so, doubts tugged at me. Maybe I was risking a great deal by assuming Sam still loved and wanted me. Maybe he'd finished his work and left. I shoved the worry aside; he would be there. He was Sam.

And if not?

I lifted my chin. If not, then God had sent him elsewhere. I'd visit with Frank, Eva, Bud, and Mary. And Poo. I'd remain to work among the villagers for a few weeks—and then I would track Sam down like a hunted animal. And if I couldn't find him?

Simple. I'd get Nelda to help. Between the two of us, we'd find him. And once I did that, I'd convince him that together we *could* make a difference. Maybe not in the conventional way, but who said life had to follow a certain plotline?

325 / LORI COPELAND

Either way, I came prepared this time. Now that I had a better understanding of the climate, I'd packed sufficient numbers of sturdy jeans, hiking boots, T-shirts, and long-sleeved cotton shirts. One suitcase held a wide-brimmed canvas hat that could be wrung out after getting soaked. I had herbal teas and flavored coffees for Eva and Mary. My third suitcase bulged with additional gadgets for the village children. I knew they would enjoy the colorful inflatable punch balls, jump ropes, and bright gaudy jewelry and books.

Lots and lots of picture books.

My heart warmed when I thought of Poo and all of the things I planned to teach her and the village children. They would use the knowledge very little in their everyday life, but as the little girls grew into women, they would remember the missionary who taught them the proper way to eat, bathe—I grinned—and apply lip gloss. Impractical things, yes, but it was spending the time together that mattered. Letting them know someone cared. That was my goal.

And I had another goal as well—to unearth one particular child's proper name.

The flight attendants began their landing routine. I straightened my seat back and rotated my shoulders to work out the stiffness. It would be good to get off the plane and move around.

I remembered the last time I'd made this flight—the anxiety, the doubt, the lack of anticipation. All that was gone. Instead, I was consumed with enthusiasm and the deep faith that what I was doing was ordained by God. I was jittery, yes, but only because I was excited!

Today was the first day of my new life, and I couldn't wait to experience it.

Once on the ground, it took awhile to collect my cases, load them on a cart, and head for customs. I heaved a mental sigh when I cleared with no resistance. Outside the building, I hailed a cab and gave the driver the name of my hotel.

As I rode along, I watched the passing scenery, thinking about my last trip to the airport. The ambulance ride was a dull, painful memory. I'd been so sick—and so certain I'd never come back. This time the modern buildings, the palm trees, and the smiling faces of people we passed strengthened my conviction: I was doing the right thing.

We drove past a shop with windows full of bright-colored sarongs and skirts in flowered prints of varying colors. I was going to bring Eva and Mary here soon. We'd spend the day shopping and then have tea.

The taxi stopped in front of the hotel Sam and I had stayed in on my first trip here. The bellhop stacked my luggage in the corner, and I handed him a tip. It must have been a good one because he bowed from the waist, smiling and murmuring, "Thank you very much, kind lady!" He left still smiling.

Memo to Johanna: learn monetary rate of exchange.

I locked the door behind him and walked over to stand in front of the air conditioner with the vents pumping out glorious cool air. Might as well enjoy it while I could.

Nothing marred my sleep that night. I woke with the daylight to shower and rearrange my bags. After breakfast I walked to the car I'd ordered the night before. That chore had been more difficult than I anticipated. After numerous failed attempts to secure a driver, one of the coffee shop waiters mentioned that his cousin had a car and might be available to drive me. He made the final arrangements, and soon a short Papua New Guinean man waited to meet me, leaning against an old model blue Ford. The driver sprang to attention as I approached.

"Miss Holland?"

"Yes, and you are Bokim?" At least he spoke English.

He bowed. "At your service."

I climbed in the backseat and he loaded the suitcases. Then we were off to the small airport, where I would board the single-engine plane that would carry me to Sam. I hoped they'd maintained the airstrip while I was gone. Correction: I *prayed* they'd mowed the airstrip. I really didn't want to be in a plane skidding and bouncing along that overgrown runway.

The drive was brief; we arrived at the tarmac, and I spotted the pilot sitting in the aircraft. Oh, yodel. It was Mike, the rude, profanity-spewing, sans gallbladder pilot I'd encountered on our first flight to the village.

Momentary horror closed my throat. My spiritual maturity sprang three steps backward and frost coated my attitude and resolve as I studied the man through calculating eyes. I didn't want to go anywhere with him. However, he owned the plane and I needed his services, so I didn't have a choice. I bit my lip, kept quiet, and climbed into the cockpit passenger seat.

Mike yanked the seat belt around his middle and glanced over at me. "You look better than you did the last time I saw you."

"When was that?"

"When I flew you out. Sick as a —" He spewed an obscenity that singed my ears. "Glad to see you're doin' better."

"Thanks." I took the remark as a compliment—albeit a salty and inappropriate one.

He reached up and put on his headphones. "Figured we'd seen the last of you, kiddo. How come you're back?"

"Unfinished business." I noticed that in addition to fluent blasphemy, my pilot spoke perfect English.

"Business, huh?" He flipped a couple of switches, the engine roared, and the aircraft started to move. "Buying monkeys or mangoes?"

I smiled. "Love, Mike. I'm going after love."

❦

We hadn't been in the air long before the rain hit. Water fell in sheets, blinding me. "How can you see to fly?" I knew I was yelling, but the noise of the rain and roar of the plane motor made speaking in normal tones impossible. The craft bounced like a rubber ball.

"Don't have to see. Know the trip by heart. The strip will be slick."

The overgrown landing strip. I would sooner face a crazed python!

The roller-coaster ride left me clutching the seat with panic-induced power, knuckles white and standing up like marbles under the force of my grasp. Lightning forked the sky in ragged bursts of white heat.

Mike looked over and grinned. "She's a real—" he spouted off a string of cuss words that curled my hair—"ain't she?"

That she was. And more. I offered a stiff smile and held on.

As suddenly as it started, the rain stopped. Sunlight burst through the clouds and scudded across a sapphire sky. Below, I spotted ocean waves rippling the surface of blue water. I could make out the tops of feathery palms. When Sam and I had come to the village, we'd taken a boat, but I had no idea who to contact for such services. Pop had made my travel arrangements to the island. The flight cost more but the plane was quicker. All I wanted was the comfort of Sam's arms.

"There!" The pilot leaned over and pointed, then spewed profanity I think he made up. "They haven't mowed again!"

Panic and desperation gripped me. "You're going to land, aren't you?"

"Not on your life, pumpkin! I told them to mow the strip or I ain't landing this baby."

Not land? He must be kidding. He *had* to land ... this baby. "I'll give you fifty dollars extra!"

"Life's worth more than fifty bucks."

"A hundred."

He cocked his head, cupping a hand to his earphone. "Can't *hear* you."

"One fifty." I bit my lip, vowing to keep my temper. This was the first day of the rest of my life; I couldn't have a slug-out with a blasphemous pilot.

He reached out, wiggling his fingers. "You're gettin' there."

"Two hundred. That's my final offer." Never did I think I would pay two hundred dollars to crash! I caught my breath as the plane took a sudden nosedive. Bingo! I'd hit the magic number.

I clutched the seat rest, watching tiny dots scurrying below. The natives had heard the growling machine, and they were gathering. I located several dots running along the jungle trail—that would be Sam and the missionaries. I strained, spying a small spot struggling to keep up.

That would be my Poo.

"Hold on, sweetheart. We're going in!"

Clamping my eyes shut, I braced myself as the pilot lined the aircraft up with the ragged strip and took it down. I'd never experienced such a rapid descent—like locusts on a cornfield. Apparently the guy was a former navy pilot. He could set the craft down on a dime and hand back eight cents' change. Over the engine's roar, I watched the ground rising closer and closer. I sucked in my breath and burst into a rousing chorus of "Amazing Grace."

"... that saved a wretchhhhhh like me!" Yikes!

The pilot's deep baritone joined me. "I once was lost, now am fooound ..."

"Was blind, but now I seeeeeee." Holy moley! The front wheels hit, bounced thirty feet, hit again, bounced twenty feet, slid, spun around twice, then slid another fifteen feet to an abrupt stop. My spine knitted to my neck bone.

I heard the sound of a blowing bubble pop.

When I opened my eyes, Mike was jotting down something in a logbook, chomping on gum.

I unhooked my belt and pushed out of the seat. I couldn't believe it. I was alive!

The pilot kicked the door open, and there he was, just as I remembered him—Sam. Wonderful, dependable, love-of-my-life Sam.

When he saw me appear in the doorway, his eyes widened, and then laughter danced in those Tom Selleck depths.

I jumped from the death trap into his waiting arms.

Whirling me around, he hugged me, kissing me, trying to ask questions that I couldn't answer. Not yet. For now, I wanted to savor everything about him. The strong feel of his arms locked around me. The scent that was antiseptic, gauze, and jungle heat.

And I wanted to savor the overwhelming knowledge that God makes good on his promises.

Sam finally lowered my feet to the ground. "What took you so long to get here?" he growled against my ear.

"Oh, Sam, can you ever forgive me?" I showered his sun-bronzed face with kisses.

"There's nothing to forgive. It just takes some of us longer to realize our purpose." He winked and kissed me full on the lips, in front of everyone.

Eva, Mary, Frank, and Bud pressed close, welcoming me home. Then the missionaries stood aside so Poo could race toward me, her smile as wide as a barn door, the blinking light around her head set on high. I scooped the child up in my arms and swung her around, so happy—*so* happy to see her.

"Jo!" She looped her arms around my neck and held on tight. "Jo!"

Excitement was slow to fade, but I finally paid the pilot the extra fare. Sam's brows raised, but he just motioned for a couple of natives to transfer my luggage. I'd tell him all about the blackmail later.

We walked across the strip, Poo holding tight to my right hand.

"Are you surprised to see me?" I grinned at the love of my life—the very center of Johanna Holland's world—besides, of course, fulfilling her God-given purpose.

"No. I knew you'd come. I wasn't sure when, but I knew you'd come."

I paused, pressing my lips against his. He felt so good. So right. "Pretty sure of yourself, aren't you?"

"Sure of God." He returned the kiss before we walked on.

"Now, Sam. You *aren't* going to tell me that you believe God answers *all* prayers to our satisfaction."

"Not at all." His smile was warm and loving. "I believe he answers prayers to *his* satisfaction."

Now was the moment I'd been waiting for—and dreading just a little: the unveiling of my thoughts and deductions. I'd intended to wait until a later time with better circumstances, but I heard myself blurting out the speech I'd rehearsed all the way across the ocean. "I'm not called full-time to the mission field, Sam. Nothing is clearer in my mind. But I *am* called to you, and I am most willing to serve you and the Lord. I can pray for you, keep a fine home waiting for you in Saginaw. I can speak to churches, nursing homes, where God opens a door. I can help raise funds and even help out with your clinic a couple of times a year. I love children—I can serve the mission children and make a difference, not as often as you are called to serve, but often." I caught my breath, then bit my lip. "I wish I could be more like Mary and Eva—support you full-time in your passion—and maybe someday God will call me to that. But it's not now—not yet."

We faced each other, and I tried to read his expression. "What do you think?"

"Good enough."

"Good enough?" Not the most romantic response I could fathom, but I wasn't proposing Niagara Falls and an endless honeymoon.

"Good enough." He grasped my shoulders, holding me away from him. His eyes — filled with open devotion — met mine. "We've been over this a hundred times, Johanna. God will let you know when and if he calls you to serve in the field. We're all given gifts. And from what I hear you're doing a fine job with your gift."

Color flooded my cheeks. "Thank you …" I paused, eyes narrowing. "Wait a minute. What do you mean, from what you hear?"

He winked. "Come on, Johanna. You don't think I would sit by and be ignorant about your recuperation? That I didn't think about you every hour, pray for you, wonder what you were feeling, how you were doing? What kind of man do you take me for?"

I crossed my arms. "I *know* what kind of man you are, Sam. But I smell a rat."

He shrugged, his smile growing. "As a matter of fact, you smell many. I've spoken to Mom and Pop once a week, and they write me twice a month. You've got a great set of parents. They love and care about you, you know. Then there's Nelda and Jim; they've become more than friends. There've been a lot of postage and satellite calls on your behalf since last March."

"I can't believe this." I'd thought I was alone in making my decisions, sorting through my thoughts, coming — with God's help — to my own conclusions. And now I knew the truth: everyone else, including God, had known all along what I was going to do.

"Well, then …" I might as well accept the subterfuge. I was confident it wouldn't be the last. "How *do* you feel about my conclusions?"

"About us?"

"About my solution to our problem. You can continue your mission work; I'll accompany you when I can, but the rest of the time I'll remain in Saginaw and raise funds for your work, support you in prayers, speak to local church groups."

He slid his arms around me. "Well, now, I don't know if I can do without you *too* often during the year."

I smiled. "I know it won't be easy, but who knows? God has a way of doing things when they're least expected. I'll keep praying for direction; I'll come with you a couple of trips a year; after all, Poo is getting to be like my own child." I grinned down at the imp who still held tight to my right hand.

The child gazed up. "Jo."

Sam cleared his throat. "Johanna . . ."

Uh-oh. I knew that tone of voice.

"What would you say if God is calling me to other places than Papua New Guinea?"

"God . . . other places?" *Oh, no. He wouldn't do this to me.* Not when I'd worked so hard to accept his will for these villagers.

"My church is opening a new mission front in Greenland."

Blood left my face. "Greenland."

He warmed to the subject. "One month, Jo. Come with me one month out of a year." He started walking, and I fell in step beside him. "Honey, are you aware that Greenland has the world's lowest population density? About 88 percent of its people are Greenlanders—Greenland Eskimos. Then 10 percent are Danish, and 2 percent are United States military. The Danish community is largely Lutheran, but few others know the Savior in a personal way. The breakdown of their

Yes, indeed. Jo. Johanna Holland. On her way to Green-land. My steps matched Sam's, and we walked together down the path.

We were together; that was all I needed.

At long last, I was home.

335 / LORI COPELAND

native culture has had devastating effects on the continent. Immorality, alcoholism, apathy, mental illness, and poverty are just a few of their problems. The gospel witness there is very weak."

"Hmm. I suppose travel conditions aren't good and living conditions are harsh ..."

"The worst!" He sounded utterly delighted. "Communities along the coasts are isolated, which makes missionary work an even greater challenge." He engulfed my hand in his own. "We can work together — run a medical clinic — "

We made our way through the winding jungle path, and I tried to absorb it all. Greenland? What about Papua New Guinea? The jungle?

Flies.

Dirt.

Heat.

I glanced at Poo. Sticky fingers.

Sam's arm slid around my shoulders. "How about it, honey? Can we do it?"

What he meant was could *I* do it? I leaned into him — and grinned. I couldn't help it. Could I do it? Well, hadn't I just discovered that with God all things are possible? My mind was open to his holy nudging ...

But *Greenland*?

I laughed. Well. With Sam, why not? Jungles. Greenland. Mars and Pluto! What did it matter, so long as we were together and God was there with us?

"Greenland, huh?" I tugged at Poo's hand. "Sounds like an adventure, doesn't it?"

The child's fingers tightened on mine and she grinned. "Jo!"